D0310904

MURDER IN HOUSE

Ellie Quicke is back

Ellie and her new husband Thomas are called to deal with student Ursula, who has staged a sit-in at church. Ursula challenges Ellie to solve three mysteries: a broken engagement, a disappearance and a death. As she investigates, Ellie suspects there is more to these events than anyone is admitting. Soon she finds her own friends and family targeted, as a powerful group hunts her down...

This book should be returned to any branch of the
Lancashire County Library on or before the date shown

OCT 11

27 AUG 2013

CPP

23 JUL 2012

1 1 JAN 2013

25 JAN 2013

1 1 JUN 2013

25 APR 2013

20 JUL 2018

2 1 MAY 2013

2 8 OCT 2014

1 6 APR 2018

SW

FG

EP

DM

aN

FM

JD

LML

MURDER IN HOUSE

Veronica Heley

Severn House Large Print
London & New York

This first large print edition published 2011
in Great Britain and the USA by
SEVERN HOUSE PUBLISHERS LTD of
9-15 High Street, Sutton, Surrey, SM1 1DF.
First world regular print edition published 2009 by
Severn House Publishers Ltd., London and New York.

British Library Cataloguing in Publication Data

Heley, Veronica.
    Murder in house.
    1. Quicke, Ellie (Fictitious character)--Fiction.
    2. Detective and mystery stories. 3. Large type books.
    I. Title
    823.9'14-dc22

    ISBN-13: 978-0-7278-7955-4

Severn House Publishers support The Forest Stewardship Council
[FSC], the leading international forest certification organisation. All
our titles that are printed on Greenpeace-approved FSC-certified paper
carry the FSC logo.

Printed and bound in Great Britain by the
MPG Books Group, Bodmin, Cornwall.

ONE

After her first husband's death, Ellie Quicke discovered that she was stronger than she'd thought. She'd coped with a demanding daughter and, by networking in the community, had solved some neighbourhood crimes. Now married to the Reverend Thomas – her best friend as well as her dear love – she was finding marriage second time round deeply satisfying, if not always easy. To add to her good fortune, she'd inherited money and moved into the big house in which her Aunt Drusilla had lived and died. This didn't mean she knew all the answers, however, especially where murder was concerned.

'Get that vodka down him!'
'I can't hold him—'
'Knock him out, then!'
'He's getting away!'
Whack! Heavy breathing.
'That's better! Now, hold his nose and pour it down his throat. Never mind if it gets on his clothes. That's right. Now, pick him up under his arms, that's it. Drag him to the balcony and heave him over.'

5

'She'll tell!'

'She's not capable of telling anyone anything at the moment, is she? When she comes round we'll say he got drunk and took a swing at you. Misjudged the distance, went over the edge. That's right, lift him up!'

'It's the top floor, for heavens' sake!'

'All the better. Come on, now. All together ... and over!'

Silence, but for more heavy breathing.

'Now,' said the leader of the pack. 'You and you! Run downstairs and yell that he's gone over in a drunken frenzy. Right?'

'What about her?'

'Leave her to me. I'll take her out the back way. Get a move on!'

Sunday lunchtime

Ellie didn't often go down with a cold, but this one had been a blinder. She wasn't the only person to go down with it, of course. Sometimes it seemed as if the whole world was suffering from it. Even her beloved husband, who was normally as strong as an ox – if you could have an ox who looked like an old-time steamship captain complete with beard – even he'd been forced to spend a couple of days in bed and had only just recovered his appetite.

The temperature had plummeted overnight, the rain had turned to sleet, the roads were black with slush, and Thomas ought to have been convalescing in the warm. Unfortunately,

6

one of his clerical friends had rung to say he'd gone down with pleurisy and could Thomas take the morning service for him. Thomas, being Thomas, had stuffed his pockets with cough sweets and gone.

Ellie decided not to go with him as she was only just beginning to feel better, so had stayed at home to drink honey and lemon and prepare roast beef, Yorkshire pudding and all the trimmings against his return. She was aware that both of them ought really to be on a diet of lettuce leaves to reduce waistlines expanding with middle age and a love of good food, but in the aftermath of a heavy cold and in such bitter weather, surely it was right to pamper oneself a bit?

He should have been back by now. What was keeping him? She tested the vegetables cooking on the stove – almost done – and wished that her daughter Diana were not bringing little Frank over for tea that day. Small boys could be overpowering when you were feeling below par. What's more, Diana had asked for a 'family conference', meaning she didn't want Thomas in on it. Diana had been known to refer to Thomas as 'the proverbial church mouse, scraping the barrel while looking for a cushy berth for his old age'. Mixed metaphors apart, the poison had worked since Thomas now refused to discuss Diana.

Conscious that her mind became a whirlpool of contradictory emotions whenever she thought of her demanding daughter, Ellie felt she could have done with some backup that afternoon as she was sure Diana was going to ask for money.

Normally Ellie would have pointed out that although she'd inherited much of her wealthy aunt's estate, most of it had been put into a charitable trust and monies could only be disbursed by agreement of a board of directors, who were unlikely to give money away to someone with a tendency to cut corners in financial and other dealings. As Diana had done.

But circumstances were not normal, since the downturn in the financial market had found many small estate agencies – such as the one Diana and a partner had gone into – going out of business.

Ellie did not like to think of Diana in serious financial trouble, couldn't imagine what advice she should give her, and deplored the timing of her visit. It would serve Diana right if she or little Frank caught this heavy cold and had to suffer with a fierce sore throat for days until finally the cold broke, and then they would be awash with tissues and wouldn't sleep properly. And even when the catarrh had cleared up, there would probably be another fortnight of nursing a hacking cough.

How she wished she could discuss this with Thomas but – apart from his not wishing to be involved – he had more than enough on his plate with a demanding job editing a national church magazine, and a paper he was due to read at a conference in Oxford the following weekend.

She would be firm and not let Diana upset her ... especially on a Sunday, which was Thomas's one day off work.

She looked at the clock. Thomas was late getting back from church, and Ellie was getting anxious. The Yorkshire pudding would spoil if left on a high heat in the oven, and sag if she lowered the temperature. The beef would lose its tenderness if overcooked. What could be keeping him?

At that moment Thomas used his keys to let himself into the house and came into the kitchen, still wearing his heavy car coat.

'Ellie, light of my life, I have a problem. Could you put lunch on the back burner? A teenaged girl has staged a sit-in at church and won't leave. She refuses to tell me or the churchwarden what's troubling her, but she might talk to you.'

Ellie was horrified. 'What, me? Go out, now?' She sneezed and said, 'No way!' at the same time. 'She's probably pregnant. Give her the number for social services.'

Thomas put his arm about her. 'I thought of that. She said it was far more serious. I know you're not feeling a hundred per cent, the weather's filthy, and we've both been looking forward to a good meal. But would it hurt to put it back for an hour? There's something terribly wrong with this girl.'

Ellie hesitated. Not only would the roast be

spoiled if she went with him, but it would also mean leaving their housekeeper, Rose, alone in the house. She noted Thomas's grave expression and sighed. Thomas loved his food, and he wouldn't ask her to defer lunch if this were not more important.

She turned back to the stove, working out how to keep the food warm without spoiling. 'She's drunk? On drugs?'

He sneezed and blew his nose, his voice thick. 'Neither. She's rational, calm and polite, but won't leave. She says she needs to stay in the church to fulfil some sort of vow.'

Ellie switched the hostess trolley on to warm up, and transferred the roast joint on to a plate so that she could make some gravy in the pan. 'Do we know her?'

'No. The churchwarden didn't know her either. She wouldn't give her name, but I judge her to be late teens or early twenties, possibly an undergraduate from a good family background, well educated. And determined. Apparently she sat at the back of the church during the service and didn't leave when everyone else, including me, trooped out to the church hall to have coffee.

'The churchwarden asked her to leave and she refused. She's brought a sleeping bag, some sandwiches and a Thermos full of coffee and says she proposes to stay the night. The churchwarden said the heating in the church was being turned off and what would she do about going to the loo, and she said she'd brought a bottle for emergencies. And indeed, so she had.'

Ellie, stirring gravy, was forced to laugh. Thomas almost smiled too. He shucked off his coat and went to help her by ladling the roast potatoes and parsnips into a Pyrex dish that could also be put in the trolley to keep warm.

Ellie said, 'I'm intrigued. Almost.'

Thomas sighed. 'I'm not. I persuaded the churchwarden to put her in the vestry where there's an electric fire and access to a toilet. He muttered about security and said she'd probably let a crowd of vandals in to wreck the church if we left her there. She thought that was funny, which was reassuring in a way. I said I'd be responsible for locking her in, and for getting her out. He agreed, eventually. So I've got the key, the churchwarden's gone off to his lunch and she's in there all alone with her problem.'

He inhaled the aroma of the beef joint. 'Ellie, it's just about killing me to leave this food. I could eat a horse and this is better than horse. Don't tell me there's apple crumble for afters.'

'Then I won't. I'll heat it up when we get back.' Ellie fitted the gravy boat into the trolley and drained cauliflower florets while Thomas mashed swedes and piled them in as well. 'Let me check on Rose and then we'll go.'

Their housekeeper – inherited from Aunt Drusilla – was asleep in her big chair, next door. The television was on, but the cup of tea which Ellie had taken in earlier had not been touched. Ellie spread a lightweight rug over her old friend and hoped she wouldn't wake in their

11

absence. Perhaps it would be best to leave a note for her, just in case?

Outside there was a nasty wind and sleet was striking the windows. Ellie shivered as she found a Post-it note and scribbled a message. She definitely did not want to go out into the cold and rain. And for what? The girl must be a hysterical little madam to devise this plan. What were her parents thinking of, to let her inconvenience so many people?

She tore off a piece of kitchen roll and blew her nose for the umpteenth time that morning. What if going out in this awful weather meant she developed pneumonia? Or Thomas did? She put a pack of tissues in her handbag.

Thomas folded her into the light but warm overcoat he'd bought her for an extra Christmas present and kissed the tip of her nose, which tickled and made her laugh. Her stomach rumbled. Oh well. Better get it over and done with.

The church wasn't one that she knew well, though she'd attended a wedding there some years ago. It wasn't anything like the pretty, mid-Victorian church in which Ellie had worshipped for many years. Far from it. It was one of those brick edifices built in the twenties, seemingly designed to keep builders constantly in work on repairs, since there were flat roofs and chapels and fiddly bits sticking out here and there. Hard to heat.

Thomas used his borrowed key on an unobtrusive door at the side of the church, and let them directly into the vestry.

The girl had made herself very much at home. She didn't look to be in any kind of distress, but was sitting on a folded-up sleeping bag, with a colourful holdall beside her. She had clear skin, innocent of make-up; was warmly dressed in jeans, a couple of heavy sweaters and good-looking boots ... and was engaged in straightening her long, honey-coloured hair with battery-operated tongs. She had the electric fire on, was hooked into an iPod, and had poured herself out a cup of something from a Thermos flask. A number of small candles had been lit and placed around the room. Ellie wondered if they were from the church's store, or if the girl had brought them with her.

Thomas gave a giant sneeze and slammed the door on the outside world.

The girl turned brown eyes from Thomas to Ellie and back again. She didn't shift her position in any way. She didn't speak, either, but she did unhook one ear from her iPod.

Thomas mopped himself up. 'This is my wife, Ellie Quicke, who is good at sorting out people's problems. She wonders if you'd like to tell us what's troubling you over lunch.' He was hungry. So was Ellie.

Apparently, the girl was not. She looked Ellie over, but her remote expression didn't change. 'You don't have to worry about me. I'll leave the place tidy and let myself out in the morning.'

Ellie blew her nose. Coming in from the cold

13

always set her off. 'I didn't see any banners up outside the church. What are you doing a sit-in for? It must be something serious.'

'I don't expect anyone like you to understand.' The girl shrugged, implying that no one of Ellie's advanced age could be expected to understand the problems of youth.

Ellie gritted her teeth. Did this young girl think no one in the world had ever got themselves into trouble before? Such arrogance! For two pins she'd sweep out and leave the girl to it.

Yet Thomas had wanted her to help. He'd foregone his lunch to get her here, so she supposed she must make an effort. She looked the girl over. As Thomas had said, she sounded well educated, she didn't seem short of a penny, and she was set on having her own way.

Thomas seated himself on the vicar's swivel chair, and swung round so that his back was towards them. Ellie loosened her big coat, and sought for the pack of tissues she'd put in her pocket. No tissues. Had she dropped them somewhere? Ah, in her handbag. She held back impatience. 'I'm dying for my lunch. So is Thomas. But I suppose if you're having a sit-in, we'd better sit it out with you.'

'No need for that.' The girl put the tongs away in her bag. 'I'm doing this for me. A sort of detox. I'd rather be alone.'

Thomas swivelled round. 'A hermit job? Isolation, peace and quiet? Trying to shut out the world's noise and listen to what God is

14

saying to you?'

'God?' She considered the matter. 'I'm not sure I believe in God. I'm doing this for someone else. Someone who did believe in God. And then I'll have closure and can move on.'

Ellie indicated the impedimenta the girl had brought with her. 'Shouldn't you be doing it properly? Without all these creature comforts?'

'Thought about that. But no. He wouldn't have wanted me to catch my death of cold or anything. I just need to be here, where he used to come. Just for a day and a night. He wouldn't have minded being left in the church in the dark, and anyway, I brought these candles with me, just in case.'

Ellie made a guess. 'He ... whoever he is ... is dead?'

The girl nodded. Her eyelids contracted and for a moment Ellie thought the girl would cry, but she didn't. Tough love?

'A boyfriend?' The girl was attractive in a big-boned sort of way. Not beautiful, exactly, but she had an interesting face. Of course she would have a boyfriend.

The girl shrugged. 'No. He's still alive, but you can go off people, you know.'

'You went off him ... when? After this other boy died?'

'Maybe.' She brought her knees up to her chin. 'I promised myself I would do this for him, and I don't break my promises.'

Ellie made her voice soft. 'Other people break their promises, perhaps?'

15

The girl closed her eyes and turned her head away from them.

There was quiet in the vestry. No one moved. Ellie could feel another sneeze coming on, and fought it down.

Thomas sneezed so ferociously that he almost fell off his chair. A gust of wind hit the window and made it rattle.

Ellie's teeth chattered. 'That's enough. Thomas, you'll catch your death if we stay here much longer. We've got lunch waiting for us back home, and I'm taking both of you home with me, right now. After we've eaten, Miss-whatever-your-name is, we can discuss your problem and, if you still want to, we'll bring you back here to finish off your vigil in peace and quiet.'

'Sorry!' muttered Thomas, into his handkerchief. 'Thought my cold was clearing up, but it seems to be getting worse.'

'Pleurisy, pneumonia, I'm not risking it,' said Ellie, bending down to pack the girl's stuff away into her bag. 'Put your coat on, girl. It's murder outside.'

'It was murder, anyway,' said the girl. 'He was murdered.'

'Was he, now?' said Ellie, startled. 'Well, you'll have two more deaths on your hands if we don't clear out of here and get warm. So let's get back to civilization.'

The girl didn't move until Thomas switched off the electric fire.

* * *

16

'My name's Ursula. That's all you need to know.' After two helpings of everything, the girl was relaxed enough to give her name, but no more.

'Coffee? Tea?'

She shook her head. 'Thank you for lunch. Shall I help you stack the dishwasher? Then I'd best be getting back to the church.'

Thomas grumbled. 'You led me to believe you'd talk to Ellie, if I got her along to the church.'

Ellie sent Thomas a wifely look, question and reproach nicely blended.

The girl looked at Ellie with a dozen doubts showing. 'That was before I'd met her. I'm sure she's a very good cook and means well, but ... well, this is not exactly the usual sort of parish problem. It was nice of you both to give me lunch, and I must say I feel better for it, but it isn't helping me get through this. I'll phone for a cab. If you'll let me borrow the key to the church, I'll pop it back to you first thing tomor-row.'

Thomas gave a giant sigh, and blew his nose. 'You know very well I can't let that key out of my possession and I really don't want to go out again, with this cold on me, but—'

'Certainly not,' said Ellie. 'You'll catch your death. Ursula, I understand that you've decided to perform some sort of penance. Only you know if that's sensible or not, but it is not sen-sible to put other people at risk of catching pneumonia, is it? Is it right for you to take

17

Thomas out into this dreadful weather when he's so unwell?'

The girl thrust out her lower lip. 'You're twisting everything. You dragged me here. I didn't ask to come.' She was stubborn, but retained her good manners. She'd been well brought up.

Ellie reflected that you could sometimes press the buttons on a well-brought-up girl by asking her to help you. 'Well, before you go, could you just help me get Rose up the stairs to her bedroom? She was my aunt's housekeeper – more of a friend, really – who stayed on to look after Thomas and me after my aunt died. She used to be such a bustling little person, but she's not well at the moment and I'm not sure I can get her upstairs by myself. Thomas would help me, but she really doesn't want a man doing things for her.'

Thomas gave her a Look, but heroically refrained from challenging the lie, and began to stack dishes.

The girl stiffened. 'She doesn't want men around her? Well, I suppose I can understand that. Of course I'll help if I can. But then I must go.'

Ellie led the girl into Rose's sitting room next door. Rose had fallen asleep in her big chair again, her plate of food almost untouched. Ellie suffered a jolt of anxiety, as she often did nowadays when she came upon Rose asleep. So frail, so tiny.

Ellie touched Rose's shoulder and the faded

18

blue eyes opened. 'The potatoes were quite nice, dear, but I must let you have my recipe for them sometime. Miss Quicke always says I make the tastiest of roast potatoes.'

'Yes, dear. Shall I help you up to your bedroom for your afternoon nap?'

'No, no. Quite happy where I am. But perhaps a cup of tea when you're making one? In a cup, not a mug. Don't bother just for me, though.'

Ellie led Ursula back to the kitchen. 'That's the first time Rose hasn't gone upstairs for her afternoon nap. I think perhaps we ought to make up a bed for her downstairs. And don't say she ought to be in a home. She looked after my aunt beautifully, and made her last years very happy. Now it's our turn to look after her till she picks up again.' Back in the kitchen, she put the kettle on. 'So, what's all this about a murder?'

Ursula tossed back her hair. 'It wasn't murder. Of course not. He fell, that's all.'

'I'll take some tea in to Thomas and Rose, then we can sit down comfortably and you can tell me all about it.' Ellie was rather afraid the girl would take herself off as soon as Ellie left the room but no, she had seated herself at the kitchen table when Ellie returned.

'Who was it who died?' said Ellie, putting sugar and milk into her coffee. 'Not a boyfriend, you said?' At first she thought the girl was going to maintain her silence, but a noisy burst of sleet hit the window, making both women look up. Perhaps this reminder of the horrible weather made up the girl's mind.

'Not a boyfriend, no. One of the crowd. A party in the new year. He had too much to drink, got into a quarrel, took a swing at someone, toppled over a balcony and that was that.'

'You used the word "murder".'

Silence. Long eyelashes were lowered, eyelashes the same colour as her hair, both true honey blonde. 'I was stupid, thinking I'd get some sort of message from God if I stayed on alone in the church. I suppose if the usual vicar had been there, he might have had something nice to say about my friend and that would have made me feel better. If you hadn't interfered ... well, it's done now, and I'll be off.'

She shook back her hair, making up her mind to some new course of action. 'Of course it wasn't murder. The police said it wasn't and they should know, shouldn't they?'

'You disagree?'

Ursula treated Ellie to a look in which calculation overlaid doubt. 'Your husband said you were good at solving mysteries. How about investigating a disappearance, a broken engagement and an accidental death which was really a murder? All in one neat little package.'

Ellie felt like slapping the girl. Her manner was almost – but not quite – insolent. 'Accidental death: the non-boyfriend? A broken engagement: you're not wearing a ring. A disappearance: the boyfriend to whom you were engaged?'

Ursula pulled a thin gold chain out from

under her sweater. She undid the clasp and slid a gold ring from it on to the table. It wasn't a modern ring by any means. Perhaps Edwardian? A lovers' knot was the only decoration, and there was no jewel on it. 'Perhaps you'd like to return it to him for me.'

Ellie blinked. 'What...? Who...? No, I—'

'Daniel Collins. Park Gardens. He'll understand. No message.'

Ellie stared at the ring. She picked it up. It was warm from contact with the girl's skin. The front doorbell rang, and someone used keys on both locks to let themself in. Ellie's attention switched from the ring and she rose from her seat. 'What...?' Only Thomas, Ellie and Rose had both keys to the front door.

'Yoohoo!' Yes, that was her daughter Diana calling from the hall. Could Diana and little Frank be arriving so early? But how could Diana have got hold of keys? Ellie glanced at the clock, and realized they were on time. It was she who was running late. The dishwasher hadn't been started, Thomas was probably having a nap in his study, and there was no cake made for tea.

Diana, fashionably gaunt and trendy, appeared in the doorway, unbuttoning her coat. She was followed by six-year-old Frank who made a dash for Ellie, knocking her back into her chair. 'Is it going to snow? I like it when it snows. Can I have a sledge for when it snows?'

Ellie laughed and kissed him, saying it didn't often snow in London. Remembering her

21

visitor, she tried to disentangle herself from Frank as Diana said, in her sharpest voice, 'Watch it!'

'Don't go, Ursula!' Ellie got to her feet. Too late. The girl was no longer in her seat, and Diana was staring out into the hall.

'She pushed past me. How rude!'

'Stop her!'

Too late. Ellie reached the hall only to see the front door close behind the girl.

'Ursula's back. Saw her in the Broadway yesterday.'

'She's not going to make trouble, is she?'

'She tried that, Dumbo. Got nowhere, did she! She won't try it again. And if she does, we'll deal with it. We can't have her muddying the water when things are so critical. The Man's in a right state with so much money tied up in the flats and buyers dropping out all over the place. We've got to keep things calm.'

'The architect's still on board, isn't he? And don't call me "Dumbo".'

'He's trying to wriggle out of it, but The Man's got him nailed. Don't tell me you fancied her.'

'Great legs.'

'Legs come and go. There's always a good supply of legs.'

'She'd brains too.'

'Not enough to shut up when we told her to. Don't look so alarmed. The police have closed the case, and she's going back to Uni. End of story.'

22

'*And Mia?*'

'*She knows better than to talk, wherever she is.*'

'*What we did to her—*'

'*Ah, shut up. She was asking for it. She was never really one of the family, anyway, was she?*'

TWO

Sunday afternoon

'Who on earth was that?' Diana was annoyed and suspicious. 'Someone in trouble.'

'Gran, what do you mean, it doesn't snow in London? Of course it does. When I got up this morning everything was white all over—'

'Quiet, Frank,' said his mother. 'I'm speaking.'

Thomas appeared from his study, rubbing his eyes. 'Hello, hello? What's all this then?'

Frank launched himself at Thomas, was caught up in the air, screaming with laughter, and whirled round. Frank approved of Thomas.

'Mother, you were expecting us, weren't you?' Diana shed her expensive black coat that was rather too fussy around the collar. 'I did say four o'clock.'

'We got held up. Diana, I didn't know you had keys to the front door. Have you had a set

23

specially made? They cost a bomb.'

'Oh, I'm using Rose's keys. She never goes out now, so it seems—'

'What?' Ellie felt her temper rising. 'You had no right. I know she hasn't been up to much lately, but she'll pick up again soon and ... Diana, you'll let me have her keys right now. She'll need them again soon, and I need them this minute because you forgot to turn the mortise lock.'

'What makes you think that?'

'The girl let herself out, which she couldn't have done if you'd remembered to use the second key after you came in.'

'Oh, don't be such a fusspot. You know perfectly well that Rose is well past doing the shopping and running this house. If she's even stirred herself to make you a cup of tea this last week, I'd be surprised. No one but you thinks she's going to see out the winter and—'

Thomas took Frank's hand and led him to the stairs. 'Let's go on a cat hunt, shall we, Frank? Midge hasn't shown up for his lunch yet. Do you think he's gone on the prowl in the attics?'

Frank trod the steps beside Thomas but looked stricken. 'Rose isn't going to die, is she? Everyone dies around here.'

Frank lived with his father and his father's second family during the week, where he led a stable, structured life enlivened by two little half-sisters whom he adored and who adored him. At weekends Diana was supposed to have him, but often didn't, and at least twice a week

Frank found himself dumped on Ellie and Thomas. All three of them enjoyed these visits, but Ellie fancied that Diana's restlessness and unreliable behaviour were beginning to undermine the little boy's sense of security.

The death of his great-great-aunt, Miss Drusilla Quicke, was the first time Frank had experienced such a loss, and he'd taken it harder than anyone had expected. It wasn't surprising that he was also anxious about Rose, who had cuddled and spoilt him from babyhood.

'Rose is all right, but she's not feeling too good at the moment. This cold, you know. You haven't had it yet, have you?' Thomas's voice faded as he led Frank through the door on the landing that led to the top storey of unused and unheated attic rooms.

Ellie opened her mouth to call after them that it was no good looking for Midge the cat up there. Midge could open any door that could be pushed open, or that had a handle that could be pulled down, but the door to the attic rooms was a knob and, so far at least, Midge had failed to master it. Thomas knew that, of course. He must be taking Frank out of the way so that the two women could talk in peace.

So Ellie shut her mouth and followed Diana into the big sitting room at the back of the house, where she set about drawing long velvet curtains to shut out the darkness outside. She hated these early dark nights. The calendar said the nights were getting shorter, but no one seemed to have told the sun about it.

Diana ran a finger across the mantelpiece to check for dust, but there wasn't any. Rose might not be up to running the house at the moment, but there were a couple of efficient Polish girls who came twice a week to take care of the cleaning.

Frowning, Diana subsided into Ellie's high-backed chair by the fireplace. 'Aren't we to have any tea, after I've taken the trouble to visit you?'

'We were delayed by our visitor. I'll make it in a minute.' Ellie switched on sidelights and removed the layer of Sunday papers which Thomas had strewn on the floor around his big reclining chair.

Ellie was worried about Ursula. Would the girl have tried to go back to the church? But she had no key to get in. No, she'd have gone home, wherever that might be. Or back to university, perhaps?

Diana sniffed. 'Some waif and stray demanding a handout, I suppose. How much did she con you out of?'

'Nothing. May I have Rose's keys, please?'

'In a minute. Now, Mother, before the others come back, we really must have a talk.'

'Keys first. Talk afterwards.'

With some reluctance Diana handed over two keys on a ribbon; a ribbon which usually hung around Rose's neck. Ellie was annoyed with herself because she hadn't spotted they were missing. She laid them down on the occasional table beside her. 'I'll make some tea now, shall I?'

'Won't Rose...?'

'She's having a little nap.'

'She should be in a home.'

Ellie hated arguments. 'Rose stays as long as she wants to. She's looked after us for years, and now it's our turn to look after her. Besides, she's bound to pick up as the weather improves. So, what do you want to talk about? Money? I thought you and Denis were doing well with your estate agency.'

'Of course we were, but nothing's moving at the moment, and how we're going to manage long term if this recession continues...'

'I suppose you'll go in for renting out properties nobody can afford to buy.'

'Renting – especially short term – is a lot of work and Denis says we've got to think outside the box in case this recession lasts much longer.' Her hands twisted in her lap. Was she nervous? 'To put it mildly, we have a cash flow problem, especially since Denis put his boys into private schools last term.'

Ellie tried to work out how much that would be costing him. While she would be the first to admit that mental arithmetic was hardly her strong point, she didn't like the total that popped into her mind.

Diana's partner in the 2Ds Agency was a steely-smiling, ambitious and ruthless individual. Harder than Diana. Denis must be getting anxious. Even desperate.

'So what is Denis proposing to do? Put the boys back into state schools? Surely that would be the sensible thing to do.' Denis would hate the loss of face involved in taking such a step. Denis was pushing Diana to find another solution to his problem. So what would that be? Ellie had a horrid feeling that somehow or other she was going to be involved in sorting out Denis's problems.

Diana got to her feet and prowled, not meeting her mother's eye. 'He thought – well, I thought, actually, that we should talk about my future. I have someone wanting to move into my flat so I wondered when you'd be able to let me have our old house. You did promise you'd transfer it to me when you moved into Great Aunt Drusilla's place, and after all it will be mine when you die. I know the fire damage last year made it uninhabitable, but the redecorations must be nearly finished by now, and if they aren't, I'm sure I could get them done more quickly and cheaply than you.'

Ellie considered what had been said, what had been twisted in Diana's mind and what had been left unsaid. Ellie's first husband had actually left the old house to her for life. After her death, half was hers to dispose of as she thought fit, and the other half would go to Diana. This was not precisely what Diana had said, but Ellie supposed it was near enough.

As to the matter of getting the house finished on time and within budget, Diana had cut corners when Aunt Drusilla had allowed her a trial period in which to manage some of her properties. If there was one thing Ellie had, sorrowfully, to admit, it was that Diana never seemed to learn by her mistakes, but went on her way regardless. Ellie hated to cross Diana twice in an afternoon, but it had to be done.

She steeled herself to give unwelcome news. 'I did say that I would let you have the house, and I stand by my word. The redecorations are well under way. The work was put out to tender, and the insurance people agreed which quotes to accept. I'm not sure how long it will be before I can let you have the keys. Perhaps some weeks? I'll enquire. Surely the buyer for your flat will wait? If not, perhaps you could move into a furnished flat somewhere for the time being?'

'How soon?'

'Three or four weeks, at a guess.'

Diana pulled a face. 'While you've got the builders in, you might as well tell them to install a loft conversion.'

'It's a three-bedroomed semi, Diana. That's what it was insured for, and that's what you'll get. Now, tea?'

Some time back she'd heard Thomas and Frank clattering down the polished wooden stairs, laughing and saying 'Shush!' to one another. Had they found Midge? Unlikely. So what had they been up to?

Diana said, 'Well, don't blame me if I'm forced to move in here with you.'

Ellie told herself not to scream. She took a

29

deep breath, held it, let it out. 'I don't think that would be a good idea, Diana.'

'Why not? You've masses of room. I could move into your guest bedroom, which has a bathroom en suite. You've already allocated Frank a bedroom, a nice big one, for the odd nights he spends here. I won't need a kitchen because I can use yours. Or, how about my moving into Rose's part of the house? That's self-contained, isn't it, with its own door to the courtyard? She's not exactly pulling her weight now, is she? Great Aunt left her well off. She can afford to go into a home, and the sooner the better. Or, if the worst comes to the worst, I could take over the attic floor. Plenty of space there.'

No way could Ellie cope with a bullying daughter under the same roof. She unstuck her tongue from the roof of her mouth. 'There's no heating up there.'

'Put in storage heaters. Why not? It's the perfect solution. I could let the old house out till the market improves, and when I leave you'd have a self-contained flat to rent out yourself. Perhaps with an outside staircase?'

Ellie got to her feet, trying to suppress her agitation. Help, Thomas! 'No, Diana. Forget it.'

'But you'll hand over the old house to me straight away? I need to move at the end of next week, or even earlier. The decorating can be finished as and when.'

Was this blackmail? Probably. Ellie knew when she was beaten. 'I'll see what can be done. Shall we have tea now?'

Thomas and Frank were busily cooking in the kitchen, both inadequately covered with aprons. There was flour all over the big table and over Frank, as he pounded some greyish pastry into submission. Rose was there as well, sitting in a big chair at the end of the table and laughing at the two men's antics. 'Wouldn't Miss Quicke have enjoyed this?' Rose's thinning hair was neatly brushed, the buttons on her dressing gown were all done up, she was wearing her bedroom slippers, and she looked more lively than she had done for many a day.

Frank waved floury hands in greeting. 'Hi, Gran! Guess what we've been up to...? Ooops!' He put his hands over his mouth, his eyes wide with laughter. 'I nearly told, didn't I? But it's a secret!'

Thomas opened the oven to take out a baking tray covered with irregularly shaped biscuits, which he proceeded to transfer on to a wire cooling tray. 'That's it, my lad. Zip the mouth.'

Rose was on her feet, almost as spry as usual. 'Tea for the workers, and juice for Frank. That is, if he'll let me into his secret.'

'I'm not telling anyone!' shouted Frank. 'Not Mummy, not Granny, not Rose, not anyone. I promised Grandpa!' He turned a flour-spattered face up to Thomas. 'I can call you Grandpa, can't I?'

'No, you can't!' Diana's ferocity froze everyone in their places.

Thomas recovered first. 'Frank, you can call

me Thomas. All my friends call me Thomas.' He rattled mugs on to the table. 'Hot biscuits, anyone?'

'Certainly not,' said Diana, removing the apron from her son. 'Look at you! I can't turn my back for five minutes. Let's get you cleaned up and returned to your father and stepmother, or you'll be in dead trouble.'

Frank's expression changed to one of endurance. 'Maria says it's all right for children to get dirty, so long as it comes off in the wash.'

'She doesn't have to do her laundry in a tiny flat with no drying facilities,' said Diana, jerking him away from the table. 'Oh, come along, do!'

'We made the biscuits specially for you.'

'Look at the time!' Diana seized a cloth to work on his hands and face.

Ellie sampled a biscuit, which was surprisingly tasty. 'Won't you let him stay for tea?' said Ellie. 'These biscuits are delicious, Frank. Well done.'

'Can I take some back for Daddy and Maria?'

'Certainly not,' said Diana, scrubbing his face. 'They've got enough biscuits. Come along, now. Where did I leave my coat?'

Ellie put a couple of biscuits into a paper bag and, while Diana was donning her big coat in the hall, she slipped the bag into Frank's hand and gave him a kiss.

It was only after Ellie had waved Diana's car goodbye that Ellie realized Diana had bested her yet again. In the old days a Yale lock had been sufficient for the big old front door, but after a disturbing incident last year a mortise lock had been added, so you needed two keys to get in and out. Diana had let herself out in the usual way and turned the key in the mortise lock behind her as well. How had she managed to do that? There was only one answer, and Ellie didn't like the sound of it.

She darted into the sitting room. Yes, Rose's keys had disappeared from the table on which she'd left them. Diana must have waited till Ellie had left the room, and pocketed them again. The thought of Diana being able to enter the house at will was unnerving. With hindsight, Ellie told herself she ought to have put them straight into her pocket, or handbag.

And ... horror of horrors ... what had happened to the engagement ring Ursula had given her to return to her boyfriend? She'd had it in her hand when she'd heard Diana arrive. Then Frank had come charging at her, and ... what had happened to the ring?

Thomas came out of the kitchen, carrying two mugs of tea and a plate of biscuits. 'I've cleaned up the kitchen, the dishwasher's doing its job, and Rose has gone to have a little nap after all that excitement. Don't look so frazzled. Whatever Diana wants, it's not the end of the world.'

She made herself smile. No, of course it wasn't. But it was bad enough. She would have to tell him what Diana had threatened to do. But perhaps not tonight. Sunday was his day off and what a day it had been so far!

Anyway, judging by past behaviour, when she did tell him, he would only smile and say he trusted her to repel boarders. Faced with this latest threat of invasion, Ellie had to admit she cringed.

And what about the puzzle Ursula had set her?

'I'll be with you in a minute.' They stored all old newspapers in a green plastic box for recycling, which was collected once a week by the council. Ellie usually remembered to pick up the newspapers from where Thomas had left them, but sometimes they lay unregarded under chairs and in the magazine rack for a couple of weeks until she had a good clear-out.

Ursula had spoken of an incident at a party in the new year, in which a man had died. If it had been local, it would have been reported in the local Gazette. Sometimes the pages of the Gazette were used to wrap bones and other food waste before they were put in the recycling box. Where to look first? There was a cache of Gazette papers on top of the fridge in the kitchen. She leafed through them. No. No mention of an accidental death in the last few weeks.

There was one issue missing; the one for the second Friday in the new year. Of course, that particular issue might already have been recycled. Ellie thought she might have seen a single copy somewhere ... yes, it had drifted into Rose's sitting room. Rose was dozing again, cosily ensconced in her big, high-backed chair, propped up with cushions and smiling in her sleep. Ellie retrieved the paper and made her way quietly back to the kitchen. She spread the paper out on the table.

There it was. 'Tragedy at Top Venue.' She scanned the paragraph. Not much information. A student called Lloyd had drunk too much at the Grand Opening of the stunning new block of flats on the North Circular called Prior's Place and fallen from the top floor. Yes, yes ... terrible accident, parents stricken. Presumably this was the death the girl had been referring to. Why had Ursula thought it was murder? There was no picture of the deceased, but there was one of the building concerned. Something futuristic with penthouse balconies.

She scissored out the paragraph, thinking she'd come across a mention of the building somewhere else recently. It would come to her in due course. It looked expensive. Flats for those with a fortune to spare, but none for the deserving poor.

She tucked the cutting between the glass doors of the spice cabinet, along with a card for a dentist's appointment and a programme for local events they might like to see. She sighed, thinking of everything she'd have to do before she could get her old house handed over to Diana and, hopefully, get her daughter off her back.

Thomas called out from the sitting room. 'Hurry up. Your tea's getting cold.'

He'd pulled forward the little table that stood

in front of their two big chairs, and was working his way through his pile of biscuits. 'These aren't half bad. Have one?'

He really ought to go on a diet. She ought to as well, for her skirts had begun to feel a trifle too snug since Christmas. She'd think about that tomorrow. 'We won't need any supper after this. What did you do with little Frank in the attics?'

'I spotted an old rocking horse up there when I was putting the Christmas decorations away. It lacks a mane and tail, but I thought he might like it, and he did. I'll get it restored for him, if you think it's a good idea.'

She nodded, smiling, wondering which child it had been bought for in the house's long history. For Frank, her first husband, perhaps? He'd been brought up by his aunt Drusilla in this house, but he'd never mentioned having a rocking horse. Perhaps it had been Drusilla's? Ellie shook her head. She couldn't imagine Miss Quicke riding a rocking horse. Not her style. If it had been an abacus? Maybe.

'Blissful Sunday,' said Thomas, stretching arms and legs. 'No emails. No visits to make. No phone calls. Time apart.' He reached across to pat her hand. 'A nice quiet evening with you. What more could a man ask?'

This from a man who'd gone out into the cold that morning to take a service for a friend, and to save a soul. Possibly Ursula didn't think of herself as having a soul, since she didn't really believe in God. Well, he'd rescued a maiden in distress. At least, Ellie presumed Ursula was a maiden. She was certainly in distress. One didn't talk about maidenhood any more, did one?

She relaxed, washing down her third biscuit with her cuppa. She told herself, I Must Not Worry. It May Never Happen.

Thomas was fidgeting. She wasn't quite sure why, but she'd noticed that just occasionally he had bouts of fidgeting, even sometimes of pacing around the ground floor as if looking for something. Maybe he needed more exercise? Perhaps that was it. But she wouldn't encourage him to go out for a long walk in this weather. Now he said, 'Is there anything on the telly, or do you want to tell me about it?'

So she told him Ursula's story as far as she understood it. 'One accidental death which might be a murder, one broken engagement, one disappearance. The papers didn't say it was murder; they said it was an accident. It happened at the new block of flats on the North Circular, Prior's Place. It seems to ring a bell.'

'Isn't that something your cousin Roy got involved in?'

Of course. Roy was a talented, hard-working architect with a loving younger wife, a baby girl on whom he doted, and absolutely no sense where money was concerned. His unmarried mother, Miss Quicke, had been unable to keep the boy when he was born, and had given him up for adoption. Roy had only traced her a couple of years ago, since when she'd helped

37

finance him in one or two projects, while steering him away from others which she considered doubtful.

Once she died, Roy had turned to Ellie for funds to put into the development at Prior's Place. The project had looked all right on paper, but Miss Quicke hadn't liked it, so Ellie hadn't been easy in her mind about it either, and had also ended up refusing to help him.

She took the last biscuit, and sighed. 'Roy and money do not make a perfect marriage. And talking of marriage, I seem to have mislaid the ring which Ursula wanted me to return to her boyfriend. At least, I think he was her boyfriend. You haven't seen it?'

His mind was on other things. 'I suppose I could ask the vicar if he knew the lad who died?'

Ellie felt a sneeze coming on. She tried to remember the name of the boy the ring was to be returned to. Daniel something? She could, she supposed, contact him and confess that she'd lost the ring which Ursula had given her. Or she could do nothing. Presumably he wasn't expecting it? Or was he? She sneezed. Thomas handed her a box of tissues. She used one, thinking she really preferred cotton hankies which were kinder to her nose.

A spot of prayer was in order, perhaps. A trivial matter. She really didn't want to bother Himself with it. On the other hand, remembering the other things the girl had said: a murder, a broken engagement, a disappearance? All very odd. Probably Ursula had been exaggerating as the young tended to do. Ellie told herself that she hadn't exactly promised the girl that she'd do anything for her.

But all the same ... *Well, dear Father, how about it? If the girl wasn't making it all up – which she could have been doing – but ... well, you do see what I mean, don't you? I haven't a clue how to ...* Oh dear, another sneeze was coming on.

She dived into her pocket for a hankie and felt something round and smooth in one corner. The ring.

She took it out and looked at it. Thomas was smiling, content. Midge, their marauding ginger tom, had arrived from nowhere and was balanced on Thomas's ample frontage. Where had Midge been all day? He hadn't touched the bowl of food she'd left for him in the kitchen, but he looked well pleased with life. As did Thomas.

'All right, dear heart?'

She smiled and nodded, slipping the ring on to her little finger. She would return it tomorrow.

'Can I speak to Ursula?' A man's voice. Youngish. Anxious.

A woman replied. Middle-aged. Brisk. 'Is that Daniel? I'm afraid she's already gone back to uni. Didn't she tell you she was going back early?'

'No, she didn't. I've tried to get her on her

mobile, but can't get through.'

'She dropped her mobile and broke it, clumsy girl. I told her to reverse the charges when she rings home, till she gets herself another. I expect she'll let you have her new number when she gets it.'

Silence. 'Well, when you speak to her, will you tell her I called?'

THREE

Monday morning
The weather wasn't any better the next day. A hard frost had whitened pools of slush in the roads. On the bright side, both Ellie and Thomas had had their first good night's sleep since they went down with the cold.

Drawing curtains and tidying rooms, Ellie considered the day ahead. Gone were the days when she'd been a housewife with time at her disposal to spend on friends, family and neighbourhood matters. Now she was a woman of property and this meant weekly meetings to oversee the small empire of housing-to-let which her aunt her left her, and monthly meetings to service the trusts into which she'd put most of her inheritance. The house more or less paid for itself, as Thomas's magazine paid rent for his workspace, as did the Trust for hers.

First on the list was to check that the dining room radiators were working; one of them produced an air bubble occasionally, which made the room too cold to hold meetings in it. Miss Quicke had used this room as an office and it still seemed to resonate with her dry wit and incisive speech.

In fact, the sitting room also seemed to hold echoes of the older woman's presence. Sometimes Ellie thought that if she turned round quickly enough she'd catch sight of her aunt, gnarled hands on top of her stick, sitting by the fire ... or with two fingers rapidly emailing someone in the financial world in which she'd swum to such good effect for so many years.

The dining room radiators seemed to be behaving today, but Ellie was happy to recall that this was not a day for meetings. Her sneezes seemed to be abating, and she thought she might be feeling strong enough to tackle the tasks Ursula had set her. Or one of them.

Don't think about Diana, and what she might be up to.

No, on consideration, it was best to face it. If it were just her own peace and quiet that was threatened, she could deal with it, but Diana's threats – and they were threats, no mistake – also involved Thomas.

She looked at her watch. In a minute Thomas would be off to deal with emails and post and the problems involved in editing his magazine with only intermittent help from a young geek on a gap year. Rose was up and about today, which was good. Rose was insisting on clearing the kitchen. And if it had to be done all over again later, then so be it.

Ellie caught up with Thomas as he was about to disappear into what had once been the morning room and was now his study. 'Thomas, I hate to worry you, but Diana's got Rose's front door keys. I asked her to give them back to me, and she did at first but then took them away with her. She's strapped for cash, wants me to hand over my old house to her straight away so that she can sell her flat. She's threatening to move in here if she doesn't get her own way.'

Thomas stroked his beard, stone-faced. 'It's your house.'

'No, it's ours. I know it sounds hard-hearted, but I really don't want her moving in here. I think, if you agree, that I should get the locks changed.'

He went to poke and prod at the heavy bolts on the front door. 'Suppose we put the bolts across? Hm, they haven't been used for decades. Suppose I get the oil can out before I start work, eh? It might take a couple of days to get a locksmith round.'

'Bless you, yes.'

'Cheer up. It may never happen.'

Well, he wasn't as well acquainted with what Diana could do as Ellie was. Diana had tried to move in on her before, at the old house. Ellie tried to smile, to pretend that she believed him. Not a good effort.

Thomas wiggled the bolts but neither would

42

move. 'My tool kit's in the cupboard in the downstairs cloakroom, isn't it? You'll have to come and go via the kitchen if I can get the bolts across, so remember to take the back door key with you if you go out.'

A hug and a kiss, and he went for the oil can while she made for the telephone in her own study.

First, she must ring Stewart. Stewart had been a highly satisfactory manager of properties to let for Miss Quicke, and Ellie had reappointed him in that job after her death. The offices for the Trust itself, and for the property management company run by Stewart, were located in a big house not far away. In addition to his other duties, Stewart was overseeing the restoration of Ellie's fire-damaged house in his usual careful way. He would hate to be hustled into doing a quick fix-it, especially if it would be to Diana's advantage ... because Stewart was Diana's ex-husband and the father of little Frank. He was now happily remarried and had sired another couple of children since the divorce but still, there was need for tact.

Did Ellie feel like being tactful today? No, not really. But needs must. The weekly meeting to discuss her properties wasn't due for a couple of days, but this couldn't wait. She decided it would be best to tell Stewart everything, and leave it to him to work out what to do. She got him on his mobile and explained what was happening. He let silence grow and then sighed. 'Yes, I understand. Don't you worry about it.

I'll drop round there this morning, see what still needs to be done and get back to you.'

Greatly relieved, she tried the next on her list. Yes, the locksmith could fit her in on the morrow. She conveyed this information to Thomas who, mission accomplished re the front door bolts, was just disappearing into the morning room. He waved his hand, his mind already on his work. Thomas would sometimes emerge for a coffee and a biscuit at eleven, but might work through till lunch. If he had no meetings planned, he'd probably take himself off for a stiff walk round the block, make himself a sandwich for lunch or some home-made soup – he loved Rose's leek and potato soup, but was quite happy to make it for himself – and then work through till supper-time.

Ellie looked at her calendar. She had no business meetings fixed for that day, but had promised to call in on Felicity, Roy's wife, with a recipe that Rose had given her some time ago and, of course, to play with their delightful baby, who was soon to be christened at their old church. How time flew! And maybe she could find out if Roy had had any involvement with the new block of flats on the North Circular at the same time? She rather hoped not but, knowing Roy ... she sighed and shook her head.

So now to Ursula's little problem. Ellie found a plastic envelope in her desk and put the ring into it, so it wouldn't get lost. She consulted the phone book, and rang the only Collins in Park Gardens. She spoke to a male voice, enquired if she were speaking to one Daniel Collins and, on receiving an affirmative, asked if she might call as she had something for him from Ursula. Daniel sounded uncertain but agreed, so Ellie decided to go there straight away.

The Collins family lived in a red-brick Edwardian terraced house, three storeys high, semi-detached but spacious. Tiled pathway, paved-over front garden with planters spilling over with ivies and polyanthus plants. So far so good, but there was a suggestion that the paintwork might need attention soon. A couple of tiles were missing from the path. A suspicion of seediness?

The door was opened by a dark-haired young man who looked as if he might work out. Standard broad-shouldered, nice-looking young college student, late teens or early twenties. An air of anxiety?

'Ellie Quicke. I rang earlier. Are you Daniel?'

'Who is it?' A husky woman's voice from the depths of the house.

'It's all right, Mum. Someone for me.'

'Oh?' The voice was coming nearer.

Daniel opened a door off the hall and ushered Ellie inside before the woman could reach them.

They were in what had once, perhaps, been a rather grand sitting room complete with ceiling rose, cornices and picture rails. It was now a student bedsitter with a divan bed doubling as a couch in one corner, bamboo blinds at the big bay window, stripped pine floor, and lots of

45

shelving which looked none too secure.

Sports equipment spilled out of a huge Edwardian wardrobe with four doors on it; a dressing-room in itself. A folding chair sat before an improvised desk, on which were piles of papers and books around a laptop. There were two armchairs, mismatched but comfortable, and a small telly on the mantelpiece of a blocked-up fireplace. Travel posters on the walls.

Holiday snaps of the girl Ursula had been Blu-tacked on to the wall behind the desk, together with some group photos: young people with their arms round one another in the garden of a pub, sitting on a beach in the sun, dressed up for a wedding. In two of these the girls were wearing evening dress, the men good casual wear. Bottles on the table, paper hats on their heads. A Christmas celebration?

Ellie seated herself, unasked.

The boy fidgeted, finally subsided into the other big chair but didn't relax. His hands were big, clean. He rolled his shoulders, trying to ease tension. 'I don't know you, do I? How did Ursula come to...?' He rubbed the back of his neck. Quality clothes. Short-sleeved blue and white checked sports shirt, pullover, grey trousers and shoes. A good haircut, traditional not trendy. 'Traditional but not trendy' probably summed him up. Not a great brain but a nice lad, sports enthusiast. PE teacher?

'I've been trying to contact Ursula for days. Her mother says her mobile's out of action. She gave you a message for me?'

Ellie had meant to tell him exactly what had happened but now, confronted by his uneasiness, she found herself probing for information.

'Ursula spoke of a broken engagement. With you?'

His eyelids contracted. A good-looking lad, perhaps not all that imaginative. He made an inarticulate sound, which might have been agreement.

'Long-standing?' Ellie made her voice soft.

He nodded once, violently. 'We've,' he coughed, cleared his throat. 'We were at school together. Always knew. It didn't matter that we were at different universities. I'm doing my teacher training here in London. It made no difference. She's home most weekends. I just don't...' His voice died away. He got up and went to look at the photos on the wall. For reassurance? 'I can't believe it.'

He'd not asked her why Ursula had broken off the engagement, which meant that he knew. 'Tell me about it.' Again, her softest voice.

This time it didn't work. He took a deep breath, focused on Ellie. 'What did she say? When did you see her?'

'Yesterday. She had lunch with me and my husband.'

'You said she gave you something for me? A letter?'

'A ring.' Ellie fished it out and tried to hand it to him. He stared at it as if it would bite him. She got up and put it on his desk, still in its plastic envelope.

He hit the wall with his fist. Once, twice. Ellie remembered that kings used to kill a messenger who brought bad news. But no, he was a well-brought-up lad and wasn't going to take out his anger on her. He swept papers and books off his desk, wrenched photos from the wall. Tore them across. Once, twice. And again. Threw the pieces in the air.

He picked up the ring and looked at it, made as if to throw it across the room, but instead held it out to Ellie with a hand that shook. 'Give it back to her. I don't want it.' His breathing was erratic. Was he going to cry?

Ellie tried to damp down the emotional tension. 'If she broke it off, then it's yours to keep.'

Silence. He shook his head. Went on shaking it. 'She shouldn't have taken it that way. I told her. We all told her.'

'Did she break it off because of the murder?'

'What?' He considered the word 'murder' and didn't like it. His chin went up and he made an effort to control himself. 'There was no murder.' His body language spoke of agitation, even of distress, giving the lie to what he'd said. His fists swung backwards and forwards. He looked like a bull about to charge. 'I've got to get out of here. I need ... I can't...' He picked up a jacket from a chair and crashed open the door, taking one step into the hall before stopping short. He said, 'Not now, Mum. I'm going out!'

He hurtled down the hall, leaving Ellie holding the ring. The front door slammed so hard it made her wince.

A woman appeared in the doorway, looking after him. 'What's got into him?' A woman in her fifties, perhaps? Pink velveteen jogging suit and white trainers, dyed ginger hair, a bright lipstick. She spotted Ellie. 'Who are you?'

Ellie opened her mouth to introduce herself, but the woman stopped her. 'Don't tell me. I've seen you before somewhere. Ah. Got it. Golf Club.'

Ellie didn't belong to the Golf Club any more. 'Ellie Quicke. I'm afraid—'

'I met you at some "do" at the Golf Club when my husband was still around. You do good works, I believe. One of our unsung heroines. You came to see Daniel? I'm afraid he's rather moody at the moment.' She gestured to the back of the hall. 'I'm having a cuppa. Want one?'

'Well, I ... all right. Yes. Thanks.' Ellie followed Mrs Collins down the hall and into a sunroom which had been tacked on to the back of the house. Here there were the same signs of a decline in fortunes; the extension had been well planned and built, but the cushions on the bamboo three piece suite were showing wear and tear. A pine table was covered with the impedimenta of life: newspapers, magazines, a small telly, a basket of washing ready to be ironed. Beside it, an ironing board, up and ready for use. A plastic-coated airer was draped

49

with more newly-washed winter wear, mostly men's. A rubber plant showed more dead leaves than live ones, but the telly was tuned to a perky cartoon and everything smelled clean. An open door led on to a galley-style kitchen, into which the woman disappeared.

'Forgive the mess. I more or less live in this room. Take a seat, if you can find one. Move the newspapers if they're in the way. Instant do you? Milk and sugar?'

'Lovely. Thanks.'

From above came the thump, thump, thump, of a stereo playing music with too much bass. Someone else in the house?

Two large mugs of instant coffee appeared and the woman seated herself, hands on knees and knees well apart, four square. Determined. 'So, what did you want with my son, and why did he take off like a bat out of hell, eh?'

'I met a girl called Ursula yesterday. She spoke of a disappearance, and a broken engagement.' No need to mention the word 'murder' as yet.

'Ursula,' said Mrs Collins, bright eyes fixed on Ellie, 'is Daniel's fiancée. They're getting married as soon as they're both through university.'

Ellie placed Ursula's ring on the table. 'She asked me to give this back to him.'

Mrs Collins said, 'What...?' without sound. She sat still, eyes and mouth open for what seemed a long time to Ellie. In shock.

At last Mrs Collins took a deep breath, blinked. 'He might have told me. I did wonder if everything was all right between them over the holidays but ... excuse me.' She took her mug off into the kitchen.

Ellie heard the glug and chink of a bottle. A top-up of brandy? Mrs Collins didn't offer any to Ellie but returned, heavily sighing, gulping down the coffee-plus.

Ellie tried to put her at ease. 'It's always difficult, youngsters tying themselves up before they're twenty.'

'I told him, wait a while. Lots of good fish. But he wouldn't listen; no, not he! Though I must say I couldn't have wished for a better in many ways. He's known her since secondary school. No money in that family, but that's not everything, as I should know if anyone should. She kept him out of the silly scrapes his crowd were always getting into. I always knew who'd wear the trousers.'

Ellie was diffident. 'Does that matter, really?'

'No, I suppose not.' She drank deep of her coffee and whatever. 'I suppose I ought to be thankful it's lasted this long. Her having the brains and him being brawn, if you see what I mean, though it's not a bad recipe for living if they're both OK about it. And you're right, it doesn't matter which of them handles the money, does it? So long as they're both happy about the spending of it. Meaning no disrespect, for he's as good a boy as you could find in this day and age.'

Ellie nodded encouragement.

'I wonder why she's broken it off now, though sooner now than later, I suppose. Give him a chance to look around, find someone more ... less...'

'Find a dumb blonde?'

Ellie thought she'd probably gone too far but Mrs Collins laughed, if a shade ruefully. 'Call me Gloria. Aerobics teacher, till the hip went. Husband's scarpered, money's short, I take in students to make ends meet and thankful that I've got a big enough house to do it, right?'

Ellie agreed, wincing at the thought of the unused upper storey at her own house. Was she right to refuse Diana houseroom there? Oh dear, but it would be torture. No peace and quiet.

Gloria drained her mug. 'Thing is, Dan may not be the sharpest knife in the drawer but he's a faithful soul, never looked at anyone else. I could see he was worried about something this last month or so, but I thought it was Ursula going off to the States for the holidays, and Lloyd getting himself killed. And of course it was the first Christmas Dan's father's not been here. Dan moped the whole time, bit my nose off ... you know how it is with teenagers, would not settle to anything. I thought everything would be all right when she got back.

'He tore out to Heathrow Airport to meet her, and she came round to give me a present she'd bought me in New York. After that we saw neither hide nor hair of her, and his temper went from bad to worse. I thought maybe she'd

52

found someone else, had her eyes opened by the talent over there. Nice girl, but I've no illusions about my son because he's no high-flyer, and she ... yes, she is. Perhaps in a way I'm relieved, if you see what I mean.'

Ellie saw.

'Kids. Who'd have them, eh?'

Ellie agreed with her. 'How many have you...?'

'Three. Girl, married. A bit quick with the sprogs; two so far in two years. Son-in-law's all right. Working for the council. Then Dan. Then my youngest – he's the one who's playing his music too loud upstairs. He's still at school, hoping for university. Wants to do medicine; not a doctor. Physio. Do you know anyone who would like to rent a room? I've a vacancy now, and could do with the rent.'

'I'll ask around. Ursula told me someone – a friend? – had died early in the new year. You knew the lad?'

'To be honest, I was really surprised when I heard. Disappointed too. I didn't think he was much of a drinker and certainly not into drugs. But maybe ... what do I know, as Dan says? End of term party, everyone having a ball, letting their hair down. Kids!'

'Do you mean ... did he lodge here?'

'Back room, top floor. Kept it tidy and kept the noise down, unlike most. He played music all right, but not the bang bang junkety sort, if you know what I mean. I'll miss him, tell the truth. Used to make me laugh; always paid his rent on time. Not like some of the others, puking up all over the place and expecting me to clean up after them. His parents were that shocked. Elderly, Welsh Baptist or Methodist, church goers, anyway. He was their bright hope. They couldn't believe their boy was just like the rest of them, but I suppose he only did what everyone else was doing.' She sighed heavily. 'Want to see his room? Then if you know of someone who might like it...?'

'I'd love to.'

Mrs Collins picked up a bunch of keys from the muddle on her table, and led the way up carpeted stairs to the first floor, and then up an uncarpeted flight to the attic rooms. It was a big house. Five doors confronted them on the top landing. Two were half open, one leading to a small kitchen, and the other to a bathroom. The third and fourth – which would overlook the road – had posters and stickers all over them. One sported a Halloween mask hanging from a nail. The fourth door was unmarked, and locked.

'Have to keep the doors locked or they pinch stuff from one another, and move their friends in overnight,' said Mrs Collins. 'If they want to bring a friend in for a night, they can pay me double rent, right?'

The room that had been Lloyd's was bright and airy, clean and tidy. The furnishings were reasonably new, and the furniture mismatched but serviceable. The window looked out over back gardens below. There was no sign of

54

anything belonging to the previous occupant, except for an intangible something that Ellie could only describe as 'serenity'. She was familiar with this, because it always hung around the places in which Thomas had been praying. Not everyone would have noticed it, but she knew straight away.

'Was Lloyd a Christian?'

'Yeah, yeah. Went to church, joined some sort of fellowship, but not a peep out of them after he died. I had to pack up all his stuff for his parents to collect when they came up for the cremation. I thought they'd want to take him back home to bury him, but they said they were too ashamed. I said no one needed to know he'd got into a drunken fight over a girl that caused him to go overboard, but they didn't see it that way. If he'd been my lad, I'd have stood by him, I can tell you that for nothing.'

'Sad,' murmured Ellie. 'He was a student, too?'

'Teacher training like my Dan, but bright with it. Maths was his subject and he could twist numbers every which way. When I got in a tangle with my bills, he'd help me sort them out. And he never brought a girl home with him, not once.'

'Thank you for showing me. If I hear of anyone...'

'You do that.' Mrs Collins relocked the door and led the way down to the ground floor. The door to Dan's room was still open. He hadn't returned yet, and he hadn't locked it behind him. Mrs Collins said 'Tck!' and sought for the right key to lock the door with, but Ellie was quicker. She slipped into the room to pick up some of the torn-up photos on the floor.

'Is this Lloyd?' she asked, holding up a picture of Ursula, with half of her face missing. She was snuggling up to a little dark-haired girl, while an attractive blond man grinned at the camera over their two heads.

'Hm? What's he torn his photos up for? Look at the mess he's made. No, that's not Lloyd. He's got a mop of dark hair, looks very Welsh if you know what I mean. That's Anthony. Or maybe it's his brother, whose name I always forget. They're not twins but do look alike.'

Intrigued, Mrs Collins began to pick up the pieces of photo herself. 'Now, here's Lloyd in the background, behind Ursula and Dan. That's Mia Prior, of course. The little dark girl, wonderful eyes, hasn't she? She's their stepsister, daughter of the current Mrs Prior by her first husband. The boys are from his first wife, who's gone to live in Spain with her personal trainer, if you believe the gossip. And yes, there's Timothy Long-legs. Well, that's what they called him, some of the time. Dumbo, otherwise. I don't know why. Nice lad. Perfectly all right, not dumb at all.'

'Here's Dan again,' said Ellie, also collecting scraps. 'And this one ... is this the one you called Anthony again? Or his brother? They look alike, don't they? Are they at teacher training college as well?'

Mrs Collins snorted. 'Chance would be a fine thing. There's money in that family. Silver spoon, know what I mean? What a shame; here's a lovely picture of Dan but his left arm's missing. I think that was taken the day they all went on the river last summer. Hired a boat and went up past Henley, all got a bit high, drank too much, someone fell overboard, can't remember who now, but no harm done, except they all came back red as lobsters from sunburn. Why has he torn them all up?'

'I expect they remind him of happier times. How did Dan and Ursula come to know this Anthony and Timothy, if they're so well off, and he isn't?'

'School. My husband that was, he paid for the boys to go to a private school at first, which is where Dan met up with the Priors. But then money got tight and our boys had to go to the nearest state school instead, which wasn't bad at all, let me tell you. That's where Dan met Ursula. Anthony and his lot, they liked having Dan and Ursula around, and some of my other lads who lodge here as well. My husband that was used to say the private school gave the lads an important start in life, because it was all about who you knew. Maybe he was right.' Mrs Collins blinked. 'It didn't do Lloyd much good though, did it?'

'Why don't you keep that good picture of Dan? You could have it enlarged, put it in a frame?'

Mrs Collins sniffed, but stowed the picture

away.

Ellie said, 'Do you think Dan will want to keep these pieces? Maybe Ursula would like them to remind her, eventually.'

'Take them if you like. And tell her from me ... no, don't bother. I wouldn't know what to say. Good luck, perhaps? I suppose I may see her about town some time. She usually comes back for weekends. I only hope my son knows what he's doing, letting her go like that.'

'I'll stick them together and take some copies so if you want one, just give me a ring and I'll pop one in the post to you.' She tore a page out of the back of her diary, and wrote down her home phone number for Mrs Collins. 'By the way, what's Ursula's surname, and can you give me her address? Dan said to return the ring to her. Unless you'd like to?'

'Ursula Belton. It might be best if you did it. She and her mother live in one of those ground floor flats along the Avenue. I'm not sure of the number, but it's in the first block of flats that you come to on the left after the library.'

'Anthony, is that you? Dan here. Ursula's sent me back my ring!'

'Good riddance. I reckon she's been looking for an opportunity to dump you for ages. Stuffed-up chick, who did she think she was, anyway? You're well rid of her.'

'I don't see it that way.'

'Get over it. She never let you have it, did she, little Miss Frigidaire? Well, now you're free to

find out what it's all about. And once you've experienced what a real woman is like, you'll wonder why you ever stuck with her so long.'

'I never thought she'd take it so hard. What did you say to her, when she went to see you?'

'What we'd agreed.'

'She was different, after that. So angry! I've never seen her so angry, not in all the years we've known one another. And then she broke down and cried and wanted me to help her find Mia and of course I told her what you said, and she said that was rubbish, and she went on and on at me and said I had to choose, which was ridiculous as I told her, so I rang off. And the next day when I tried to phone her—'

'Her mobile got broken.'

'She wouldn't answer the landline and when I went round there, she wouldn't come to the door. That went on all week and now she's gone back to Portsmouth and sent her ring back and I feel like getting drunk.'

'Why not? Come round this evening and we'll sink a few.'

'I suppose I might. What else is there to do?'

FOUR

Ellie put Ursula's ring in her coin purse for safe keeping and made her way across the park to the house that her architect cousin Roy had revamped for his wife Felicity and their baby Mel.

The weather wasn't improving, but Ellie stopped on the way to buy some bits and pieces for supper. Her new grey skirt was getting decidedly tight around the middle, and as for Thomas, he'd always had an ample frontage, and the sooner he went on a diet the better. It was no good pretending that one could lose weight without dieting, but Thomas wouldn't eat a plain salad without a lot of dressing on it, so she must make a salad dish appetizing with red, yellow and green peppers, chicory, and tiny red tomatoes to add to the usual lettuce and cucumber. He might well enjoy that with some good balsamic vinegar over all.

He'd probably want a good solid soup, beforehand. He really ought to have a non-fattening soup made without potatoes or cornflour, but the weather was awful and he must have something starchy to keep him going. She found a soya ice cream that would do for afters; tasty but not fattening.

It started to rain again as she reached Felicity's. She'd done more walking than usual, which might be good for her but was somewhat tiring, so she looked forward to a good sit-down and perhaps a bite of lunch.

Only, Felicity was not alone. She had recently made friends with Caroline Topping, a neighbour who'd also come late to childbearing, and they often popped into one another's houses for a coffee. Felicity, ripely blonde with a figure that was filling out in response to a happy marriage and her own love of cooking, let Ellie in while jiggling little Mel in her arms.

'Come on in. What filthy weather. I'd forgotten you were coming, but I've just made a mushroom risotto that can easily do for three. You know Caroline, don't you?'

Ellie did. She blew her nose. Coming in from the cold always started her sneezing. Caroline's toddler held up his arms for Ellie to pick him up, which she did with only the slightest of groans. Her back was twinging again. This cold weather...

A chaotic lunchtime passed with the three women fielding food and toddlers, spooning in food here, supplying drink, mopping faces and hands, and managing to eat a few mouthfuls themselves between whiles. Ellie enjoyed it, but she had to admit it was blissful when Caroline took Duncan away and Mel was settled down for her afternoon nap. Felicity wiped down surfaces while Ellie stacked the dishwasher.

61

Felicity sighed. 'It's so dark. I hate January.'

Ellie said, 'Buy some daffodils, or one of those sun-effect lamps. Don't you want a rest when Mel's asleep? It was the only way I could make both ends of the day meet when Diana was young.'

'I would normally, but I wanted to talk to you before Roy gets home. It's a something and a nothing. Probably a nothing.' She made some coffee and sat at the table, stirring the coffee in her cup but not adding any sugar. 'What do you think about jinxes, Ellie?'

Ellie tried not to smile, because Felicity was looking so serious. 'What sort?'

'Prior's Place.'

Ellie refrained from comment. She'd a bad feeling about it too. 'Roy got involved, financially?'

'The building was designed by a much bigger practice, but Roy designed the health centre on the ground floor and basement. It's really striking, very upmarket, designed to appeal to people with lots of money. I know Miss Quicke advised Roy against putting money into it and you did, too, but—'

'He went and did it, anyway?'

Felicity nodded. Was she going to cry? 'He wants to, and I can't talk sense into him.'

'Your own money's safe?' Felicity had been left a wealthy woman when her first, extremely unpleasant, husband had died, and her affairs were now managed by Kate, Ellie's neighbour at the old house. Kate was much younger than

Ellie, of course, but was something of a financial wizard and the age difference didn't seem
to matter.

Felicity said, 'Roy has made enquiries about
selling or mortgaging the block of flats that
Miss Quicke left him in her will, so that he can
buy into Prior's Place. I think he's mad! He
says the flats in Prior's Place will sell like hot
cakes and he'll be able to pay the mortgage off
in no time, but of course nothing is moving because of the recession. Also, a couple of people
who were going to buy into Prior's Place have
backed out at the last minute, and the gym's not
making a penny yet, and I have the most awful
feeling that it's going to be a white elephant and
Roy will lose his inheritance and everything
he's worked for.'

Ellie refrained, with difficulty, from saying
that in her opinion no bank should trust Roy
with a credit card for over fifty pounds. He was
a kind and generous man, a loving husband and
father and a talented architect, but in money
matters he had no sense of danger.

'It's like ... like they're cursed,' said Felicity,
in a rush. She blushed. 'Of course I know that's
nonsense, but when I think about that place, it's
like a dark cloud came down from the penthouse that night and it hasn't moved, hanging
over everything. I do totally understand why
people don't want anything to do with it.'

'You were at the Grand Opening when the
boy died?'

Felicity shuddered. 'All dolled up, four-inch

heels, wearing the latest fashion with a skirt well above my knees – which in this weather is stupid, but I did it because Roy wanted me to look nice and smile at all the important people who might want him to work on something else. So of course I did just that. By eleven o'clock most people had gone. I was tired and wanted to go home, because of getting up in the night with Mel. Only, Roy wanted to stay to the end, so of course we did. There was this horrible man who kept putting his arm around me and squeezing. But that's nothing, really, is it? I mean, not compared to...'

'No. Did you know the boy who died?'

'I saw his picture in the paper after, but there were quite a few young people, not waitresses but college students, friends of the young Priors, showing would-be clients around. Someone said – I think it was Caroline's husband, he works for the Town Hall you know, and it was nice to see a friendly face among all those important people – anyway, he said the young things were there as sucker bait, and I did see what he meant, because they were concentrating on the middle-aged and elderly people with money to spend.

'The party started off in the Health Club in the basement and the show flat just above it. Lots of important people, councillors, everyone. Speeches, you know. I got stuck with this man who ... I've told you about him already, haven't I? All I know is that after eleven, after the bigwigs had gone, someone said the young people had gone upstairs to continue the party in the penthouse suite. Apparently they were drinking heavily, things got out of hand and this lad went over.

'It had been such a good party, too, until that happened. I mean, the building is fabulous, and I can see why Roy thought it would be a good investment. Only now he's so determined to have his own way and won't see sense, saying what do I know about it because I've never had to handle big sums, and of course that's true because my first husband did it all, and now Kate. I think he's made verbal promises, maybe even signed something, and I believe he knows he's being stupid, but won't admit it.'

'Just like a man.'

'I asked Kate if she could help. She said she'd tried to steer some City money into the project ages ago, after Miss Quicke had said she wasn't interested in it, but she stopped when Roy told her he could fund it himself. She says it's un-likely Roy will get a mortgage on reasonable terms for his flats at present, and if he does try to sell them he's likely to lose on the deal.' She took a deep breath. 'You aren't bothered by my silly notions about a jinx, are you? So would you get your Trust to consider buying into Prior's Place, to keep things moving in the right direction?'

Ellie had seen this coming, and didn't like the sound of it. Her Trust fund was meant for chari-table purposes, not to bail out rash relatives. Besides, the other members of the Trust would never agree to such a scheme. 'What does Kate advise?'

'She says I can't raise enough to help Roy out at the moment without selling shares at a huge loss, and selling my shares would reduce my income drastically. I mean, I will if all else fails, but ... you see the problem?'

'Don't sell,' advised Ellie. 'Not yet, anyway. I'll have a word with Kate and with the other members of the Trust to see what can be done, but I can't promise anything.'

'Bless you. If only that young man hadn't thought he could fly! I'm sure the flats would be selling if he hadn't.'

Ellie asked Felicity to ring for a cab for her. It was still raining, she had shopping bags to carry, and it was just that bit further to her 'old' house, than to the 'new'. Or rather, her own 'old' house – the one in which she and her first husband had lived for so many years – had been built in the 1920s, long after the Edwardian grandeur of the Quicke family house in which she was now living, but the words 'new' and 'old' didn't always mean exactly what you intended to say, did they?

She was grateful that at least Felicity owned her own house outright, which was a blessing in view of Roy's imprudent financial dealings. Theirs had been a love match and remained one. The marriage was solid, and it was only Roy's flights of fancy that cast an uncertain glow over their future. How could Roy's finances be saved? And how could he be persuaded never to risk his capital again in future?

Miss Quicke had managed to keep him on an even keel by backing one or two of his enterprises with her own money, and refusing to consider others. At her death he'd been left without a guiding hand, and look at the result! It was a puzzle, and Ellie had no idea how to solve it.

Well, there was one other little job she could manage before she went home. When her cab came, she asked the driver to take the road past the library at the end of the Avenue, and slow down when they came to the first low block of flats. Had Mrs Collins described Ursula's flat correctly? The sooner Ellie got rid of the ring, the better. She asked the driver to wait while she stumbled through the rain to the first of the communal doors, and checked the names on the intercom system. Yes, there was the name Belton. She rang the bell but there was no reply. Mrs Belton must be out, at work, shopping, whatever. She was on the point of returning to the cab when a disembodied, rather hoarse, voice said, 'Yes?'

'Mrs Belton? My name's Ellie Quicke. Would it be possible for you to spare me a minute? I have something your daughter left with me.'

'My daughter's not here.'

'No, I realize that.'

'Oh, very well.' The door latch clicked open.

'Just a minute. Got to get my bags from the minicab.' Ellie put her handbag down to stop the door closing and went back to the cab to fetch her shopping. Since she'd never learned to drive, she used the minicab agency regularly, and kept a monthly account with the firm. With some difficulty she hauled her shopping bags out of the cab and through the front door into the foyer.

A tall, well-built woman held the first door on the left open for Ellie, smothering a cough in a man-sized tissue. At the moment her hair – blonde going grey – was lifeless, but it had been recently well-cut and tinted. Ellie recognized the drawn, greyish look of the skin, the lack of make-up, the reddened nose. Clearly Mrs Belton was yet another victim of the prevalent feverish cold. The downturned mouth might also be a result of the cold, or it might be a permanent indication of Mrs Belton's attitude to life.

Ellie was ushered through a tiny hall into a square, all-purpose living room. Neat and tidy, the furnishings were a muted symphony of creams and greens. The furniture was not new but pleasantly functional, with magazines and papers neatly aligned on a coffee table. One or two bits of pewter, some Bristol blue glass, a bowl of daffodils, a couple of photographs of a young Ursula in silver frames. Nothing outstanding, except for two large pictures on the walls – or rather, one collage in blues and greens of an underwater scene, and a portrait of her hostess in pastels. Both showed considerable talent.

'Ursula's?' Ellie peered at both. Was she beginning to need glasses, or was the daylight fading already?

'Do be careful.' There was a snap in her voice. 'One of your shopping bags is about to split.'

'Oh dear.' Ellie let them down on to the floor. 'I am so stupid. I came out without thinking about shopping, and then, as one does...'

The woman smothered another cough and produced a stout plastic bag from the next room along, which must be the kitchen. 'Take this.'

Ellie took stock of her hostess as she transferred her shopping to a stronger bag. Mrs Belton was a different type from Mrs Collins. Also fifty plus but looking younger. Better educated. A slightly self-pitying approach to life? None of Ursula's bright-eyed, manipulative intelligence, but no fool either.

'Thank you,' said Ellie.

Mrs Belton didn't offer refreshments but let herself down on to a chair, indicating that Ellie do so too. 'I've seen you before, haven't I? At church fêtes? Someone said you'd given a local Holiday Club money for a children's outing. Didn't you marry our last vicar, the one who's just left?'

'That's so. Your daughter didn't mention that we met yesterday?'

Mrs Belton shook her head. The downturn of her mouth appeared to be a fixture. 'She went back to university early yesterday, leaving me barely on my feet and hardly able to fend for

69

myself. Not that I'm complaining, you understand.'

She was complaining, of course. Ellie sought for a tissue and blew her nose.

Mrs Belton said, 'You have something of hers? You're lucky to find me at home. I should have been at work today, but I've been laid out with flu.'

'It takes it out of you, doesn't it?'

The woman bridled with importance. 'I'm a speech therapist. Mustn't risk passing on germs.'

Ellie blew her nose again. 'Ursula didn't go straight back. My husband found her in St Mary's Church—'

'My daughter doesn't go to church. Hasn't been to church since she was in the Brownies.'

'I daresay, but let me tell you what happened.' Ellie told the story as she knew it. Mrs Belton sat very still, surprise and some disbelief showing. Even anger. When Ellie came to Ursula's saying, 'A broken engagement, a murder and a disappearance,' Mrs Belton shook her head. 'What absolute nonsense! What on earth's got into the girl?'

Ellie said, 'Let me tell you what happened when I visited Daniel today.' At the end of her recital, she took the ring in its plastic bag out of her coin purse and laid it on the coffee table in front of her.

Mrs Belton looked shocked. 'Oh no! Oh, how could she!' She stood up with a jerk, to twitch net curtains at the windows into more even folds. The nets were fresh and very white. The room overlooked the road. 'I can't believe it. They've been engaged for years. They bought that ring on a day outing to Brighton when they'd just left school. Ursula paid for it with some birthday money her grandfather had given her. Far too young, of course, but Daniel's a nice boy, and I was glad to see her settled. So ... why? After all these years?'

'I think something happened at a party they were both at in the new year.'

Mrs Belton stared. 'What do you mean, "something happened"?' Her eyes shifted and she frowned. 'You mean, the accident? Well, that happened after she left the party. She left early to fly off to America. I should explain that her father and I divorced when she was little; he went back to America and married again. They have two little boys, but he's always kept in touch. He paid for her ticket to go over there for a visit in the new year. Naturally she didn't want to leave me alone, but I'd got a bit of leave coming so went to stay with my sister in Leeds and we had a good time until I started to get a sore throat. I got back just before Ursula and went straight to bed with a temperature. This is my first full day up.'

She started to cough, fished out a lozenge and put it in her mouth. Ellie did the same, saying she'd had the cold, too, and it was a right terror wasn't it?

'Ursula never catches colds, she doesn't understand how much it pulls you down. She was very good, I suppose, doing the shopping and cooking, not that I fancied anything much. We didn't see Daniel at all, but I wouldn't have expected it. The young always avoid you when you're poorly, don't they?'

Mrs Belton pounded one fist against the other. 'I should have been the first to know. These young people, they get an idea into their heads and before you know where they are, they're committing themselves to a lifetime of loneliness.'

Like her, did she mean?

Mrs Belton straightened the already neat pile of papers on the coffee table. 'She ought to have told me, we could have talked it over. How she could have thrown over a nice boy like that! Daniel must be terribly upset. The trouble with Ursula is that she's always been so quick to pass judgment. Ten to one, she's broken it off over something quite trivial.'

So Ursula hadn't taken her mother fully into her confidence? Well, considering that her mother had been in bed ill, her decision seemed reasonable. 'You say Ursula wasn't there when the accident occurred?'

Mrs Belton sniffed. 'I told her, be sensible, you can go to parties any old time, but you have to be at the airport in the early hours of the morning, so why not give it a miss? But she wouldn't listen. Off she went to the party with her rucksack, wearing a minidress that showed far too much, but there you are, they will do it, won't they? Daniel took her to the airport, and she texted me when she got there, saying that her flight was on time.'

'When did you hear of Lloyd's death?'

'It was in the local papers, wasn't it? Ursula showed it to me last week, got really worked up about it. I had to tell her not to shout. My ears hurt! Honestly! These young people take things so hard, wind themselves up with conspiracy theories about people not drinking when he obviously had. I told her, when she's seen as much of the world as I have, she wouldn't get into such a state about a young man falling off the wagon. These things happen, big party, everyone at it. If he wasn't used to drink, then the vodka probably had more of an effect than it would have done otherwise.'

A note of grievance entered her voice. 'I thought she was settled with Daniel, that they'd be married and I'd be having the place to myself next summer. I had plans to ... I deserve a life of my own now, don't I?'

'Your daughter also talked about a disappearance. Do you know anything about that?'

A shrug. 'She had a friend called Mia. A little dark girl, almost gypsyish to look at. Tiny little thing. She was quite bright, studying some strange language, it may have been Japanese. Apparently she went off with some unsuitable man or other after the party, as girls do. Ursula wouldn't accept that, oh no! Tried to ring her, went round to see the family, but the girl's dropped out of sight. Youngsters...' She sighed. 'They never think that we worry about them. A shame, really. Mia might have talked some sense into her, instead of this.' She gestured to the ring.

'So Mia really has disappeared. Have the police been informed?'

'She's old enough to decide what to do with her life. I suppose the group is breaking up now. Pity. They have so many advantages that I never had. I had to work hard from the moment I left school. Nowadays they have these gap years and travel all round the place, having a whale of a time.'

'New York for a holiday...?'

'We should be so lucky.' She gave Ellie a twisted smile that morphed into a coughing fit. Ellie waited while Mrs Belton dragged herself into the kitchen for a glass of water. She reappeared, holding a packet of pills. 'Time for a pill.' Her voice was fading from exhaustion.

'You shouldn't think of going back to work this week, and you shouldn't go out in the cold. Do you have a neighbour who can do some shopping for you?'

'Oh, her. We don't speak.'

'Well, can I fetch you something from the shops?'

'I'll go back to bed for a bit, I think. Ursula left me with a whole lot of frozen meals, not that I fancy them in the least. Junk food! I can still hardly believe what Ursula's done. They've been together for so long.'

'Better to break it off now than after they're married.'

'I suppose.'

'I'd like to ring her, if I may. Tell her what's happened about the ring.'

'She's got no mobile at the moment. Dropped it, clumsy girl, will have to get another, though I should think she's fairly broke at the moment, what with the trip to America and all. I'll let you have the emergency number for students at the University, if you like. You can leave a message for her there.'

Mrs Belton consulted a telephone book and wrote down a number on a piece of paper for Ellie. At the same time, Ellie wrote down her own home number for Mrs Belton. 'Just in case she rings you before I can get hold of her.'

Mrs Belton gave Ellie's phone number one glance, and screwed up the piece of paper, saying she only needed to look at telephone numbers once to remember them.

Considerably intimidated by this evidence of a superior intellect Ellie, who had been known to forget her own phone number at times, got herself out of the flat, pulled out her mobile and asked the cab company to send someone round to pick her up straight away. Then she tried the number Mrs Belton had given her and left a message for Ursula to ring her, reversing the call.

'Daniel's not going to do anything stupid, is he?'

'I shouldn't think so, Dumbo. He wants a job in the Health Club when he finishes college.'

75

'He got rat-arsed last night. I've never seen him so drunk.'

'The problem with him is that little Miss Frigidaire refused to let him grow up. He'll soon find out the joys of living in today's world. She scratched me, you know.'

'Well, you did break her mobile.'

'The least she deserved.'

'I worry about Mia. I mean, she left so suddenly, and we don't know anything about the man she went off with. She could be anywhere, out on the streets, starving.'

'You've an overactive imagination. I'm not bothered, and the parents certainly aren't. She never fitted in, did she?'

'Yes, but suppose she's, well, you know. In real trouble. Because of what we did. We don't want her going to the police.'

A pause. 'I don't think she'd dare, but I suppose I could ask around. Once I'd put my mind to it, it was easy enough to see who helped her get away. I'll have words with the woman tomorrow when she comes.'

'Who, Anthony? The cleaner?'

'Who else? See if you can get Daniel to come along tonight. We've got hold of a really hot video. Might put some ideas into his virginal head. Take our minds off the financial situation. If The Man doesn't pull something off soon, we'll all be down the Job Centre.'

'I thought the architect—'

'Not as solvent as The Man thought.'

76

FIVE

Monday evening

Ellie got home to find the house dark except for a light in the hall. She remembered just in time that she couldn't use the front door because Thomas had bolted it, so made her way past the coach house that Roy had converted into his architect's offices, and let herself into the kitchen quarters through the back door.

What a sight! A splendid party was in progress round the kitchen table, with Rose presiding over their biggest teapot. Thomas – girded in his favourite apron with cats on it – was grilling a couple of pounds of sausages, while a frail-looking man in a dog collar sliced buns lengthways. Hot dogs were in the course of preparation, presumably. Ellie thought of the salad stuffs she'd bought to make them a sensible meal, and accepted she'd lost the battle for dieting before a shot had been fired.

'Just in time!' cried Rose, who looked tinier than ever, but was flushed with enjoyment. She'd even dressed herself, after a fashion, in a purple cardigan over a fuchsia pink T-shirt and a decent skirt. No stockings, but she did have her bedroom slippers on. Ellie smiled, because

Rose was obviously feeling so much better.

A large, fair-haired man backed out of the larder, holding up various jars. 'Is this the right mustard?' Stewart: little Frank's loving father, Diana's ex-husband, and the invaluable manager of the Quicke properties to let. He saluted Ellie with the Dijon mustard. 'I dropped in to see you with an update on the old house, and got roped into making tea. Hope you don't mind.'

'Of course not. Especially if you've got some news for me.'

'All the utilities are back on. The decorators started two days ago, and are scheduled to finish within three days if we promise overtime.'

'Promise anything you like. Well done, Stewart.'

'I wish I could stay to eat with you,' said Stewart, looking longingly at the sizzling hot dogs, 'but Maria will kill me if I fail to do justice to supper at home.'

Maria wouldn't, as they all knew, but Ellie smiled forgivingly as he retrieved coat and briefcase and made his way out of the kitchen door into the night.

'Feed a cold, and starve a fever. Comfort food coming right up!' Thomas pierced sausages to make sure they were cooked all through. 'Shed your coat, Ellie. I'm cooking tonight. Oh, and this is my friend Peters from St Mary's.'

'It's good to meet you at last,' said the dog collar. 'I rang to thank Thomas for taking the service yesterday, and he invited me round. He said you'd want to ask me about Lloyd.'

She did, indeed. So after a fairly raucous high tea, which finished up with lashings of Rose's Bakewell tart and cream, they adjourned to the peace and quiet of the sitting room.

The Reverend Peters swallowed pills. 'The antibiotics are kicking in at last, thank the Lord. Pleurisy's no joke, especially at my age. Forgive me if I leave soon. I still tire easily.'

'I'll run you home,' said Thomas, patting his frontage as a signal to the cat Midge to make himself at home there.

'Of course you mustn't overdo it,' said Ellie, handing them both a cup of good coffee. How many cups had she had that day, and would she be able to sleep on them? 'Can you tell me about Lloyd before you go?'

'A bright mind. Old for his years. Thought for himself. He'd been brought up a strict Methodist by Welsh parents. In their late teens, some youngsters slough off whatever religion they've learned at their parents' knee, in favour of experimentation. Sometimes they turn their backs on religion altogether. Lloyd had gone through such a phase and come out the other side. He approached me after a morning service about a year ago and started asking questions. I run a discussion group for young people on Wednesday evenings and he joined that. He knew his parents would have preferred him to go to a Methodist church, but he felt at home with us. Just before Christmas he asked me to prepare him to take communion, and he was thinking – I don't know whether he'd have gone through with it – but he was thinking that one day he might train for the ministry.'

'Did he drink at all?' asked Ellie.

The Reverend Peters shook his head. 'A half pint occasionally. He said he'd tried getting drunk and it hadn't done anything for him, so he didn't bother nowadays. As for drugs: never. And, of course, as he was a student he had to be careful with his money.'

'Sex?'

Again, a shake of the head. 'I don't think so. He said there was a girl in the group he went around with – something to do with his digs? Anyway, he said he really fancied her, but she was already spoken for. He said there'd be plenty of time later to find someone he really liked, someone he could commit to. He had – not tunnel vision exactly – but I would say he was a remarkably single-minded young man. He had two goals: to get a good degree and teach, and to find out what God wanted him to do in life. He said everything else could wait.'

'What did you think when you heard he'd got drunk and dived off a high roof?'

He looked anguished. 'When I saw the paragraph in the local paper, I thought it must be some other person of that name. I rang his digs and was told that yes, it was him, that he was being cremated. We couldn't even have a service for him at our church. Human nature never fails to surprise me. He's the last person I would have thought ... well, it's all over. I suppose I misread his character, that the front he put on for me was a false one.'

'Ursula didn't believe the official version, either. Was she the girl he liked so much, do you know?'

He shook his head. 'He didn't give me a name. Old-fashioned in some ways. I liked him all the better for it. Ah me. I must admit, I grieve for him and for myself that such a bright star should have fizzled out like ... like a damp squib.' He tried to laugh, coughed, blew his nose. Stood to depart. A stooping, elderly cleric, disillusioned but soldiering on. 'Must go.'

'I'll run you home,' said Thomas, dislodging Midge to get to his feet.

When he'd gone Ellie cleared up in the kitchen and saw Rose settled in front of her television set.

Turning the volume up, Rose said, 'Wouldn't Miss Quicke have enjoyed it this evening? She always said that what this house needed was filling with lots of people.'

Lots of people. Ouch. Again Ellie thought of the vast, unoccupied attic storey and wondered if she were being selfish in not allowing Diana and Frank to take over there.

She was restless until she heard Thomas return and let himself in through the kitchen quarters. He was unsettled, too, though he took her arm and made her sit down in the big chair in the sitting room, saying, 'Now, tell me what's going on.'

She told him, watching his face the while. She told him about Daniel and his reaction to the return of his ring, and then what had happened when she spoke to his mother ... and finally about the conversation with Mrs Belton.

'...Oh, and Roy's in deep trouble financially. He promised to put money into Prior's Place and now he's trying to raise a mortgage on the block of flats that my aunt left him, or to sell it. In the current state of the market, he's going to lose hand over fist. Felicity wants the Trust to bail him out, but I'm not sure that I should. I don't think the trustees would let me, anyway.'

'No, I don't suppose they would, but I suppose you'll want to try.' He fidgeted, frowning, sighing, shaking his head. 'This Ursula business, though. What a mess. I don't know what to think.'

'She impressed me. I thought at first that she was a manipulative little madam, but sincere in her belief that something had gone very wrong. By the time I'd finished with the two mothers I'd decided that Ursula was imagining things, that Lloyd's death was an accident, and that her sit-in at church was her way of grieving over lost innocence. She said her friend had gone missing. Well, young girls do get carried away and run off with unsuitable men and leave their families without a forwarding address. I convinced myself that I didn't need to take the matter any further. I've got a call in to her to ring me, and I thought I'd say that I'd done as she asked, and that that was the end of the story.'

'My friend Peters made you rethink?'

'Yes. What do you make of it all, Thomas?'

He pulled a face, rubbed one hand over his beard. He stood up, his eyes wandering around as if looking for something. 'I don't know, I really don't. I need to ... is it still raining? It was when I came in. I wonder if...'

He wandered out into the hall, opened the door to the dining room, which had been set up for Ellie's next business meeting. Closed that door. Went along the passage to his office, opened that door, and stood looking at the piles of work, the computers, the books. Closed that door. Didn't touch the door of the room which was now Ellie's study.

Ellie followed him, wondering what on earth was wrong. He seemed frustrated, looking for something. But what?

He said, 'I used to be able to pop across to the church to sort myself out, and it never occurred to me, now I'm no longer a parish priest, that I'd want to ... I mean, with all the vandalism that's around, it's quite right that churches are locked up out of hours, but...'

Ah-ha. Ellie understood, at last. He needed a space in which to be by himself and pray. Of course he could, in theory, pray anywhere. And, in fact, he did. But every now and then he need-ed to go away by himself to a quiet place and put in a bit of concentrated one-to-one at the feet of the Almighty. She knew he was capable of praying for an hour at a time. She hadn't that rigorous concentration herself. She was all for action in a flurry of arrow prayers. But Thomas was different.

She caught hold of one of his hands, led him back along the passage and up the stairs to the first floor. Past the master bedroom they went, past the pretty guest room and the room in which Frank occasionally slept, to the unused bedrooms at the end of the corridor. The house had been built to hold a large family, and there were five bedrooms on this floor, not counting Rose's bedroom and bathroom, which were over the kitchen quarters.

Reaching the end of the corridor, Ellie threw open the door to the first of the two unoccupied and unused bedrooms. Miss Quicke had had the furniture in these two rooms piled into the centre and covered with dust sheets, while the walls had been painted magnolia. There was an ancient blind at the window, and surprisingly little dust.

Thomas looked bewildered as Ellie dived under the piled-up furniture to retrieve a high-backed wood-framed Windsor chair, a roll of carpet and a small table. She pushed the chair against one wall, laid the carpet before it, placed the table at the side of the chair and stood back. 'There you are, your own chapel. I'll have the cleaning women move the rest of the furniture out tomorrow, and give the place a good hoover.'

'I don't need—'

'Yes, you do. You've always needed a space of your own in which to pray. You should have said, sooner. I thought you were sickening for something.' She looked around, frowning. 'You'll need a cross on the wall, won't you?'

'Ellie, I can pray anywhere, in my office, anywhere.'

'No, you can't. Well, you can, of course. But not without distractions, the emails, the unanswered letters, the phone calls. Here there's nothing but you and the cross. If only I can find you a cross. Ah.' She had had a thought. 'One minute.'

She hurried down the stairs. A while ago she'd found a Victorian religious picture worked in wools in the cupboard under the stairs, which probably hadn't been turned out in decades. It might have been worked by some distant member of the Quicke family – though certainly not by Miss Quicke, who had despised all womanly arts. Perhaps it had been bought on impulse at a church fête and immediately consigned to oblivion as being both ugly and of no value? Ellie had dusted it down, resolved to put it on the bric-a-brac stall at the next church fête, and forgotten about it.

It was definitely not her cup of tea, but perhaps it wasn't quite as hideous as she'd remembered it to be, and maybe Thomas would like it.

She fished it out, and had to laugh. It was even worse than she'd remembered. The Good Shepherd was in a beige coloured nightie, trying to balance a black sheep across his shoulders and looking distinctly unhappy about it. She took it back upstairs with her to show to Thomas, who was still standing in the middle of the room, looking stunned.

She said, 'I thought this might do for the moment, but I'm afraid it's past it.'

'No, it isn't,' said Thomas, smiling. He took the picture from her and balanced it against the piled-up furniture. 'See, he's got a beard like mine, and a comfortable figure, and he's finding it hard to carry that awkward and very naughty sheep across his shoulders. I'm sure that sheep is trying to wriggle down, but he's holding on to it for dear life. Just like I have to hang on to my faith at times.'

He was actually laughing! He put his arm around her shoulders and held her tight. 'Thank you, Ellie.' Was his cold getting worse again? 'You are a pearl of great price. You give me so much more than I ever dreamed possible. Yes, I can pray here. And I will. If I'm late coming to bed, you'll know where I am.'

Ellie made her way downstairs, thinking how strange matrimony could be. It wasn't all cuddles in the bedroom, or companionship, or facing problems together. It was about adapting oneself to someone else. It made her smile – a trifle wryly – at the idea of her first husband Frank wanting space and time apart from her. If he'd wanted it, he'd have taken it without reference to her wishes. By going out to play golf, for instance. But he'd expected her to be at his beck and call whenever he condescended to come home.

Thomas was different. He needed his quiet times; times in which to pray. It was part and parcel of what made him what he was. She was extremely glad that she'd worked it out at last, because he would never have asked for it himself.

As she reached the ground floor, she heard the telephone ring and smiled again, thinking that there was no way Thomas would hear it up in his new room. She glanced at her watch. Whoever could it be at this time of night?

It was the operator, asking if she would pay for a call from Ursula in Portsmouth. Of course. The line was poor; background noises indicated dance music and people talking, laughing.

'Hi, Mrs Quicke. I'm ringing from the Student Union. It's a public telephone. You wanted to speak to me?'

'Very much so. I returned your ring to Daniel, who refused to accept it. I spoke to Mrs Collins, who gave me your mother's address. I left the ring with her.'

'How is she? I've been really worried about her.'

'Improving.'

'That's all? You're satisfied with the official verdict on what's happened?'

'Ursula, will you please stop playing games with me? Give me one good reason why I should look any further than the end of my nose.'

'Gut reaction doesn't count?'

Ellie sighed. 'It might. Tell me in words of one syllable what you know. Not what you've been told by others, but what you yourself know.'

'Half the time I think I'm going crazy, but ... well, all right. Our crowd was asked by Anthony to act as "hostesses" and "guides" for the Grand Opening of Prior's Place. We were to dress up prettily, and show would-be buyers around the flats and the gym. We were sucker bait. We chatted them up, gave out leaflets, and so on. Anthony said our crowd was going to continue the party upstairs when the guests began to leave, but I had to shove off to the airport to catch my plane. Daniel came with me to Heathrow, so we actually missed what happened.'

'Then whatever you've heard about Lloyd's death is hearsay. Inadmissible evidence.'

'True. I had a brilliant time in New York, texted Daniel and Mia – she's my best friend here – from time to time, but only got one text back from Daniel, and none from Mia. I didn't worry too much, thought my battery was run down, hadn't got my charger with me. I bought presents for everyone; Daniel met me at Heathrow on my return. He told me then that Lloyd had got drunk, messed about with Mia, had tried to fight someone who interfered and, in taking a swing at them, had gone over the balcony to his death. He said Mia had subsequently run off with another man.'

'Did Daniel see any of this happening him-

88

self?'

'No, it happened after we left. So yes, what he told me was hearsay too. I was so shocked, I couldn't take it in. Lloyd drunk, dead? Mia playing around, running away? No way! Daniel dropped me off at home where I found Mum really poorly, so I couldn't talk to her about it. I put her to bed, made hot drinks for her. The next day I tried ringing Mia but her phone was out of order. I phoned her parents but they said she'd left and they didn't know where she'd gone and what's more, after the way she'd behaved, they couldn't care less. It was like dropping into Alice in Wonderland; everything had changed.

'I met Dan at the café; didn't want him coming to the flat with Mum so ill. I tried to discuss it with him but he lost his temper, said didn't I believe him. The awful thing was that I didn't. He looked ... guilty. I realized then that he knew something, but he wouldn't tell me what it was. That was a terrible moment. I knew he hadn't been there when it happened, but I thought he must know something, have been told something. I said I needed to talk to someone who'd actually been there, and he went all huffy on me, said if I didn't believe him I could do what I liked.

'He wouldn't come with me, but I knew Anthony and his special friends would probably be at the new gym that evening, and so they were. Anthony said there were eye witnesses to Lloyd's getting drunk, that there was vodka all over his clothes and in his stomach, and that

Mia was a little slag and I'd been deceiving myself if I thought she wouldn't lift her skirts for anyone who fancied her.'

Ursula gulped. 'It's not true, Mrs Quicke. Lloyd hardly drank at all, and he wasn't the sort to lose his head just because the others were overdoing it. Mia wasn't a slag; we told one another everything and she'd only tried once and that hadn't worked because she was tiny, you know? She'd decided to wait till she met someone who really turned her on, and as of eleven o'clock on the night of the party, she was fancy free. I'd stake my life on it. Besides, where is she? No one seems to know.

'I was so angry, so miserable, I went to the police. They said, like everyone else, that boys will be boys and Lloyd's death was an accident. Case closed. As for Mia, they said she was over eighteen and if she chose to leave home that was her prerogative, and if she wanted to get in touch with me then no doubt she would.'

'That sounds sensible.'

'So I'm not sensible! But I tell you...' Her voice rose, and she brought it down again with an effort. 'Mia is Anthony and Tim's stepsister, right? Mrs Prior had Mia by her first husband, whom she divorced ages ago. Then she met Mr Prior, and married him. He'd also been married before and brought the two boys to his second marriage. So what sort of stepbrothers are they, not to care when Mia goes missing? All right, they weren't a very lovey-dovey family, but ... you see what I mean?'

90

Ellie was silent. Ursula had a good point, there.

'Nothing made sense any more. When I tried to find out what happened, I got nowhere. Daniel let me down, big time. I'd always thought it didn't matter that I was the strong, stable one in our relationship. When he chose to side with Anthony rather than back me up, I realized what sort of future I was letting myself in for, always nursing him along, always having to be the strong one, the one who made all the big decisions. I told myself that it didn't matter, but it did. It took some time, but eventually I realized that however much I loved him, I couldn't go on being engaged to him. Breaking it off was really hard...'

Her voice wobbled. She cleared her throat. 'I was stuck, like. I didn't know what to do next, but I felt I had to do something. That's why I pulled the church stunt. I needed space to grieve for Lloyd and Mia and I couldn't do that at home, with Mum being so poorly, and I thought ... I'm not sure what I thought. I'm not sure even that I believe in God, but I felt the need to get away, to be quiet, to think. I told Mum I was going back early to uni, and I took my gear to the station and left it there while I went to church. Then you came, and everything went wrong.'

Ellie thought about this. 'You haven't given me one fact to disprove their story. Except ... what happened to your mobile phone?'

'Anthony smashed it.'

'Anthony Prior smashed your phone? Why?'

'To show me who's boss. I don't want to say what he did next, but it wasn't nice.'

'He hurt you?'

'He tickled me. The others held me, and he ... I thrashed about, I couldn't help it. In the end ... he made me cry. That's what he wanted, I suppose. They all laughed.' Humiliation leaked out through every broken phrase.

'You told Daniel?'

'He said Anthony would never do anything like that.'

'He probably did believe you, but was afraid to admit it. Daniel is one mixed-up kid.'

'I don't need a mixed-up kid. I need someone I can rely on.' She sounded a lot older than her years.

Ellie held back a sigh. 'Did you report them to the police?'

'Anthony said that if I tried that, he'd say I was gasping for him to take notice of me, and they would all back him up. Believe me, they would. He also said that if I went round making trouble, my mother would lose her job with the health authority.'

'What? But he couldn't—'

'Oh yes, he could. His father is on all the right committees. He could put in a lying report saying she'd been racist or anti disadvantaged people or something. Never mind that she works with all sorts and they think she's brilliant. But if she lost her job then we'd lose the flat, because she had to mortgage it to give me a debt-free run through university. Oh yes, he meant it all right.'

'Very well. I believe you. So what is it you want me to do?'

'Find Mia. The Priors must know what's happened to her. I can't believe they just let her walk off into the blue. Do you know their address? It's Prior's Place, off Mount Park Road. Mr Prior gave the new block of flats the same name. Shows what a big head he's got. If Mia really doesn't want to see me again I suppose I'll have to accept it, but I need to know that she's all right.'

Ellie thought this was another familiar story: nice girl kicking over the traces.

Ursula was overreacting, from grief and shock. Anthony's tickling her was a mild enough punishment for being called a liar, though humiliating, yes. He shouldn't have done it, but it was no grounds for thinking him capable of murder, was it?

There was only one thing that disturbed this picture of modern youth at party time, and that was the smashing of Ursula's phone. That had been malicious, especially when Anthony must have known that Ursula wouldn't be able to replace it easily.

And what about Mia's phone being out of service? Could the same thing have happened to hers?

Ellie said, 'What makes you think I can find Mia, when you couldn't?'

'You're on the spot and your husband says

93

you have a reputation for solving mysteries. Then again, you've enough cash behind you that you don't need to be afraid of what the Priors might do to you.'

Ellie blinked. Hadn't she enough on her plate at the moment, what with a demanding daughter and grandson, Rose's gentle decline, and a nasty little ache at the back of her shoulder – which might be due to her having lain in an awkward position in bed, but might be the onset of rheumatism or arthritis? She hadn't a clue what the difference was between rheumatism and arthritis, but gathered the effect was probably the same.

'Ursula, I need to think about this and get back to you. Are you returning to London this next weekend?'

'I ought to. I'm worried about Mum but ... you'll laugh ... I'm a bit scared of running into the old crowd.'

'How would it be if I dropped in to see your mother, checked that she was getting on all right, and rang you back? Oh, how will I contact you? Are you getting another mobile phone?'

'Can't afford it. I had to get a new laptop this term. The old one died on me.'

'I've got a mobile phone to spare because I was given a new one at Christmas. Let me have your address.'

'You there, Dumbo?'

'What do you want, Ant? You're interrupting—'

'She'll wait. Listen up. The Man has got a buyer for Prior's Place.'

'Sure. The architect.'

'Nah, it turns out he's got to raise the ready by mortgaging another property, or selling it or something, and who knows how long that will take. No, a real player's popped up, a Middle Eastern prince or sheikh or whatever he is. You remember him from the Opening?'

'Who could forget? He gave the girl a rough ride, and it was only after she threatened to go to the police that he paid her off. Is this a good idea?'

'It's him or bankruptcy. Only, there's a catch. He took a fancy to the long legs and blonde locks of our beloved Ursula at the party. He's annoyed that she left early, and is hinting – more than just hinting – that he'd be happy to sign the papers if she's delivered to him on Saturday night.'

'What? But Ursula won't play, will she? I mean, she doesn't ... does she?'

'She's always short of cash. We can make sure she gets a cut.'

'But I don't think—'

'You're not required to think. Just deliver her on time. If it's a choice between the Job Centre and a new sports car for you, you'll do it.'

'There's no way to contact her. You did her mobile in, remember? Plus, she's gone back to uni.'

'So you ring and leave a message for her to contact you, Dumbo. Make sure she gets the

95

*invitation. Promise her a new dress. Honestly,
you'll be asking me to brush your teeth for you
next.'*

Silence. 'Did you find Mia?'

*'I know where to look. But she didn't appeal
to His Highness even then, and she's no good
for that sort of thing now, is she?'*

'Is she all right?'

*'Give it a rest, will you? I know what I'm
doing.'*

SIX

Monday night

Ellie put the phone down, thinking about a
mobile for Ursula. Diana had given Ellie a
brand-new, all-speaking, all-dancing mobile for
Christmas, so her old mobile was, in theory,
redundant.

All that was true. What was also true was that
Ellie was frightened silly by the new instru-
ment, which was sleek and slender and would
show you television programmes and doubtless
also put you in touch with the moon and the
stars, if you so wished. There were so many
functions on it that you needed a degree in
further mathematics even to turn it on.

Her old phone also had a lot of programmes
she had never learned how to access, but she

did at least know how to make a phone call on it, and how to switch it on to receive one, though texting was still a foreign language. And, in fact, she'd still gone on using it to this day.

How would it be if she sent Ursula the new one? The girl would probably be able to master its intricacies in ten minutes, whereas Ellie knew that she'd never get beyond 'the cat sat on the mat' stage in a hundred years.

Diana had said that Ellie must learn to live in today's world, face up to the new technology, and embrace the opportunities it offered.

Ellie didn't see the point of owning a gadget which was a lot cleverer than she was. All she wanted was to send and receive phone calls on the odd occasion when she was out of reach of a landline. She was dearly tempted to send her clever box of tricks to Ursula ... except that, sigh, Diana had given it to her, and it had doubtless cost more than was reasonable for her daughter to spend. And so ... what we do for our children! ... Ellie must learn to master at least the basic functions on it. She'd send her old one to Ursula tomorrow, which would force her to come to terms with the new.

This settled, Ellie sat in her big chair by the fire, and patted her knee so that Midge understood he could leap on to her lap and spread himself out. Rubbing his head to make him purr, Ellie listened to the sounds every old house makes. A whisper in the central heating, the faintest of murmurs from the television in

Rose's sitting room, the wind gusting around the conservatory. The rumbling purr of the cat.

No sound from upstairs, where Thomas would no doubt have rolled up the carpet she'd laid down for him, and seated himself in that hard chair to pray. In another age, perhaps he'd have spent his life in a monastery, except – Ellie grinned to herself – that he was satisfactorily enthusiastic in bed, had two grown-up children living in the North to show for it, plus two grandchildren on the way.

Midge pushed his chin at her hand to remind her to continue rubbing. Midge only came to sit on her nowadays if he couldn't get at Thomas, but the room she'd chosen for Thomas's retreat had a doorknob and not a handle. Midge could handle handles, so to speak, but doorknobs were, so far, beyond him.

The room was dim and quiet around her until Thomas stole in to sit beside her and reach out for her hand. As usual when he'd been praying, he brought serenity into the room with him.

'All right?'

She nodded. 'And you?'

'I'm good.'

She grinned, knowing he hadn't meant it literally. 'So you are.' Teasing him.

He laughed; slapped her hand lightly. 'You know what I mean. You've talked to the girl?'

'She wants me to find her friend Mia, who's gone missing.' She told him what Ursula had said.

He stirred, sighing, shaking his head. 'Smashing her phone was vindictive. The man's a bully.'

Ellie discovered that her own doubts about the girl's story had dissolved. 'Her mother, Dan's mother, and your friend the Rev, all accepted that boys will be boys and that girls do go astray. Ursula didn't. She spoke up, and got clobbered. And now she's scared.'

'Whistle-blowers do get hurt.'

'She's safe enough now she's back at university, but she's worried about her mother, who's had flu. I think I might drop in to see how Mrs Belton's getting on tomorrow. Am I being naive, Thomas? Ursula said the Prior boys had threatened to throw her mother out of her job, because Mr P sits on the right committees. Can he really do that? I hate to think that he can.'

Thomas stroked her hand. 'It happens. I hear tales, sometimes. What would you like me to do to help?'

She wanted to say that she hadn't a clue, and that she had never understood why he thought she could tackle problems of this magnitude when she was really only just able to cope with being a housewife. Oh, and grandmother. And a part-time business woman. But deal with crime? Everything she'd achieved in that direction had been done by chance, by asking around in the neighbourhood and occasionally being able to put two and two together.

Thomas had moved on. 'Silly of me. Of course you'll want to find out if the tales about the Priors have any truth in them. And I suppose you'll want to check with the police that they have definitely closed the case.'

It was the last thing she wanted to do. Her relationship with Detective Inspector Willis had started with mutual mistrust and gone downhill from there. Ellie swallowed. What Thomas said made sense, but she wasn't sure she could bring herself to tangle with the woman again. It required a vast expenditure of energy even to think about it, and at the moment she felt completely and utterly limp, without a working muscle anywhere in her body.

Thomas had cocked his head, listening. Rose must have turned her television up, for they could hear it quite clearly now. 'My dear, do you think it's about time we reorganized things for Rose?'

Another anxiety. 'I promised she wouldn't have to go into a home.'

He patted her hand. 'Of course not. But the stairs are getting too much for her, so couldn't we rearrange her sitting room to make it into a bed-sitting room? There's a washbasin and toilet in the cloakroom off the hall, which she could use temporarily, but perhaps we should put a shower in that little room off the kitchen that we only use for storage?'

'I didn't want to make any changes while she could still get up the stairs to her bedroom, but you're right. I'll ask Stewart to get things moving.' She sighed. 'Some days she brightens up and is almost her old self again. We've been friends for so long, and she made Aunt Drusilla's last few years so happy that I feel really bad about this. I did think I could do everything for her myself, but I can't and now I worry about leaving her when I go out shopping or to see people. Now there's this troublesome affair of Ursula's to worry about. I agree. It's time to do something.'

'Don't lay a guilt trip on yourself, Ellie.' He was right, of course, but facing facts was never comfortable. Ellie got up to turn off the side-lights and put the day's papers into a tidy pile for recycling. 'The other day she said she was sure she could hear my aunt's bell ringing for her to take in the tea. Then she laughed at herself, and I laughed with her. Five minutes later she'd cupped her hand around her ear, listening for it again. But she's not unhappy, is she?'

'No, my dear. She's not. Now, come to bed?'

Tuesday morning

It was past eleven the next morning before Ellie had attended to various business matters and got herself out of the house. As she nerved herself to push open the door of the police station, she told herself that helpful and intelligent members of the police force did exist, and that not all the officers at this station treated her as a bumbling idiot, although she could think of several who did.

She fantasized that in response to her request to see DI Willis they would say that the DI was away on a sabbatical, or had been transferred to another division – perhaps to the moon? – or

101

even, of course, that she had been demoted and was therefore no longer available to reduce Ellie to the quivers.

'Detective Inspector Willis?' The desk sergeant raised his eyebrows. 'You might just be lucky. Who shall I say?'

'Mrs Quicke. Ellie Quicke. It's about the student who was killed early in January.'

His eyes sharpened. It was clear he'd heard of her, and that what he'd heard failed to amuse him. He accessed an internal phone. 'There's a Mrs Quicke here to see you, about that student who killed himself.' He listened, flicking a glance up at Ellie, smoothing out a smile at what he was hearing from the DI. He put the phone down. 'I'm afraid she's not available. Perhaps you'd like to talk to one of our WPCs?'

Ellie reddened. 'I'll wait.'

'Perhaps you'd care to sit over there?' He was being elaborately polite. Ellie wondered if forced politeness were worse than rudeness, but now that she was here, she would wait and see what she could find out. So she sat. And waited. The seat was hard. Several people came in from outside and spoke to the desk sergeant. And left. Policemen and women drifted in and out of the building. Some were in plain clothes, others in uniform. Some looked over her head, one or two of those leaving the station glanced her way and then averted their gaze. She imagined those might know who she was, and have been told not to pay her any attention. Or was she getting paranoid? No one came to speak to her.

102

Perhaps DI Willis thought Ellie would give up and go if she ignored her? Ellie was annoyed with herself for not having brought a book to read.

How long should she wait? *Please Lord, is this where you want me to be right now? Because if not, there's a thousand things I need to be doing.*

She got out an old envelope on which she'd made a list of things to do. Some of them she'd already done, and she ticked them off.

Rose. Rose had not gone upstairs to her bedroom last night, but had curled up in her big armchair downstairs. In consequence she was so stiff this morning that she could hardly move. Oh dear. Ellie tried to help Rose get her circulation going again, but wasn't a nurse and didn't know which bits to rub.

Rose herself had been flustered and upset, worried that she was causing Ellie more work, and saying that she'd be up and climbing those stairs again in next to no time.

'Dear Rose.' Ellie was much distressed. 'We can't have this. How would it be if we got your bed downstairs and set it up over there in the corner, so that you can watch your telly in peace and quiet when you want to go to have a rest? Just until you feel like climbing the stairs again.' It was a big enough room to take the bed, with a little reorganization.

'What luxury to watch the telly in bed.' Rose was greatly relieved, as they both skated over the fact that she was probably not going to climb stairs ever again. 'But won't it be a lot of trouble for you to arrange?'

'I shall enjoy it,' said Ellie, laughing to see Rose perking up. Ellie fetched down some of Rose's clothes, helped her to the toilet, and got her dressed. Then, with some tea and toast inside her, Rose settled down at the kitchen table to make a shopping list of food for the week. Ellie guessed she'd probably have to do the list all over again in due course since Rose, once such an efficient housekeeper, was now inclined to ask for onions when she meant potatoes.

Ellie blew her nose fiercely once she was out of the kitchen. When their two splendid cleaners arrived – only five minutes late but keen to get on with it – Ellie took them up to Rose's bedroom, only to discover that the bed she'd been using there had an iron frame that refused to come apart and therefore couldn't be taken out through the doorway and down the stairs. Luckily there was a divan bed among the jumble of furniture in the farthest of the unused bedrooms, and they managed to manoeuvre that, and a small cupboard with hanging-space, down and into Rose's sitting room. Old-fashioned pieces, but practical.

Ellie made sure that all Rose's favourite bits and pieces were taken downstairs, plus her clothes. She asked if the cleaners might stay on that afternoon, to clear out the room that Thomas had taken over for his prayers. The odd bits of furniture he didn't need could be stored in the only other unused bedroom, which was rapidly taking on the appearance of a junk room.

Ellie had her own personal assistant who helped her deal with correspondence that could not be handed over to her Trust fund. Pat had, however, also gone down with this flu-like cold, so there was a stack of mail, which Ellie opened and then decided to ignore for the time being.

After that she checked on Thomas and his secretary, whom she left hard at work but listening out for the locksmith, who'd said he'd come at half nine and hadn't arrived by the time she left at ten.

Before she'd left, Ellie had spent some time with glue and Sellotape, fitting together the torn-up photographs she'd taken from Dan's room, and making photocopies of them. The more she'd looked at the pictures, the more her eyes had been drawn to the smiling face of the little dark-haired girl called Mia. Mia the missing.

On her way out, she'd phoned Stewart to say she'd like to check on the progress at her old house in person, and could he meet her there this afternoon? And then perhaps he could come back with her to the big house to see about putting in a shower downstairs? Stewart would probably have to rearrange his day to do this, but she didn't often interfere in his schedules, and he made no demur.

When she'd finally got out of the house, she'd

stopped by the post office to put some more money on to her old mobile phone and send it off to Ursula. Now, looking at the new one as she sat at the police station, she hadn't a clue how to make it work. It seemed to be leering at her, thinking no doubt that she'd never be up to taming it. Which was probably true.

Suppose she were to buy herself another plain and simple one? Diana need never know. Oh dear, Diana. Problems. And what about Roy overreaching himself financially? She really ought to get out of there and tackle him.

A puff of air stroked her cheek as the inner door opened again. DI Willis: her hair now more ginger than mahogany, her mouth tight with displeasure. 'Are you still waiting, Mrs Quicke? I heard you had a query for me. I can only give you a few minutes, but I'm sure ... would you like to come through?' She issued the invitation through gritted teeth, but held the door open for Ellie to pass in front of her.

Ellie told herself not to be intimidated. The DI was an intelligent, hard-working officer who had a lot on her plate, and if she thought Ellie a bumbling, ineffectual waste of space who happened – most unfortunately for the DI – to stumble across cases that Ellie hadn't the training or intelligence to solve, then so be it.

Ellie in turn thought the DI had had a charm bypass, but told herself that this was not in itself a good reason to dislike the woman.

'I hear you've got married again,' said the DI, implying that this was the oddest thing she'd heard in a fortnight.

'And you?' enquired Ellie, who was pretty sure no man had ever invited the DI into his bed. She was sorry, as soon as the words escaped her, but admired the DI's restraint as she showed Ellie into the usual small, grey interview room without further comment.

'Oh, well...' The woman was actually blushing?

Ellie was astonished. Was she going to have to revise her opinion of the DI? Well, well.

But to the matter in hand. Settling herself, Ellie said, 'I wanted to talk to you about the young man who took a dive off Prior's Place early in January.'

The DI raised both eyebrows in a don't-waste-my-time gesture. 'It was an accident. Case closed. Is that all?'

Ellie hadn't expected anything else, had she? 'I'm also interested in the case of the disappearing student.'

The upright line between DI Willis's eyebrows deepened, and for the first time she looked uncertain. 'Name?'

'Mia Prior.'

The DI exhaled loudly. 'Mia Prior? Oh, now! Come on, Mrs Quicke! You cannot be serious. I have the greatest respect for you,' she lied through her teeth, 'but Mia's disappearance is no mystery.' She got to her feet. 'Now, I'm very busy, so if you have no fresh information?'

'I believe I do.'

'What is it?'

107

'A girl called Ursula Belton—'

'The name rings a bell.' She sighed. 'I'd better fetch the files.'

She wasn't away long. Ellie had got out her new phone and tried to ring Thomas to tell him she'd be a while, but couldn't even work out how to switch it on. She did hope the locksmith had come. And that the cleaners had made up the bed for Rose downstairs. And that Diana hadn't tried to get in.

The DI returned to slap a couple of files on to the table. Seating herself, she leafed through the thinnest one, and looked up. 'Ursula Belton called at the station last week, to report that a girl called Mia Prior had disappeared. The parents were interviewed by one of my sergeants. The parents said that although Mia had an innocent face she slept around, that she'd been finding the restrictions placed on her at home too much for her, and so had packed her things and lit off with a bike-riding boyfriend.'

Ellie gaped. 'Mia's not like that. Why would her parents say she was?'

She shrugged. 'There it is. Dead end. The girl's old enough to kick over the traces if she wants to.'

'What you're saying is that if a girl is given a bad name, no one cares if she disappears?'

'Fact of life.'

Ellie winced. 'Yet I've been told that as of the night of the party during which Lloyd died, Mia had no particular boyfriend and was definitely not sleeping around. Surely you can check this

108

out with other people; perhaps with fellow students at her university?'

The line between her eyebrows deepened. 'The parents should know what goes on with their daughter. Besides...' She focused on a note in the file, then closed it. 'We can't waste time on girls who choose to disappear. End of story.'

'I don't understand why you've closed the case without investigating it properly. Or do you know more than you're saying? You've some information that I haven't?'

A momentary expression of discomfort passed across the DI's face. 'No comment. You have no fresh evidence, so that's it.'

'I know that Mia and her best friend, plus best friend's fiancé and their friend Lloyd, were invited to the Grand Opening at Prior's Place. Young and pretty things of both sexes were paraded before prospective buyers. Heady stuff, influential circles, money no object. Drink flowed. My informant—'

'This same Ursula Belton, whose take on Mia is contradicted by her parents?'

'She's a strong, stable personality from a middle-class professional background. Struggling to make ends meet as a university student, but nobody's fool. Ursula says that up to the time when she left for the airport with her fiancé – she was going abroad for a holiday – all was well. She says that Lloyd was a strong, practising Christian who hardly drank at all, and that Mia was her best friend, a hard-working student, a good friend, and fancy free.

'I think the party got out of hand after Ursula left. The youthful sales staff moved upstairs, away from restraining adult influences. And then something happened. I'm not sure what, but Lloyd went over the balcony and Mia dropped out of sight. My question is: were the two events connected, and if so, how?'

The DI raised her eyes to the ceiling. 'Very well. Let's go through the motions. You think that Lloyd made up to Mia at the party, and that his death upset her enough to take off into the blue?' She opened the second file, read, and frowned. 'Statements were taken from three young men. Lloyd didn't normally drink much, but he'd guzzled some vodka that night. He was out of his tree, got into a fight, took a swing at someone, missed and went over the balcony. All three lads were duly horrified, expressed regret, etcetera.'

'No one asked Mia to make a statement?'

The DI rifled through the pages. 'Names were taken of those present at the time.' She ran her finger down the list. 'No, she wasn't among them.'

Ellie tried to think straight. 'Mia was there at eleven. When did Lloyd fall, and how long did it take for the police to get there afterwards?'

'After midnight ... they seem to have sent for an ambulance first. Yes. The ambulance men called the police, but it all seemed straightforward. Yes, there was time for the girl to leave before the police got there, but in view of the other witnesses' statements, I see no point in

110

taking the matter further.'

Ellie took a deep breath. 'I don't want to think the worst, but did Mia die, too? How do we know that she did make it safely home after the party? Or did she just disappear into thin air?'

The DI consulted the file again. 'She didn't leave home for a week after that, the parents said.'

'How can we be sure of anything they say, since they lied about what she was like?'

'Allegedly.'

'All right, allegedly. Did anyone else see her back at home? You see, if she'd been mixed up in something, her stepfather would want to hush it up, wouldn't he? He would want to avoid a scandal at all costs, after having invested so much money in Prior's Place.'

'Step...? There's nothing here about his only being the stepfather.'

'Both Mr and Mrs were married before. Mia was her daughter, the boys were his sons. Were the boys asked about her disappearance?'

'Not that I can see. Mrs Quicke, what makes you think violence was involved?'

'When Ursula confronted the Prior boys about what had happened to Mia, they manhandled her and destroyed her mobile phone. Isn't that indicative of something not quite right? What's more, Ursula believes Lloyd was murdered. Not accidentally killed, but murdered.'

The DI folded her arms on the table. 'According to her own version of events, Ursula wasn't

111

there when things went wrong, so how can she say it was murder?'

Ellie sucked in her breath. 'I know, I know. She says it's gut reaction, and I know that's not evidence.'

'If the girl wishes to make a formal complaint about her treatment at the hands of the Priors, then we will of course investigate. Is she likely to do so?'

Ellie shrugged. 'I don't think so.'

The DI continued to frown. 'You're wasting my time, Mrs Quicke.'

'I have some pictures of her.' From her bag Ellie took photocopies of the torn-up photos. 'The blonde is Ursula, and the little dark girl is Mia. The handsome lad leering down Mia's shoulder is her stepbrother, Anthony. He seems to be the leader of the group.'

The DI took the photos, looked at them for a couple of seconds and then pushed them back to Ellie. 'Bring me some new evidence, something to convince me that I should get permission to reopen the cases. Otherwise...'

'May I ring you, if I do come across anything?'

'Of course.' She stood, waiting for Ellie to go.

Ellie decided she would not apologize for wasting the DI's time. The DI, however, was intent on driving the message home. 'Forgive me for keeping you waiting so long, but we do have rather a lot of real crime to solve at the moment, and conspiracy theories are ten a penny.' She smiled. Falsely.

'Oh, yes. Of course.'

'You being such an expert on what goes on in the community–' buckets of irony – 'I had hoped you might have been coming in to tell us something about the muggings that are keeping householders indoors at night. Now, there's something I could do with some help on. A real community problem, right up your street.'

Ellie shook her head, trying to remember. There'd been something in the local paper, per-haps? A gang wearing toy masks had been rob-bing people out late at night, snatching bags, jewellery, mobile phones?

'Ah well,' the DI said, showing her out. 'You never know. Have you got your car nearby? It looks as if the weather's turning nasty again.' The DI knew very well that Ellie didn't drive. What's more, Ellie hadn't brought her umbrella with her. If only she'd a mobile phone which she could use to summon help! Well, she hadn't. So she'd better put her head down into the wind and get on with it.

'You there, Dumbo? I thought you were ringing me back.'

'I tried, didn't I? You weren't taking calls.'

'I was working, didn't want interruptions – not with that particular customer – if you get my meaning. You got hold of Ursula all right?'

'I left messages, urgent, for her to ring me. First at the Student Union, and then later I got through to the office and got the phone number of the house share she's in. Someone there said

he'd leave a message for her but she might not be back till late.'

'You haven't the brains you were born with. Have you tried her mother? She'll know how to contact the girl. Ring her, now! Understand?'

Mumble, mumble.

'What was that?'

'I said, if you hadn't done her phone in, we wouldn't be having this bother.'

'I had to show her who was boss, didn't I? Get on with it.'

SEVEN

Tuesday lunchtime

Ellie's new phone hadn't rung once that morning – but then, she hadn't given anyone this number, had she? If she couldn't ring out, they couldn't get hold of her, either. She wasn't sure if this were a good thing, or not.

Anyway, the rain was holding off so far, and it was lunchtime. She would return home by way of the shops, picking up some of the delicatessen's fresh quiches for herself, Thomas and Rose. Not that Rose was eating much nowadays.

Musing over a display of cold meats, Ellie wondered how Ursula's mother was faring. Not a particularly attractive personality, but there ...

114

a heavy cold did tend to bring out the worst in one, didn't it? Mrs Belton had had a week in bed, and she hadn't fancied the frozen meals Ursula had left for her. Perhaps Ellie could drop some bits and bobs of dainty, easily-digested food round to Mrs Belton on her way home? Something to tempt the appetite?

Ellie bought more than she'd intended, but consoled herself by saying that whatever Mrs Belton didn't want, Thomas would eat.

Mrs Belton's flat wasn't far out of her way.

Ellie rang the doorbell and waited, checking her watch. Her stomach was rumbling because it was long past her lunch hour. Perhaps Mrs Belton was having an afternoon nap? For which Ellie couldn't blame her. A splendid idea.

Ursula's mother came to the door at last, hugging herself into a large mohair cardigan in a strident shade of salmon pink. Ellie didn't think young Ursula would have approved of it, but it would keep its wearer warm in a flat that was not particularly well heated.

'It's only me,' said Ellie. 'I was in the deli and bought far too much, so I wondered if you'd take some of it off my hands.'

'Come in, quickly, or I'll start sneezing again. It's true, I can't seem to fancy anything much at the moment. Yes, kind of you. Forgive the mess, I was lying down when the doorbell rang. Oh, if you really mean it, this way to the kitchen.'

Ellie followed her hostess, who seemed distracted. 'Is anything the matter?'

'No, of course not. Well, yes, but ... do you fancy a cup of camomile tea? I can't seem to taste anything else at the moment, but ... is that one of the deli's quiches? They're wonderful, aren't they? Thirty seconds in the microwave, and fit for a king. Forgive me, but I have to listen out for the phone. Ursula promised to ring every day though she couldn't be sure what time she'd be able to make it, and there's this urgent message for her, which means I can't go back to bed until she's rung. It's so inconsiderate of young people nowadays. They think all we have to do is wait on them hand and foot.'

'No tea, thanks,' said Ellie, handing over the quiche she'd intended for her own lunch. 'I should have brought you some honey and a lemon. My husband swears by it. Do you have Ursula's timetable?'

'She usually rings just before supper, but now she's got to use a public phone she might call any time. After she'd gone I did wonder if I shouldn't have given her my own mobile phone, but I need it for work: contacting patients, changing appointments, that sort of thing. Besides, if she was careless enough to drop her phone, she only has herself to blame. They don't think of the worry they cause us, do they?' She popped the quiche into her micro-wave.

Ellie told herself it wouldn't do her any harm to wait for her own lunch. So Ursula hadn't told her mother how her mobile had got broken? An understandable omission, considering that Mrs Belton was still most unwell. And unsympathetic?

Ellie divided her little packets of food into two, and pushed one half over the table to Mrs Belton. 'There you are. Keep you going for a bit. I know Ursula stocked you up with frozen food, but little treats help when you're convalescing. You won't try to go back to work this week, will you?'

'I really must try to get out today. I feel as if I've been indoors for ever. Was that the phone?' It was. Mrs Belton hurried back into the living room as the microwave pinged, announcing that luncheon was served. 'Hello?' Mrs Belton picked up the phone.

Ellie didn't exactly mean to listen in, but she couldn't help overhearing what was said as she hovered in the doorway.

'No, Tim. She hasn't rung me yet. Give her a chance. She said she'd ring me every day, and I'm sure she will ... yes, yes, I'll make sure to tell her ... yes, I said I'd let you know when she phoned and I will, but ... I don't see quite what else I can do ... no, don't ring again this afternoon. I'll ring you when I've heard from her.'

Mrs Belton put the phone down, looking flushed. 'Young people, nowadays. They seem to think an invitation to a party is more important than work. I don't know, I really don't. Expecting me to take messages for Ursula, expecting her to come running back here when she should be making the most of her opportunities to socialize down in Portsmouth. It's more important than ever that she gets to know some nice young men down there, now that she's broken off her engagement to Dan.'

'That was one of the crowd? Anthony Prior?'

'Younger brother, Tim. He's got some stupid nickname, can't remember what. Would you believe, there's some big party this weekend, and they want Ursula to come. Apparently she's caught the eye of some jet-setter or other, who wants to get to know her better. She didn't say anything to me about attracting a wealthy man, but I suppose I really wasn't taking in much of what she did say, I was so poorly.'

'Your lunch is ready, and I imagine you'll want to have a little rest this afternoon,' said Ellie, trying to make allowances, but finding that she really didn't like the woman much.

'Stupid boy,' said Mrs Belton, looking at once annoyed and, surprisingly, a lot more capable. Maybe she was over the worst of her flu. 'You'd think he'd be wanting Ursula to get back with Daniel, instead of pushing her into the arms of a stranger, however much money he has to throw around. Tim even offered to go down to Portsmouth to fetch her back on Saturday, can you believe it?'

Ellie shook her head and said it was a sad day, which she wasn't sure that she really meant, but it seemed to satisfy Mrs Belton.

Once outside she found that the wind hadn't dropped, but that it was too late for her to return home and have lunch before she met Stewart at her old house. Luckily it wasn't far. She wondered if Stewart would know how to use her new phone. Thomas didn't. She supposed that in the end she'd have to go into a specialist shop where she'd be treated with condescension by some young thing hardly out of nappies, and be bombarded with facts that she wouldn't be able to take in. More likely than not they'd call her 'dearie' or 'luvvie' and it would drive her insane.

She crossed the road and turned the corner, smiling as her little semi came into view. The outside had been repainted and looked better than ever. Luckily, the fire hadn't touched her next door neighbours' house. Were either of their cars there? Armand would be at work, but Kate was usually at home during the day, looking after the children, but ... no, neither was there today.

Kate and Ellie had become close friends despite the age difference, and they still had frequent contact since Kate had a formidable financial brain, helped Roy's wife Felicity to keep her affairs in order and was one of the directors of Ellie's Trust.

Ellie surveyed her own house. The front garden had suffered when the firemen had trampled all over it as they extinguished the fire. It needed attention; nothing a bit of tender loving care wouldn't put right. Then Ellie stopped smiling, for there was a 'To Let' sign nailed to the front wall, put up by the 2Ds Estate Agency. Diana's agency.

Someone tapped on a car horn, and Stewart drew up beside her. He got out, clutching keys and a clipboard. He treated the noticeboard to a long stare, his face wiped clean of expression.

Ellie said, 'Stewart, you may not be aware of this, but my husband left me half this house outright. The other half is mine for life and only goes to Diana on my death. I had told her I would make it over to her to live in, but I'm not letting her have it to provide her with an income.'

He gave her a look full of unspoken thoughts. He had the unfashionable virtue of loyalty and probably wouldn't speak ill of Diana, even though she'd treated him badly when they were married, during their divorce, and ever since.

It was clear to Ellie that he knew something he wasn't sure he should tell her. Questions buzzed around her head, but it was too cold to stand still outside.

'Let's go in.' Stewart ushered her into the house; her well-remembered, much-loved house. Her first husband had brought her here soon after they were married, and despite all their ups and downs and his early death, it had been a comfortable home, and a welcoming one.

It was no longer her home.

The downstairs rooms had been emptied of furniture, some of which had been removed to the big house, some sold and some put in a skip. New double-glazed windows kept out the weather, while the ruined carpet had been replaced with laminated wood flooring. The walls were being painted magnolia, because that was the way Miss Quicke had always had her properties painted; a decision Ellie saw no reason to change.

There were painters working upstairs and down, and a workman whistling away as he fitted tiles on the kitchen floor. Stewart took out his clipboard to make notes about the odd things that still needed attention, while Ellie wandered around in a daze. She was surprised to find everything so much smaller than she remembered it; no doubt because she'd been living in a bigger house for months.

Her much-loved conservatory had been stripped of plants and what had once been a terracotta tiled floor had also been given the wooden treatment. Cold and noisy, but all the rage.

Going up the stairs she clung to the banister for a moment or two, remembering how Diana had pushed her down those stairs so many years ago, not meaning to hurt, of course, but still ... that fall had caused the last of her miscarriages, the one they had hoped that at long last ... ah well.

The bedrooms and bathroom were almost finished. She looked down on the back garden; that pretty little garden on which she'd lavished so much love over the years. No one had touched it since she'd moved to the big house, and it hurt a little to see it neglected.

Miss Quicke had never taken any interest in

the garden at the big house, though Rose had loved to potter about in it. Ellie hadn't wanted to trespass on Rose's territory, but she missed getting her hands dirty, cutting back here, encouraging there, sweeping up leaves, planning a new border. Perhaps Rose would let Ellie work in her garden now that she herself was so frail?

Stewart appeared at her elbow. 'They've serviced the boiler, checked out the electrics, the gas, put in a water meter, smoke alarms, etcetera. I've put extra men on to finish the redecorating, and barring accidents, we should be able to hand over the keys in a couple of days' time, maybe even tomorrow night.'

She blew her nose, stiffened her back and led the way downstairs. 'It's no longer my home. I thought I'd feel sad to see it go to someone else, but I'm not.'

'What do you want me to do about the "To Let" sign?'

'Take it down. I'll have a word with Diana this evening about it. If she isn't going to live in my house, then I'll let it myself. You can find me a tenant, can't you, Stewart? Now, let's go back to your car and get warm. My feet are frozen.'

He made her comfortable in his car, switched on the ignition, and started the heater. Then he got out again, carefully closing the door behind him. She watched him tussle with the 'To Let' sign and got out her iPhone. She really must tell Thomas she was going to be late. But how to switch it on? There was no obvious button to

122

use. Was there a switch at the top? Which way up was top?

Stewart got back into the car and settled himself, but didn't drive off.

She said, 'Do you know how to work one of these? I ought to ring home.'

'My father-in-law the councillor, Maria's dad, he's got one. He was showing us its tricks over Christmas. You need a computer to enable it, he said. Perhaps it's been done for you? Shall I have a look?'

She handed it over, and he pressed on the surface to produce a set of icons. 'Think of it as a computer screen, like a microwave panel. Touch and go. You want to make a phone call? You press this one and ... there you are.' He was going to hand it back to her, but froze. 'There's a lot of telephone numbers on this already. Your home number included.'

'How kind of Diana,' said Ellie, surprised but pleased. 'She gave it me for Christmas, and must have known I'd need—'

'Hang about. Let me just...' He touched this and that. Sighed. Handed it back to her without comment.

'Spit it out.'

'Diana set it up for herself. All those phone numbers are connected with the 2Ds Agency.'

A second-hand gift. Right. What else had she expected? An expensive gift, though. She handed it back to Stewart. 'I'm thinking of getting myself one of the old-fashioned ordinary kind of mobile and junking this one. Can you get it to ring through to home for me?'

He did so and handed it back to Ellie, who heard the phone ring and ring, unanswered. She left a message that she'd be back soon, and put the phone away. Stewart still hadn't started the car, but he had set the windscreen wipers working on the sleet which was now battering the world outside.

'Out with it,' said Ellie. 'There's something you think I ought to know? Let me guess. In a housing recession, estate agents often go to the wall. The 2Ds Agency is in trouble?'

'I wasn't going to say anything, but...' He threw up his hands. 'I've always admired Diana: her drive, her ambition. I was amazed when she decided to marry me, and shattered, though perhaps not particularly surprised, when she moved on. I thought it was my fault for not being man enough for her. Maria says it isn't.' He wiped a grin off his face. 'Maria is something else.'

Ellie tried to decipher the code. 'This is not about money but about sex? I know Diana's highly sexed.'

He nodded, fiddled with the ignition key. 'Being in the same line of business, you hear things. The 2Ds overvalue properties, their fees are slightly more than they should be, and they drive customers away with a hard sell. So yes, of course they're in trouble and may go to the wall. It's not that. A couple of days ago I had a visit from a woman wanting a job in my office. She'd just been sacked by Diana. Her tale was so lurid that I didn't believe her, but if half of what she said was true ... I think you need to talk to Diana as soon as possible.'

Having said as much as he thought was needed, he put the car in gear and drove smoothly off.

Well, if he wouldn't talk, he wouldn't. She tried something else. 'Your father-in-law knows everything that goes on at the Town Hall, doesn't he? What committee does he head up? Planning? Has he said anything about a Mr Prior?'

The car jerked as Stewart momentarily lost concentration. 'What do you want to know about the Priors? They're not good people to tangle with. Mr Prior has a finger in every pie going and there's talk of corruption. It's true that some rather surprising planning permissions have got through the council lately. Father-in-law is very concerned about it.'

He signalled and turned into the driveway of the big house. 'I used to be naive about politics, thinking it was all about people trying to do their best for others, but I've learned a lot since I've been working for Miss Quicke, and for you. Father-in-law wants me to consider standing for the council myself. He's been getting me to help him out with this and that. I'm beginning to see that it's all about finance and the art of the possible...' His voice trailed away. His eyes were fixed on a well-known car parked by Ellie's front door.

Ellie cleared her throat. 'Now, who's come

calling?' Though they both knew, didn't they?

There was no sign of the locksmith who had been supposed to arrive early that morning, and the front door was ajar. Ellie pushed it open, hoping, dreading what she might see.

The reality was worse even than she'd feared.

The large entrance hall was crowded with people and everyone in it seemed to be shouting or crying or doing both. Her architect cousin Roy was there, red in the face, and yelling at Diana ... who had glued herself to Thomas, and was sobbing into his shoulder. Thomas was showing signs of fright. The whites of his eyes were visible and he was ineffectually trying to pull Diana's arms away from round his neck. There was a pile of Diana's belongings at the foot of the staircase.

Roy's wife Felicity was there, hanging on to Roy's arm. She was crying, too, and at the same time trundling the baby buggy to and fro to satisfy her toddler, who, of course, was yelling.

Ellie's two cleaners were halfway up the stairs, mouths and eyes wide open. Of course. What a tale they'd have to tell!

Perhaps most distressing of all was Rose, holding a tea towel in one hand and a mug in the other, also weeping.

To add to the confusion, a burly man pushed into the hall past Ellie and Stewart. 'This the right house, missus? Sorry I'm late. Got held up.'

Everyone in the hall automatically turned to see who had come in. On seeing Ellie, there

126

was a general surge towards her. Ellie took half a step back, coming up against Stewart's stalwart form.

Ellie saw that Diana was trying to wind her legs around Thomas and in that instant she shed all her inhibitions, and gave way to the age-old instinct to fight for her mate. If Diana thought she could make a fool of Thomas, she had another think coming! Everyone else could wait.

Ellie thrust past Roy and Felicity to grab Diana by one wrist and haul her off Thomas. 'How dare you!' With a strength she hadn't known she possessed, Ellie whirled her much taller daughter across the hall till Diana's head snapped and she cried out.

Ellie flung the sitting room door wide and pushed Diana inside. 'Wait there! I'll deal with you in a minute.'

Ellie slammed the door on her daughter's indignation and turned to face the others. Who was next?

The locksmith. She pointed her finger at him. 'You should have been here hours ago. You can fit a spyglass in the door so I can see who's trying to get in, and then make yourself scarce. Thomas – attend to him, will you?'

Thomas was pulling his sweater straight. 'So sorry, Ellie. I was on the phone, didn't hear her.'

'Never mind that now.' Ellie prodded Stewart in the region of his heart. 'Tell me now, this minute, what you heard about Diana!'

Stewart looked dazed, not having been exposed to Ellie in this mood before. 'I'm told

Denis gets his leg over anything that moves.'

Ellie's eyes went to the sitting room door. 'I know that he once...'

'Of course. And recently too. Also the girls in the office. And clients. I hear his wife's thrown him out.'

Cousin Roy thrust his face at her. 'Ellie, this is urgent—'

Felicity wailed, picking up baby Mel, who was also red in the face. 'Ellie, I didn't want to—'

Thomas had taken the locksmith aside and was telling him what to do, accompanied by forceful gestures. The locksmith was protesting that it wasn't his fault that he was late, and that he couldn't stop now, not on any account. The volume of noise failed to decrease.

Except for Rose, who'd been reduced to whimpering. Ellie put her arm around Rose and held her tightly, while facing up to the rest of them.

'Roy, you are a good architect but an idiot with money. Take your wife and child home and calm them down. Do nothing, do you hear? Neither buy nor sell nor mortgage till you hear from me again. I'll phone you tomorrow, right? Not another word! Go!'

Rose was quivering within Ellie's arm, mopping up the tears running down her face with her tea towel, which had got itself wrapped around the mug she'd been drying. 'Sorry, so sorry, Ellie. She got in somehow, I don't know how, and I know you didn't want her to—'

Ellie said, 'Shush, dear. Hush a bye. I'm angry because she's upset you, that's all. Diana is my problem, and I'll deal with her. Now, darling Rose, can you do something for me? I'm desperately hungry, have missed lunch and really could do with some soup or, well, anything. Can you find something for me to eat, now? And have you had something yourself? And Thomas?'

The one thing guaranteed to drag Rose out of her tears was an appeal for her to cater for hungry people, and it worked. 'Oh, what must you think of me, hanging around here when you're hungry. And yes, we had a lovely fry-up, a full English breakfast for our lunch. Thomas is such a good cook, isn't he?'

Ellie made a mental note to talk to her husband about going on a diet; but not at that moment. She urged Rose towards the kitchen. 'I'm dying of hunger, dear. And a nice cup of tea, as well?'

Once the kitchen door closed behind Rose, Ellie turned on the two cleaners, who would have a good tale to carry back to Maria at the end of the day, wouldn't they? She only had to raise her eyebrows for them to discover they were halfway through tasks upstairs, and vanish.

Stewart next? But Stewart didn't need hinting away. He winked at her as he helped Felicity to settle Mel in her buggy, and followed her out of the house. Ellie saw Roy open his mouth to start arguing, but she held up her hand, giving him such a strong signal to desist that he actually did so. And took his family off without further demur. The locksmith had already departed.

And then there were two.

Thomas wiped his hand across his forehead. 'Apologies. Diana let herself in while I was on the phone, Roy came in through the kitchen and upset Rose, and then Felicity arrived with the baby. Diana says she's homeless, wanted me to promise to help her. She was trying to...' He rolled his shoulders. 'Sorry, Ellie. I should have been more careful. No one would let anyone else speak. I've never been more thankful in my life than when you come through that door.'

Ellie nodded. He made as if to put his arm around her, but she fended him off. She couldn't afford to be tender and loving at the moment. She was on a high, and needed to stay that way, in order to cope with Diana. 'It's all right, Thomas, I understand. Now let me deal with my daughter.'

She marched into the sitting room and closed the door behind her. Diana was sitting on the big settee, handkerchief to mouth. Waiting for Ellie.

Ellie knew that this interview could go one of two ways: she could try to be patient and understanding, as always, or she could precipitate a rip-roaring row. She supposed Thomas would be all for the quieter procedure, being a forgiving sort of person. Ellie wasn't sure she could be that self-controlled.

The room was darkening at the corners; dusk

was descending early. Ellie ignored Diana to switch on a couple of sidelights. The room was not quite warm enough with background central heating, so it would be pleasant to have the fire lit as well. Ellie bent to put it on.

Diana watched, over her hankie. 'You know something? You're beginning to turn into Great Aunt.'

'Well,' said Ellie, sinking into Miss Quicke's high-backed chair by the fire, 'we both know what she thought of your carryings-on, don't we?'

Diana started to laugh and sob at the same time. 'Who else can I turn to? Denis and I ... well, you know! His wife's thrown him out, so...' She flapped her hankie. She really was crying, but also trying to smile. 'Naturally, he came to me for help.'

'And moved into your flat? Why aren't you cosying up to him in your own bed, then?'

'You don't understand. He needs his own space and somewhere to see the boys after school and at weekends. I'll visit him in the evenings, when they're not there.'

'A businesslike arrangement. I don't see what you get out of it, though.'

'Well, you've never had a strong sexual urge in your whole life, have you?'

Ellie set her teeth. Perhaps with her first husband sex might have been routine rather than deeply pleasurable, but with Thomas...

No, she was not going to go into detail about her sex life with Diana. On the other hand, the recent scene in the hall was engraved on her mind's eye. 'I understand very well what you were trying to do to Thomas just now.'

Diana half smiled. 'Well, what of it? He's a man, isn't he?'

'Just this. If I ever find you trying that on again I shall put you over my knee, and don't think I couldn't, because the way I feel at the moment I could happily slap you into the middle of next week.'

Diana jolted upright. 'You? Don't be stupid! You've never laid a finger on me.'

'A mistake. Your father and I believed sweet reason would prevail, but—'

'I could always wind him round my little finger.' Diana shrugged. 'Oh well, if I promise to leave poor ickle Thomas alone in future, you'll help me out, right?'

'You're going too fast. Suppose you fill me in on what's been happening.'

'Well,' Diana leaned forward, tears forgotten, 'Denis and I have been an item off and on ever since we started the agency, which is not to say that we didn't both of us look elsewhere from time to time. Oh, don't look so shocked, his wife hasn't been interested in him forever.'

'Remind me how many children they have? Three or four?'

Diana frowned. 'They're part of the problem. Their school fees are horrendous. Denis raised a mortgage on their house to start the agency, but what with everything falling apart in the housing market, and his wife throwing him out,

132

we're in real trouble financially. The agency is all we've got left. Somehow or other we've got to keep it going until things improve.'

'Do you suppose Denis will ever marry you?'

Diana shrugged again. 'I don't care about marriage. I'm not defined by a wedding ring.' Did she mean that Ellie was? 'Anyway, Denis said that if we keep our heads and maximize our assets, we'll be all right.'

'By which he meant moving into your flat instead of buying one for himself when his wife threw him out? By which he meant taking over and letting out the house that I was giving you to live in?'

'Well, you don't need the income from your old house, and we do. I know that I can always rely on you to keep me off the streets, even if you don't always like the way I behave.'

'No, I don't like the way you behave, and no, I'm not giving you an easy way out. You've intentionally made yourself homeless, and I've changed my mind about handing over my old house to you. As you say, the housing market has taken a dive, and my income has been reduced. So if you're not going to live in it, I must maximize my assets and let it out myself.'

'What!' For the first time a shade of uneasiness crossed Diana's face. 'You don't mean it. You're just trying to frighten me. All right. I'm sorry if I took you for granted, but I'm desperate for somewhere else to live, and you are my only hope ... as if you didn't know it. You really shouldn't try to play hard to get. People

133

will think you're more interested in money than in your own family.'

Family? Thomas was more her family than Diana had ever been. Ellie remembered how Diana had rubbed herself up against Thomas and the thought drove her to her feet, itching to send Diana flying into orbit around the world. 'You can't expect me to let you stay after what you tried to do to Thomas. I don't know where you're going to sleep tonight, and I don't care. So long as it's not here.'

'What?' Diana couldn't believe what she was hearing. 'Mother, you can't be serious. I'm relying on you.'

'Just go, will you?'

Diana looked undecided. She jiggled her lips, frowned, unable to comprehend her mother's unexpected defiance. 'You can't turn me out. Where would I go?'

'Go back to your flat. Tell Denis to make it up with his wife. If he takes his boys out of private school, he could save himself a fortune.'

'He thought of that, but he had to sign up for a year and ... no, I'm not going back to the flat. It's too small, too cramped. I outgrew it ages ago. I need—'

'You need a dose of reality, my girl, and that's what you're about to get. Sleep in your car, if you wish, but not on my doorstep.' Ellie marched out to the hall where she seemed to remember Diana had left her coat, briefcase and handbag in a pile. Yes, there they all were. Ellie opened Diana's handbag, sought for, found and removed Rose's keys.

Diana hovered in the doorway, frowning and then smiling. 'Mother, you can't do this. I'm not going to let you—'

Ellie drew back the bolts on the front door, used Rose's keys to open it, and flung it wide. The chilliest of winds rushed into the hall, and someone exclaimed something about the draught. Thomas, coming out of the kitchen with a tray in his hands? Ellie, still on a high, picked up Diana's belongings and threw them out into the drive.

Diana screamed, high and thin, and went after them. 'What on earth do you think you're doing?'

Ellie slammed the door behind Diana, and drove the bolts home. She dusted her hands off, one against the other, and said, 'Ha!'

Thomas laughed. 'Would madam have time for some food now?'

Ellie was too angry, too tired, to be reasonable. The fact that he was offering her some food on a tray was, in some way she couldn't explain, an insult. Food? In this crisis? No way.

She snatched the tray from him and threw it with all her strength across the hall. Soup splashed richly across the panelling. Sandwiches flew across the floor. Plates broke. Cutlery scattered.

She screamed, as loudly as she could. 'Aargh!'

'Ursula here. Tim, is that you? I got a message

to ring you, urgently. Is something wrong? My mother? Dan?'

'No, no. They're both all right. It's just that—'

'I've been imagining all sorts; accidents, fires, mother in hospital.'

'No, it's nothing like that. It's—'

'It's Dan then, isn't it? I'm desperately fond of him still but—'

'It's not Dan. He's perfectly all right. Having all sorts of fun now you've let him off the leash.'

Silence. 'So, what's the rush?'

'We don't want you drifting away from us. Of course you were upset about Lloyd and Mia. We all were. But losing two of our members makes it even more important for the rest of us to stick together, and I always thought you could have done a lot better than Dan. Now there's a special someone who's been hanging around, waiting for you to get over Dan ... are you still there, Ursula?'

'I'm still here.'

'Well, The Man's throwing a drinks party at home this Saturday, and we want you to come, to show there's no hard feelings, right?'

'After what you lot did to me? No, I don't think so.'

'Look, Ursula, we all got upset, didn't we? We did things that maybe weren't too clever—'

'Tim, you held my hands up in the air while Anthony assaulted me.'

'Not "assaulted", not really.'

'You laughed, Tim. You all did. You made me

136

beg to be released. You made me cry. Do you think I'm going to forget that?'

'I'm sorry, yes. It was bad. Destroying your mobile was wrong too. I don't quite know what got into us that night. It's something I don't like to think back on, now. Look, I'll buy you another phone, shall I? As for Anthony, I'm sure he'll apologize, if that's what you want.'

A sigh. 'Sorry, Tim. You were always the best of the bunch, after Dan. I wish you could learn to think for yourself sometime, and not always rush to obey Anthony's slightest wish, but there it is. We are what we are. If Mia had still been around perhaps ... have you any idea what happened to her?'

'I ... no, I don't. She packed up and took off when we were all out one day. I must admit I miss her, but life goes on.'

'Yes, it does. That part of my life's over, and I've got to move on too. Let me know if you ever hear from Mia, will you? I wish you well, but I won't be coming to your party.'

'But Ursula—'

'Goodbye, Tim.'

EIGHT

Tuesday evening

Silence assailed her ears. She could almost feel the astonishment of the big house, which had never, in all its hundred years of existence, been subjected to anyone screaming in that unladylike way.

And Thomas? Undoubtedly he would be shocked by her behaviour, so she didn't look at him. She turned on her heel, pounded up the polished wooden staircase and went straight into their bedroom, slamming the door behind her. If he dared to follow her, she'd ... she didn't know what she'd do, but he'd better not!

She threw herself on the bed and told herself it would do no good at all to cry as it would only give her a headache and then she'd be fit for nothing, and someone was going to have to clean up that mess in the hall, and she'd upset Thomas, too, and she didn't care! Not she! They could all go to ... wherever. So long as she didn't have to see them or talk to them or ... well, not tonight, anyhow.

She sobbed a little, pressing her face into her pillow. She was not going to allow herself to cry. Certainly not.

She reached for a box of tissues and blew her nose. Her throat was dry and sore. It would serve everyone right if her cold turned to pneumonia. Perhaps she really was sickening for something serious. Well, that would teach them all not to count on her to pick them up every time they fell over and hurt themselves.

It was getting dark. She didn't bother to get off the bed to draw the curtains. Too much effort.

She pulled the duvet over her, fully dressed as she was, and sighed. Let the world go hang.

She woke when one of the bedside lights was switched on.

Whatever time was it?

And oh ... how appallingly badly she'd behaved. She'd had a full-scale tantrum, how awful! She felt as if she'd been run over by an express train. Her head ached, and her eyes were puffy and she was, astonishingly, hungry.

She tried to sit up, and failed. She felt hot and sticky and horrible. And she needed to go to the loo.

Thomas was bending over her, looking anxious. She avoided his eyes, reached for a hankie, couldn't find one, connected with a box of tissues, blew her nose and sat upright. More or less.

'I'm sorry,' she said. And then, 'Are you all right?'

'I'm all right if you're all right.' He wasn't smiling, either. There was another tray of food on a table in the window. He'd put it far enough away so that she couldn't hurl it across the room. Oh dear. How awful of her to behave so badly, to make so much trouble for everyone else. But how satisfying it had been to throw Diana out! Ha!

Thomas drew the curtains against the night and then stood watching her, stroking his beard. 'Light of my life! Whatever will you do next? Am I allowed to kiss you now? You look like a white owl, all big eyes and ruffled feathers.'

She tried to laugh and almost made it. 'I'm sorry. I shouldn't have taken it out on you. I don't know what came over me.'

'Flu, followed by too much pressure from everyone – including me – leading to an extreme reaction which I, for one, fully endorse.'

She got off the bed. 'But how awful of me, to throw out my only daughter.' Her mouth curled into a grin. 'I actually did it, didn't I? But I feel so guilty, having all these rooms in this big house and I could easily have said she could stay. Except that I didn't want her to because it would mean an end to our peace and quiet, and of course that's a bad reason. But no, she went too far.'

He knew what she meant. 'Yes, she did. And no, I didn't handle it too well. It's not as if I haven't had experience of women coming on to me. Pop stars and the clergy often get it, and I suppose it means as little to the pop stars as to the clergy. The pop stars can often get a minder to prise the groupie off their back, but a clergyman can't risk manhandling a woman, so we usually send an experienced woman to deal with the problem. Which you did, very neatly.'

She tried to smile. Not a great effort. 'I feel all hot and sticky. I think I'll have a shower. It might improve my temper.'

'I didn't know you had a temper.' He didn't seem to mind. 'It's good to know there are limits to what you'll put up with.'

'Actions speak louder than words?'

As she came out of the shower she heard the landline ring and Thomas laughing. She shrugged herself into her white towelling robe – another present from Thomas – and joined him, murmuring, 'Who is it?'

'Stewart,' he said, and into the phone, 'I'll hand you over to her now, but before I do so, tell me, how did Maria react? Ellie broke two plates!'

'What?' Ellie snatched the phone from him. 'Stewart? What...?'

Stewart was laughing. 'I was just telling Thomas. You won't believe this! Diana turned up here half an hour ago, hung herself round my neck and demanded that I supply her with bed and board. So I yelled for Maria, who was more than equal to the occasion.'

'What? How did she...?'

'Maria said that Diana might doss down on the settee in the sitting room tonight if she'd take over the day nanny's job tomorrow, but Diana should be warned that the baby's got diarrhoea and will need her nappy changing every half hour. Diana was so incensed that she upped sticks and drove off, fuming.'

Ellie was enchanted. 'And did Maria break anything afterwards?'

'She tidied the room ruthlessly, and then – er – well, she dragged me upstairs, not that I needed much dragging and ... what a woman! She's making a late night snack for us now, so I'll cut this short. I thought you'd like to know the latest.'

Laughing, Ellie put the phone down. And then blenched. 'Rose. She was upset! I must go to her at once. How could I have forgotten—'

'Rose is fine, tucked up in bed downstairs with a sandwich, watching telly, thrilled that you threw Diana out. The cleaners finished turning out my new quiet room and have gone for the day. I cleared up the mess in the hall, so you don't have to worry about that, either. When did you eat last? I put up some more sandwiches, and there's soup in the Thermos.'

Ellie allowed herself to grin. 'Spoils for the victor? Thank you, Thomas. I appreciate it.' But as she relaxed, other thoughts crowded in on her. 'Oh, I'm so sorry, you should be working on your paper for the weekend and you've been rushing around after me, instead. And there's Roy, and Felicity's so worried about him, and if he's coming round tomorrow, what am I going to say to him? And then there's Ursula. I went to see DI Willis, but ... Thomas, I should be doing all sorts of things, ringing up people ... Thomas, calm me down. What do I do first?'

'Eat, my little pigeon. Soup first. Don't talk.

142

When you've cleared the plates, then you can tell me all, and we'll decide what – if anything – you need to do tonight.'

Good advice, if she could have taken it. She started on the soup, but her brain was whirring with doubts and worries. 'What of your day?'

'I've printed off the paper I'm giving, and it's all right, I think. And the magazine? Submissions include something old, something new, something borrowed, something blue.'

'How blue? Can you print it?'

'Eggshell blue. And no, I can't. Sometimes I worry that I might be losing my ability to be shocked by human nature. Sometimes I think plagiarism offends me more than the occasional swear word.'

'Thus speaks a good editor. But copying someone else's work is stealing, and it's right to be offended by it.'

He sighed, passing her the plate of sandwiches. 'Surely at my age I ought to be past getting angry at such things?'

She laughed. She was surprised at herself for laughing, after all that had happened. A gust of hail struck the windows, and both glanced towards it.

Thomas said, 'Diana can take refuge in her office, if the worst comes to the worst.'

'In the office she'll have the keys to all the houses they have on their books to sell. I'm not sorry I threw her out,' said Ellie, ready for a fight if he disagreed.

'I must admit to enjoying that moment too. I

only wish I'd been a fly on the wall when Maria worsted Diana. You'll want to discuss it at your usual property meeting tomorrow, anyway. Is it one of the ones that Kate comes to?'

Ellie took the last sandwich, sighing with content. 'I love you, Thomas.'

'Ditto,' he said. 'And when you've finished making your phone calls, perhaps we can have an early night.'

Ellie grinned. One of Thomas's 'early nights' meant they'd sleep well.

Wednesday morning

Ellie did not want to think about Diana, but couldn't stop doing so. Where had she spent the night? Had Ellie's actions been sensible, or sinful? On the whole she still felt pleased with herself, but with an undercurrent of guilt.

Turning her mind from an unproductive debate with herself over Diana, Ellie found herself worrying about Rose's gentle decline. If she were to follow Aunt Drusilla into the grave ... no, it didn't bear thinking about.

Ellie psyched herself up to enter the kitchen and found Rose already there, humming to herself as she made breakfast for them all. What a nice surprise! Rose said it had made all the difference not having to climb the stairs, and she'd had a lovely night's rest though she was afraid she'd left the telly on all night, but that didn't really matter, did it?

No, it didn't. What an enormous relief to see Rose dashing about, almost as spry as ever!

Ellie told herself that she'd been worrying unnecessarily about, well, everything. Not that that did much good. If you were the worrying sort, then you'd find something to worry about, even if you didn't need to.

Thomas took the last piece of toast and final cup of coffee off into his office, even as the phone rang. Ellie took it in the sitting room where she'd gone to do the morning tidy-up.

It was Ursula, speaking high and fast. 'Mrs Quicke, we just got the mail. However can I thank you? When I got your parcel, I was so surprised I nearly dropped it. It was so thoughtful of you and I can't tell you how much better it makes me feel. My mother will be pleased, too, knowing she can contact me easily. I do worry about her, you know.'

'I dropped in to see her yesterday. She's not fit to go back to work yet, but she's coming on nicely.'

'Of course she's not fit to go back yet, but if I know her she'll probably try to do so, because she worries so about her clients. She's ultra-conscientious where they're concerned. I'm going to ring her in a minute to give her this number, set her mind at rest, about contacting me at any rate.'

'Talking of setting your mind at rest. I saw Detective Inspector Willis yesterday, but I'm afraid—'

'I know. They've settled it in their minds that Lloyd got drunk and fell, and that Mia was a slag who went off with another man. Thanks for trying. I'm sorry I dragged you into this. I've been talking to some of my friends down here and they say that these things happen and that I really must put the past behind me, get on with my life. They say I've never really tried to get the most out of university because I was always going back up to London to see Dan and the rest of the gang. They're right. I've missed out on a lot here. I've made a resolution to change all that.'

'Sensible girl.'

Ursula sighed. 'I don't feel very sensible. Too many loose ends, I suppose. You won't believe this, but Tim Prior phoned yesterday asking me to go back up to town this weekend for some party or other. He says they don't want to lose any more friends, and there's someone they want me to meet. As if! I wanted to ask how they could forget it all so quickly, but I didn't. I suppose I ought to have gone to the police about the way he and Anthony treated me, but–' she tried out a laugh – 'I won't, because it would only prolong the agony. Evidence of a new maturity on my part, do you think?'

'Probably, yes.'

Ursula sighed. 'My friends here want me on some committee or other, something to do with the Student Union. I said I'd give it a try. So think of me discussing fund-raising, instead of partying this weekend.'

'If you're short of a few pence any time...'

'No, thank you, Mrs Quicke. You've done enough, and more than enough, and I appreciate it. And especially I appreciate the mobile. But I pay my own way; usually, that is.' This time her laugh seemed genuine. She rang off.

Ellie should have been heartened by this phone call. After all, how many young people nowadays bother to say 'thank you' for gifts? Ursula was a nice, sensible girl and Ellie wished her well.

So why couldn't Ellie be just as sensible?

She stared out of the window, twitching at the long velvet curtains to let more of the drab winter's light into the sitting room. She noticed that the little silver bell, which her aunt Drusilla had always used in order to summon Rose, had drifted back into the sitting room. A nuisance. It was supposed to be left beside Rose's chair nowadays, but seemed to have a life of its own. Ellie supposed the cleaners had moved it again.

She checked her watch. Time for the weekly meeting to deal with the properties left her by her aunt. She checked the radiators in the dining room. Yes, they were warming the room nicely.

Stewart was the first to arrive, smiling a little. He'd obviously had a good night's sleep too.

Pat, Ellie's middle-aged and efficient assistant, had come back to work for the first time for a week. She was still sniffling and not quite as sharp as usual, but then who was, on a dark January day? Kate, their financial whiz-kid, arrived with a tiny posy of daphne and winter jasmine plucked from Ellie's old garden to cheer her up. Actually, it made Ellie feel more like crying, because there was neither daphne nor winter jasmine in the garden at the big house. Ellie put the flowers in a silver vase that she couldn't remember ever having seen in use before, and hoped it wouldn't leak. Then she chid herself for allowing such a depressing thought.

Ellie tried not to think about Diana more than once a minute as the four of them moved into the dining room and settled down to discuss the housing situation and the possible effects on their tenants. Stewart gave his weekly report, and pointed out that in the present climate many of those in Ellie's properties were going to find it hard to keep up the rental payments. Ellie could, of course, resort to the small claims division of the County Court to try to recover any money owing.

Kate shook her head. 'Time-consuming, costly, and probably counterproductive. Might as well turn ourselves into a charitable housing association and be done with it.'

'I'm thinking along those lines anyway,' said Ellie.

'Ouch,' said Kate. 'I wasn't serious. Doing that – and it would take months to set up – means you'd reduce the income for the Trust. If you reduce the income for the Trust, then you'll have less money to distribute to those in need, and the directors of the Trust wouldn't be happy about that.'

'Suppose we lower our rents for those in trouble financially?'

'Tricky,' said Kate. 'We'd have to bring in

means-testing. We'd still have high maintenance bills to pay and we'd have to pick up the slack.'

'Could we ask appropriate families to downsize? After all, we have properties of all sorts in different neighbourhoods.'

'We could. It would be a lot of extra work for Stewart and his team, but it would save our tenants from being thrown out on to the street. Any properties we can't re-let immediately might benefit from a good wash and brush-up.'

Stewart was frowning. 'Someone once said that the poor are never grateful, and in my experience that's true. It would be like stirring porridge to get them to downsize, but yes, it's worth trying, and there are quite a few properties that could benefit from updating, particularly in the bathroom and kitchen areas.'

Kate lifted a finger to attract attention. 'There is one more thing we ought to consider. In a recession, the price of houses falls dramatically. It's true that Ellie is worth much less on paper now than before this happened, but she's not short of a penny and doesn't need to sell any of her properties at lowered prices. Instead of selling she might consider buying, as and when suitable properties come on to the market.'

Ellie's mind leapt to Prior's Place, and from that to the block of flats which Roy had inherited. Kate looked at Ellie in her frowning way, as if expecting Ellie to pursue the subject, but Ellie wasn't sure what she thought about either, so merely nodded and closed the meeting.

On the point of leaving, Stewart took Ellie aside. 'Do you still want to rent out your old house? I've got some possible tenants in mind. Shall I take them round?'

Ellie nodded. No one had mentioned Diana during the meeting and no one did now. Oh Diana, where are you?

Stewart gave her a quick, absent-minded kiss on her cheek and left. Their relationship had always been formal in the old days when he'd been married to Diana, but since then they'd become good friends. Perhaps one day she'd even ask him to call her by her Christian name.

Kate had taken her time putting her papers away, but was now ready to leave too. Ellie walked her to the door.

'Kate, what do you think of the mess Roy's got himself into?'

'We could take the flats off him, but you've decided against that already, haven't you? You want me to try the City, see if anyone would care to buy Prior's Place outright? I'm not sure that's going to be easy.'

'It would solve a big problem for me if you could. Have a try, yes?'

Ellie helped Pat tidy the dining room and transfer their papers to Ellie's study. It was good to have her back. Pat was fiftyish – like Ellie – and also fairly substantial in build. Divorced, with two children now more or less off her hands, Pat had good IT skills, and was also not averse to a gossip. Today she blew her nose, brewed coffee and made a start on the mail which had accumulated in her absence.

'You're hardly fit yet,' said Ellie. 'And I'm so ... I don't know. Can't concentrate. I keep thinking about Ursula and her friend Mia. Oh, sorry. You don't know about them, do you? Let me fill you in.'

When she'd finished Ellie said, 'Pat, do we know anyone – maybe a student – at the university here? I promised to make some enquiries, but I don't know where to start.'

Pat sniffled and thought. 'I know someone in the Admissions Office slightly. If a student's dropped out, she'd know. Shall I ring her for you?'

'Bless you. I don't know all that much about Mia, apart from her name and the address of the family home which she seems to have left in a hurry. It's a second marriage for her mother, no shortage of money, seems to have run with a fast set headed by her stepbrothers. I suspect she had private schooling. It's not much to go on, is it?'

In the old days she'd have gone out herself to enquire about Mia, wouldn't she? Well, actually – no. She wouldn't have known where to start. The world of the student was a closed book to her.

Worry, worry. She was such a useless sort of person today, not knowing what to do with herself. She collected the silver bell from the sitting room and took it out to the kitchen, where Rose was humming away to the food mixer. Rose seemed to have recovered her spirits and there was even a little colour in her face.

'You look so much better, Rose,' said Ellie, relieved.

Rose pointed a wooden spoon at her. 'Go away and do something useful, such as getting in something for supper tonight. I haven't the time to go shopping, have I? And take that bell back to the sitting room where it belongs, for I don't need it.'

Ellie made herself scarce. She couldn't think of anything she really wanted to do. There were plenty of things she *ought* to be doing, of course, but that was not the same thing at all. Maybe she'd get round to the shopping later.

She went to see how Thomas was getting on. He was muttering away to himself, concentrating on his computer, but managed to recognize her after a few seconds, and even broke off long enough to remind her that he had a meeting up in town that afternoon and would be late for supper if that was all right with her. Of course it was; whatever suited him would suit her.

'Oh, and Ellie. I've been thinking. A gift is a gift, isn't it? I mean, if you give someone something you can't specify what it's to be used for. What do you think?'

Ah. He meant that although she'd given Diana her old house on the understanding that her daughter intended to live in it, she couldn't take the gift back now just because Diana wanted to let it out. Perhaps he was right but no, she wasn't ready to admit it.

She went upstairs to check that the cleaners had done a proper job on the quiet room she'd set aside for Thomas, and found it just that: quiet. He'd moved the big chair a couple of feet along the wall. She wasn't sure why, but when she sat in it, she saw that he now had more space in front of him. He liked a bit of elbow room. Perhaps he was the tiniest bit claustrophobic? She sat in his chair, thinking about nothing very much. She'd noticed before that any room in which Thomas prayed soon collected an air of peace. This one had, already. She wasn't feeling particularly peaceful, herself.

She supposed she could try to pray. She didn't think she was much good at it. She certainly wasn't any good at listening, she knew that. *Dear Lord.* She couldn't get any further, she was in such a tangle. Oh well. She'd tried. Sort of. She thought she might have dozed off for a while, but something woke her, and she sprang to her feet smoothing back her hair, tugging her skirt into place.

What was she thinking about, wasting time like this? That poor child Mia was out there somewhere, if she weren't lying dead in a ditch. Ursula wasn't an alarmist, but a very practical person. There must be something that Ellie could do to help.

There was.

Downstairs, Pat held out some slips of paper. 'My contact at the University says that Mia does seem to have dropped out, though it's early days to be sure. Term only started last week but she hasn't turned up yet. I asked about her friends – who might be in her class, that sort of thing. They said only her tutors would know and they hadn't time to worry about that at the moment – the start of term, you know; they're really busy.

'Then I thought that if Mia went to a fee-paying school, well, there aren't that many, and so I rang someone I knew who taught drama at the nearest one. She's retired now and we both belong to the Ealing branch of the National Trust, but she remembers Mia well, though of course the girl left school some years ago. I said Mia had gone missing and she's anxious to help, so you might like to contact her.'

Pat hesitated, and Ellie raised an eyebrow. 'A problem?'

'Well, no. Not really. It's just that...' Pat made up her mind to be frank. 'Grace Woodyates had a long-term relationship with a married man for many years, and it was always understood that when his wife died ... you get the picture? Just as Grace retired, his wife died. Only he went and married his secretary instead, who was a much younger woman. It was quite a blow to Grace and it's turned her, I'm not sure how to put it but, well, she's a bit lonely, I suppose. She plunges into things left, right and centre. She can be a bit embarrassing.'

'I've been warned,' said Ellie, taking the telephone number.

* * *

'Dumbo, drop everything. Small problem. I've been on to Mrs B and she says Ursula's decided against coming back this weekend.'

'Told you so.'

'Don't interrupt. There's no way we can disappoint our client, so I've been working out how to get the girl back and in the right frame of mind.'

'Ursula's still livid with what we did to her. An apology from you might help.'

'Apology nothing. She needs teaching the facts of life.'

'No, Anthony, no! Not again! I've had nightmares about—'

'Forget Mia. I think I know where she is, and she certainly isn't walking the streets. Now, shut up and listen. You say Ursula's a different kettle of fish, and of course she is, or she wouldn't be attracting His Highness. What he does to amuse himself with her is no business of ours. Remember, he's got diplomatic immunity, so the police can't charge him with anything. He'll buy the flats as an investment, we get paid off, and we'll let her have a couple of hundred for her trouble, right?'

'She won't be as easy to control as Mia.'

'So we start conditioning her now. This is what I want you to do. When the pubs close tonight...'

155

NINE

Wednesday noon

It didn't seem likely that a retired teacher who'd been out of touch with Mia for some years could be of the slightest assistance, but it was as well to check, wasn't it? Ellie tried the number Pat had given her, and heard a well-modulated voice say that she would be delighted to help. Would Ellie like to drop in some time, perhaps that very morning?

Mindful of the appalling weather, Ellie summoned a minicab and had herself conveyed to a narrow street of modern terraced houses at the back of the town centre. Ms Woodyates was an over-the-top anorexic blonde living in over-heated, over-furnished surroundings decorated with photographs of old playbills. Ms Woodyates was powdered, painted and well over sixty, but was dressed in a bilious green silk suit with a décolleté neckline.

'My little collection,' said Ms Woodyates, waving towards the playbills and trying to be modest about her hobby. 'You are a theatregoer aren't you, Mrs Quicke? Most intelligent people are, aren't they? Theatre is the very pulse of life in society, don't you agree?' She didn't wait for a reply, but continued, 'I've heard lots about you, so kind to so many, we really must have you on our Ealing branch of the National Trust committee.'

Coffee was offered. In fact, had already been prepared against Ellie's coming. Coming in out of the cold, Ellie dived for her paper tissues and blew her nose. She remembered Pat's words of warning, and prepared for a lengthy visit and a lecture on the benefits of the National Trust and all the good it did. It was no use saying that she was convinced and already a contributor, for Ms Woodyates – 'call me Grace, please'– did seem lonely and was delighted to have a visitor. The coffee was good, anyway. At last Ellie managed to insert the name of Mia into the conversation.

'Mia,' said Ms Woodyates, 'a delightful child. Bright but polite with it. Most bright children are not polite nowadays, have you noticed? I am surprised to hear that she's gone missing. Not the sort to get into trouble, I would have thought.'

'We're not sure that she's in trouble, exactly. It's just that she seems to have dropped out; left home without leaving a forwarding address. Her friends are concerned – one in particular. I'm trying to get a picture of what Mia was like. I suppose girls change enormously after leaving school, and it's hardly fair to ask you for your opinion, although–' as Ms Woodyates arched pencilled eyebrows – 'I would certainly welcome it.'

'You are referring to those girls who can't wait to experience life to the full, the ones who are ruled by their hormones from an early age. They may "blossom" out – or "bosom out" as I like to put it – but you can usually see the signs before they leave school. Mia was not like that. I don't mean that she was underdeveloped physically, because she wasn't. She was beautiful in a quiet way, with lovely eyes and long dark hair, much longer and thicker than most. Have you met the mother?'

Ellie shook her head.

A frown disturbed Ms Woodyates's smooth brow which had, Ellie thought, probably been treated with Botox. 'A trifle, shall we say, flamboyant? She was quite a beauty in her day, she tells me, though I'm not sure she realizes how many years have passed since that time. Mia was her daughter by her first marriage, you know, and perhaps ... the Snow White syndrome, you know? I think she was jealous of the girl's beauty, because she used to put her down at every opportunity. In spite of what her mother said, Mia was a bright girl, currently studying some foreign language, I believe. '

Well, that was an interesting sidelight on the mother and daughter relationship.

'Perhaps it's an odd question to ask nowadays, but do you think Mia was still a virgin when she left school?'

A moue of distaste. 'In the staff room we believed you could count them on the fingers of one hand. But yes, I would say that Mia was still a virgin when she left school.'

Ellie sighed. 'So many years ago; so much may have happened to change her.'

'Oh, I don't think so. I don't know if it's scientifically proven but we used to say in the staff room that, after a girl has experienced sex, her lower eyelids appear more prominent, almost pouched. I can honestly report that Mia's eyelids showed no sign of it when I last saw her. Now when would that have been?'

She closed her eyes and lifted her chin, holding up one hand to prevent Ellie from interrupting. 'Ah, I have it. It was just before Christmas; carol-singing in the tube station. Someone had bought the choir these adorable little red Father Christmas caps, and the boys were all wearing them but the girls!' – a shrug – 'I suppose they didn't want to crush their hairstyles. Mia was wearing one. I was coming back from town and got out my purse to make a donation. I don't remember exactly what charity they were singing for, but Mia recognized me. I put the money in her tin, she smiled at me and said "thank you". I remember thinking then that she hadn't altered at all from when she was at school. I'm sorry to hear she's missing. What do you think happened?'

'That's what I'm trying to find out. Can you work out which day it was that you saw her? Perhaps I can trace her companions through the choir she was with.'

Ms Woodyates sought for her last year's diary. 'The Saturday before Christmas. I'd been

159

up to town for a matinée. I suppose it would have been half six or a quarter to seven in the evening. And, let me think ... if I could only visualize the banner they had with them, or the stickers on the collecting tins...'

Again she closed her eyes and lifted her hands in an effort to recall the occasion. 'Was it Help the Aged? No. The Hospice, I think. Now what choir was it? I recognized one or two faces, didn't I? Yes, yes. My old friend Ronald was with them. Shall I ring him, see if he can cast any light...?'

She didn't wait for Ellie to agree, but attacked her phone book and pressed numbers. 'Ronald? Yes, it's Grace here. Grace Woodyates. Yes, long time, but perhaps some time soon ... oh yes, of course I understand. Well, what it was, I wondered, one of my past students seems to have got herself into a bit of a pickle; left home under a cloud ... yes, in this day and age, but really she's not like that. At least, I don't think so. Now I spotted her in your choir at the tube station just before Christmas, and I wondered ... Mia, a nice, quiet girl, with long, dark hair ... no, I don't know exactly what...' The phone quacked on and on. Grace Woodyates gave a comically despairing gesture to Ellie, but continued to listen.

Ellie studied the tips of her shoes. Were they getting shabby? She wasn't much good at cleaning shoes, but did try to keep them free of mud. Though when they developed cracks across the leather, you might just as well give in.

160

Finally Grace Woodyates put the phone down. 'He doesn't know anything, is very surprised to hear, she wasn't involved with anyone in the choir that he knows about except for the lad who brought her along last term to sing with them, and of course, she joined in the session at the tube station. The boy's name was Lloyd; sang bass. Ronald will look up the address, if you're interested.'

'That's a dead end. He was killed in an accident early in the new year.'

'Oh, that Lloyd? I read about him in the paper. Ronald says Lloyd wasn't a boyfriend, not the kissing kind. Just a friend, he thinks. Anyway, she sang second soprano with them, hadn't much of a clue about choral music, but had a pretty little voice, helped make the tea, that sort of thing. The only other thing he can remember about her is that she said she could get some posters put up in the Avenue for their concert, since she knew someone who worked there. The Palladian Singers, they call themselves. He's always after me to join them, and maybe I will now I'm retired and have some time on my hands. I'm afraid I haven't been very helpful so far. Now, who else can I ask who might know something? Do you know the Priors socially at all? Shall I arrange an introduction?'

'So kind, but perhaps not at the moment,' said Ellie, being polite. 'And now I think I should...' She made as if to rise, but her hostess stopped her with a dramatically raised hand.

Grace was anxious for Ellie to stay. 'Do you

have to go straight away? It's so strange the way we've been thrown together. I feel we're going to become great friends. I could rustle up something tasty for lunch, and we could talk some more, if you're not too pressed for time? I'd like to tell you about our special spring programme for—'

'I'm so sorry, but I really need to—'

'I quite understand, but if I think of anything else I'll ring you straight away, shall I? Are you in the book? Oh, but Pat can give me the address, can't she?'

'Of course, of course.' Ellie made her escape, thinking that a little of Ms Woodyates went a long way.

Wednesday afternoon
The Avenue was always busy, even on a wet and windy winter afternoon. It would be even busier shortly, when the children came out of school. There were sixty odd shop units and, unless you wanted Marks & Spencer or WH Smith, you could usually find what you wanted there. One of the things you couldn't find there was a new mobile phone, but Ellie decided she couldn't face going into Ealing Broadway for one at the moment. Something was urging her on to look for Mia. It wasn't a premonition, exactly. Just a feeling of unease.

Ms Woodyates had not thought she'd been very helpful, but Ellie – who knew the Avenue well – considered that, from what she'd been told, it shouldn't be too difficult to locate Mia's contact in the Avenue. For a start, there were only a certain number of shops that would put up advertisements for local events. The newsagent's would, but they charged for the service, so they were out. The chain stores wouldn't as a matter of policy. The pharmacies wouldn't. This cut down the number of shops in which Mia might have known someone who'd do it for her.

Ellie decided to visit all those currently advertising spring sales, Open Days and concerts, to see if they knew anything. She could do her food shopping at the same time. Oh, and buy a birthday card for a friend, collect her shoes from the repairers and see if the bookshop had managed to locate the biography she'd ordered for Thomas.

But first: lunch. She had a choice of several coffee shops that served paninis and rolls and soup, but which of them also allowed posters to be put up? Not her favourite, unfortunately. The Sunflower Café had offered this facility in the past but, under a recent change of management, had done away with the board for public announcements in favour of a garish reproduction of one of Van Gogh's Sunflower pictures.

There were other cafés which she liked to visit now and again for lunch, but two of them never put up local posters. She settled for the only one that did and, blowing her nose again, ordered a panini, which dripped luscious cheese no matter how carefully she tackled it. Plus a cappuccino. Stirring sugar into her coffee, Ellie

163

planned her campaign.

Now, what fliers were on display here? Only after she'd eaten did she realize that the community notice board, which usually sported numerous posters, had been cleared in favour of a protest about a street-widening scheme. There was a new, very blonde girl – Polish? – serving behind the counter, and the place was heaving with customers. Eventually, Ellie managed to catch the attention of the manageress to ask if she happened to know where Ellie might contact Mia Prior, as she'd heard of a job that might suit her. The manageress shook her head, but somewhere – was Ellie imagining things? – she felt there had been a reaction to Mia's name. Possibly in the queue behind her?

It was raining again. When she got to the door to put up her umbrella, she looked back into the café, but no one seemed to be paying any attention to her.

The cobbler next. Her only pair of high-heeled shoes was ready for her. The cobbler did put up local notices now and then but he said he hadn't had any posters from the Palladians, and who were they when they were at home. He said he hadn't heard anything of a girl called Maria, and hummed the song from *West Side Story*, laughing at his own joke.

The bakery had some fresh almond tartlets and Ellie bought some from the usual girl, a merry-faced Pole whose ample girth encouraged everyone to indulge. There were two local posters up, but the girl said the boss would only

164

allow posters from the local schools now, because Blu-tacking them to the wall took the surface off the paint, and no, she didn't know anyone called Mia. There was a new girl cleaner there, a depressed-looking wisp of a girl with short, dyed blonde hair. Ellie didn't think she'd last long as the baker was reputed to be something of a martinet.

Ellie collected the tome she'd ordered for Thomas from the bookshop. Their policy was to take every local poster offered them. The owner rather thought they had put up posters for the Palladian Singers some time ago, but couldn't remember who'd brought them in because they did get so many. He had a couple of bright young things in training, but they were called Jessica and Mandy and looked like it too.

The gift shop took posters but were so busy – school had just come out – that they misunderstood Ellie and told her to leave her poster with them, and they'd see if they could put it up later. And no, they didn't know anyone called May or Mira or whatever, and could she please let the little girl standing behind her come to the front to buy her chocolate rabbit or whatever it was she was clutching in her hot little hand?

Ellie was so flustered by this that she left without buying a birthday card for her old friend.

The butcher was relatively new – and good. Ellie bought lamb chops and sausages. A middle-aged man and his partner served. No posters, on principle.

The fish shop: two men, some posters, though not for the Palladians. Yes, they'd take any local posters but couldn't remember who'd brought in what.

There were men putting up a new awning above the optician's. The queue at the bus stop was alarming, but two buses came along in tandem and removed it. The women serving in the greengrocer's were both heavy smokers in their forties; they did put up posters sometimes, but neither knew anything about a girl called Mia.

Someone had left a bicycle chained up outside the post office, but the front wheel had already been stolen. Oh dear.

The launderette; Ellie was getting tired. The manageress was brusque but kindly. No Mia. Yes, they took posters of all sorts, but only kept them up till the date of the event. The shoe shop; three young things serving, but one was heavily pregnant, one was black and the third was a big strapping lass, nothing like Mia.

The owner knew Ellie, and waved her over, asking how she was doing. Ellie said she was looking for a lost girl who'd had a friend who worked in the Avenue.

'Polish? Czech? Serbian? Croatian? Japanese? The world and his wife are here.'

'Japanese would be good,' said Ellie, remembering that someone somewhere had talked about Mia taking a course in a foreign language.

'They keep to themselves. Look for the most

166

expensive baby buggies and the largest cars. Have you tried the Japanese school?'

Ellie shook her head. It was another line to follow but she didn't know anyone there, did she? She was getting depressed. She decided it was time to take the weight off her feet. She went into the Sunflower Café, ordered a lemon tea and sat down to think about this and that. About how multicultural Ealing had become over the years, partly because the airport was so close and their local schools were so good. She'd heard that there could be as many as forty different native languages in just one school hereabouts. The Welsh, of course, had been here forever, and the first lot of Poles had arrived during World War II and stayed. The second lot had arrived more recently, of course. There were immigrants from every quarter of the globe: Pakistan, Middle East, Far East, Africa ... lots of Somalis, and a new influx from the Balkans.

She let her mind rove over the number of people running shops in the Avenue who were probably British born, but whose families had arrived in this country knowing no English and without a penny to their name. Singhs, Patels, Mohammeds.

There were Polish people everywhere. Builders, waitresses, cleaners. They had their own newspaper in Ealing; their own church. Their own shops.

Ellie thought of the frisson she'd felt at the café at lunchtime. Of the way that immigrants hung together. Some would go out of their way to help others less fortunate than themselves; others took advantage of those less well off. Human nature, really.

She began to see a pattern.

When she'd finished her tea she went back to the bakery. The merry-faced girl was pulling the empty racks forward for the inefficient cleaner to swab down the floor behind them. Ellie pushed at the door.

'Closing now!'

'Fine,' said Ellie. 'Ursula sent me with a message for Mia. I'll wait for her outside, shall I?'

The girl with the mop flung it down and fled to the back of the shop.

'Now look what you've done!' said her friend.

It was impossible to talk in the bakery as it was due to close, so Jackie – the fat girl – proposed they adjourn to their flat above the pharmacy on the other side of the road. It was a big flat on two floors, currently shared by five European girls who had come to seek their fortunes in London – and Mia. The communal sitting room became crowded as the other girls arrived back from work – including the blonde from the café where Ellie had had lunch. So hers had been the reaction to Ellie's enquiry for Mia?

Ellie sat beside Mia on the settee, and held her hand. Mia sat with eyes down, awkwardly posed yet still graceful. The left side of her jaw was puffy and discoloured, there was a healing cut just above her right eye, and there were fading bruises on her wrists. She didn't speak at all, and every now and then she shivered so convulsively that Ellie could feel her distress. She wore a black sweatshirt and skirt that were too big for her.

The girls in the flat were not all Poles; one was from Slovakia, another from Albania. They spoke English with varying degrees of fluency. All were currently employed and all were nervous, though some showed it more than others. Several wore jewellery and items of good clothing, which Ellie fancied she'd seen in Dan's photographs of Mia.

Ellie introduced herself. 'My name is Ellie Quicke. One of Mia's friends asked me to see if I could find her. Here is a photograph of the two of them, taken some time last year.'

'Who's that?' Jackie pointed to the man leaning over their shoulders. 'That's the man who comes asking for Mia.'

They all looked and nodded. 'That is the man,' said the blonde, handing the photograph round. Each girl in turn looked at the laughing, glamorous Mia in the photos, and then at the depressed scarecrow sitting next to Ellie.

Jackie was the one most distressed by the contrast. 'I will tell you everything. It is my mother's friend Malgosia who asks us to look after Mia for a few days. Malgosia is cleaning for this rich family up the hill; big house, lots of parties, very messy. They do not ever pick anything up or look when they speak to her, or say "thank you" ... except for Mia. Mia is always nice to Malgosia. Mia gives Malgosia her old clothes for my little sister back in Poland. Really nice things, my sister is so pleased. Before Christmas Mia came herself into the shop, with some posters for her choir's concerts. So I know Mia.

'Malgosia is away over Christmas and the New Year and when she goes back to clean, Mrs say Mia not well, and not to do her room. Then boss woman goes out. Malgosia is worried about Mia and goes to her room to ask if she would like a hot drink. The door is locked, but Malgosia know all the keys in the bedrooms are the same, so she goes in and there is Mia in her bathroom, trying to clean herself. Crying. She's been – how you say? – beaten up. See the marks, even now?' Jackie's glance invited Ellie to inspect Mia's bruises.

'She's been worked over, good and proper,' a sharp-faced girl said. She was wearing earrings studded with diamonds, not glass. Her clothes were cheap and flashy, but she sported a leather handbag that bore a famous couturier's name.

Mia didn't react to what was being said about her. She was like a broken doll.

Jackie patted Mia's shoulder. 'Malgosia say, "Who do this to you?" Mia cries and will not say. Malgosia thinks it is her stepfather or brothers. Hard choices. Malgosia says "Mia, go to the police!" but Mia says they will find her and kill her. There is no phone in her room, and her mobile is smashed into pieces. Mia asks Malgosia to help her get away, says to leave the window open, pretend she went out that way.

'But where to go? Malgosia has one small room with a bed that is also a settee, so she cannot take her in. Malgosia phones me at work and says can we give Mia a bed on the settee here for two or three days and I say yes, because Mia has sent me so many good things for my sister. Malgosia packs a bag and lifts up the window, and locks the door after Mia and puts the key back. Then she rings a friend who brings his van, and so Mia comes here and I let her in at lunchtime, and give her a key.'

'At first she is almost all right,' said Sharp-face. 'She says she will stay only till her face heal, and then she try for a job. It is her idea to cut her hair and dye it, to look different. And we think this is OK, though not so nice for us, with another person always in the shower in one of the bathrooms. But she cleans and cooks for us, and that is good. And she lends us some of her things.'

They all turned to look at Mia's down-bent head.

'Then,' said Jackie, heavily, 'we hear a man is asking for Mia in the Avenue. He says he knows his sister is hiding nearby. In the shops we talk one to another, hear everything, you understand? It is the man in the picture. He say he is her brother, but he is blonde and she is dark and we are not sure. Is he really her brother? He has very expensive car, and parks where he likes and stops all the traffic. Also, he is not nice to us. He looks down his nose – so – at us who work in the shops. We think he is maybe the one who beats her. No one says anything to him, but we worry. We tell Mia that there is this man looking for her, and after that she is so frightened that she does not eat any more.'

Sharp-face said, 'Maybe she did something to deserve the beating, and we are the ones who are in trouble for keeping her here. Maybe the police will arrest us all for hiding her.'

There were various nods of agreement.

Jackie was worried too. 'We ring Malgosia, say what to do. She says the brother hit her, saying "Where is Mia?" So now she will not work there any more. She says he is clever; he knows Malgosia helped Mia to run away and he says he will look for her where there are Polish people living nearby. Malgosia says Mia must go to the police, but when we say that to Mia, she takes a knife to cut her wrist and now we cannot leave her alone any more. I take her to work with me and the boss says she can clean the shop, but he will not pay her for she is not much good. Yesterday the man in the photograph comes and looks into the shop from the street. He comes to look but not to buy. Mia runs and hides at the back of the shop, and now she will not speak at all. We do not know what to do. And then you came.'

Ellie considered what had been said and what had been left unsaid. She didn't think Mia had handed over her belongings to these girls out of the goodness of her heart. Earrings, handbag, an expensive T-shirt, a leather jacket. No. But it wouldn't help to say they'd robbed a girl who'd come to them for help, because after their own fashion, they'd kept her safe. So far.

The blonde spoke up next. 'The man – her brother – is saying he will give a hundred pounds to find Mia. Malgosia says "no", but she needs the money.'

And so, thought Ellie, do you. Each one of you – except perhaps for Jackie – has already considered what they could do with that money and soon one of you will convince herself that telling the man is justifiable. Mia's head drooped, but she said nothing.

Sharp-face said, with care, 'Of course we wouldn't tell, not for such a small sum.'

In other words, if Ellie offered a larger bribe, they'd keep quiet. Sharp-face couldn't be trusted not to give Mia away, so Mia must leave. Besides, Mia needed a doctor and possibly a psychiatrist. She needed a safe place to hide until she could be nursed back to health. At that moment Ellie wondered, grimly, exactly what the girl had been through, and whether she would ever recover.

Ellie considered that the girl had witnessed Lloyd's death and been beaten to prevent her telling what she'd seen. Or ... no. Ellie didn't want to think what else might have happened to the girl.

The blonde said, 'He also say that he will come back and find where we live, and if we have been telling lies, and do know where she is, then he will not pay the money, but he will punish us.'

Jackie pleaded with Ellie. 'So now you will take Mia?'

'About time, too,' said Sharp-face. 'We don't want a visit from her brother, do we?'

More nods. At least they were agreed on that.

Ellie tried to think through various possible courses of action. Yes, she must remove the girl, but where to? A doctor first? Yes, but what then? If Ellie took Mia to Accident and Emergency at the nearest hospital they'd admit her, of course, but would want her to see a psychiatrist. If she continued to be silent, they'd transfer her to a psychiatric unit. Would that be in her best interests? Possibly.

But would she be safe there? If she was admitted under her own name, how long would it be before the family discovered her whereabouts, and what action would they take?

Suppose Ellie took her to the police first? But unless Mia talked, the police wouldn't be able to help her.

Consider what the brother would do. Stepbrother. He was not her actual brother. At some point – maybe even that evening – he was going to find out where the girls were living and come looking for Mia. Would the girls deny they knew Mia? They might. But more probably one or other of them would tell him that a Mrs Quicke had taken the girl.

And then he'd come after Ellie. Ouch. Ellie

had visions of mayhem back at her house; of frail little Rose being pushed around, of bold Thomas defending his womenfolk with a walking stick. Thomas was a big bear of a man but no longer that young, or particularly fit. No, no. She couldn't risk either of them being put into danger. So she couldn't take Mia home with her.

She would phone Thomas and ask for advice. Ouch. She remembered that he had some meeting up in town that day and wouldn't be back till late. Who else could she ask? Ah, but she only had that wretched iPhone on her at the moment, and if she asked to use one of the girls' mobiles, the call could easily be traced and the information handed to the stepbrother. What on earth was she to do?

Ask for help, of course. Well, she hardly had time for a proper prayer, but perhaps, when you were in desperate straits, it didn't matter what words you used.

Help, Lord. It was the best she could do.

'Dumbo, I told you to ring me back. Where have you been? Is it all arranged?'

'Can't say I like it. Beating up an old lady.'

'Nothing to connect them with us, is there?'

'Well, no.'

'It'll bring Ursula back in no time, nicely softened up.'

'Hope you're right. Did you find Mia?'

'What did I tell you? Piece of cake. I can lay my hands on her any time I like. But not this

evening. One of His Nibs's charity dos up in town. Best bib and tucker, drinks at eight, carriages at one. He's presenting the police with some bauble or other in consideration of this and that. Joy to the community and all that. You've arranged yourself an alibi too?'

'Darts match, down the pub. Picking up Dan and Bullseye from their place at seven.'

TEN

Wednesday early evening

Mia seemed catatonic. Ellie lifted the girl's chin to make eye contact. Mia's eyes were like pebbles: dark and unrevealing. She was not focusing. She was in a faraway place, driven there by terror.

Ellie made her voice soft. 'Ursula asked me to find you. She's really worried about you.'

The brown eyes flickered into life for a second, and then the eyelids dropped.

Had there been a slight lessening of tension?

Ellie said, 'If one of you can lend me a mobile phone, I'll order a minicab and take Mia away. At some point the police will have to be involved, but more immediately, I think you should prepare yourselves for a visit from Mia's stepbrother, who sounds a very nasty piece of work indeed.'

176

The blonde had a bright idea. 'So we say it is not Mia, but a cousin from Poland, who was with us for a few days only.'

'That might work. But suppose he catches sight of something of Mia's: a credit card, a scarf, a piece of jewellery? I suggest you pack up everything that might give him a lead to Mia, and I'll take it away with her. We don't want him getting the idea that you've been stealing from her, do we? Or he might start on you too. As and when the police come round, they'll be looking for traces of her, too, won't they?'

Trying not to see the dismay and fluster that greeted her speech, Ellie got to her feet, and beckoned Jackie away from the others.

Jackie was hiding a smile. She said loudly, 'We can put everything back in Mia's bag, can't we? And find her some nice clothes to wear?'

Ellie looked out of the window. They were high up here, over the shops. Even in the dark, the Avenue had plenty of people in it, coming and going from the Co-op and the pharmacy below. She couldn't see a really expensive car anywhere, which didn't mean, of course, the brother wasn't lurking in a side street.

Ellie said, 'Jackie, do you know what time of the month it may be for Mia?'

Jackie's breathing quickened. 'She has not said, or asked for ... Mother of God. You think...?'

'Let's hope not. Can you make sure nothing of hers is left behind?'

'Mia had some money, not a lot, but I think—'

'Forget it. But if someone has been using her credit cards—'

Jackie looked across at Sharp-face, who was bad-temperedly removing her things from Mia's designer handbag. 'I am stupid. I do not think.'

'You have done wonders, but now Mia must see a doctor. When the police come, tell them the truth. When the brother comes—'

'I can lie but the others may not.' A shrug.

'If he makes himself unpleasant, you must refer him to the police and say they know where she is.'

'I can do that, but—'

'I know. You need a number where you can reach me.' Ellie took out her diary, tore a blank page out from the notes section and wrote on it. 'Here, this is my home number. Leave a message if I'm not in.'

Jackie produced a mobile phone. 'You want a minicab? Where do I say they take you?'

'I will give them the address when we leave.'

Ellie thought, *Good try, Jackie, but I'm not so stupid as to let you know where I'm taking Mia.* And indeed, where could she take her? Ellie tried to think. She needed a place where she could use a phone that nobody could overhear. The offices of the Trust and Stewart's lettings office would be closing about now. She had keys to both offices – back at home. But not on her.

She couldn't involve Stewart, with his precious family. Nor Felicity with baby Mel. Too many hostages to fortune. She could ask Roy ... but his office was next door to her own home, and using the phone there would be leading the stepbrother straight to her front door.

The blonde led Mia into the room, wearing a mid-blue sweater, jeans and her own leather jacket. The clothes were her own, but she'd lost weight since they'd been bought. The leather handbag hung from one shoulder. She wasn't wearing any make-up. So where had her make-up gone? On to the blonde girl's face?

Forget the make-up, thought Ellie. It's not worth worrying about. Sharp-face tugged in a good quality suitcase on wheels.

'Credit cards, evidence of identity, driving licence?' asked Ellie.

Sharp-face grimaced. 'All there, except money for our trouble. We earned that.'

'So you did,' said Ellie, trying not to think about misuse of credit cards. Well, let the police deal with that later.

Jackie was looking out of the window. 'The minicab is here, I think.'

Ellie collected her bags of shopping, gave one bag to Mia to carry and then took it back again. The girl wasn't capable of walking in a straight line to the door, let alone carrying shopping. Jackie took Mia's hand from Sharp-face and, trailing luggage, they went down to the cab together.

'Where to, Mrs Quicke?' The cabbie knew

her, of course.

'The police station,' said Ellie, and waved goodbye to Jackie, who had registered the destination, of course. But then, Ellie had given them her name and telephone number right at the start, hadn't she? Easily traced.

Once round the corner, Ellie leaned forward to address the driver. 'I've changed my mind. Can you take me to my old house? You know where I used to live?'

'Will do.' He made a U-turn and took the shortest way. The house was lit up, with workmen putting the finishing touches to the interior. The driver helped her out with her shopping and Mia's suitcase, and volunteered to see them safely into the house before he drove off. As Ellie guided Mia down the driveway, she noticed that the 2Ds Estate Agency board had been put back up again. Well, she couldn't bother about that now.

A painter clattered down the stairs, accompanied by the sound of muzak from his transistor. 'Everything all right, missus? We're pretty well done here, now. Just tidying up, a coupla things left for tomorrow morning. Want a look before we go? There's been someone looking around today. It should let pretty quickly, eh?'

Ellie looked at the space on the floor where her telephone used to be, and caught her breath. It was no longer there. What was she to do now? Ask the painter if she might use his mobile? She couldn't trust him not to talk if the stepbrother tracked him down. She made herself smile. 'Everything looks perfect. Are you on your way, then? I'll drop the latch when I go. Just wanted to use the bathroom before ... you know?'

He laughed, called to his mate that they must be off now, collected his radio and an armful of dust sheets, and made it to the outside world.

Mia stood where she'd been left by the door. Ellie gently urged her to sit on the bottom stair, and swiftly went through the downstairs rooms, hoping against hope that somewhere a telephone might have been left, to be connected at a later date. No telephones anywhere. She supposed Stewart would have considered her old phone obsolete and decided that a tenant would want the latest cordless gadget.

There was nothing for it but to ask to use Kate's phone next door. As they'd drawn up outside the house, Ellie had spotted Kate's car already parked in their driveway, with her husband's close behind it. Red-headed and foxy-faced, Armand was head of department at a local secondary school, although Kate was the real breadwinner in the household, or would have been if she didn't have to pay for a day nanny every time she was needed to sort out someone else's financial tangles.

Kate and Armand were the proud parents of two noisy toddlers, whom Ellie could hear shouting even through the party wall. Ellie reflected there were compensations to one's only grandchild having passed beyond the screaming stage.

Ellie decided she wouldn't tell Kate and Armand the extent of her problem; just ask to use their phone for five minutes. She gathered her shopping together, and pulled Mia to her feet. 'I'm going to let us out the back way into the garden and then cross into next door to use their phone. If I take your suitcase, can you manage, because I'm going to turn out the lights in here as we leave?'

Ellie helped Mia out of the back door, down the steps and on to the path.

There was a lamp in the alleyway that shone across the bottom of the gardens thereabouts so it was possible to see where one was going, if one took care where one put one's feet. Mia stumbled and Ellie, burdened with shopping and Mia's suitcase, was unable to help her except with a rushed prayer, and a word of encouragement.

'Not far. Can you see the gate between this house and the next? It's a bit overgrown, but we used it a lot when I lived here.'

The gate squeaked and caught on the ground, but finally Ellie got it open, only to find herself floodlit from the house. A sensor had triggered a light on the patio next door. Mia was crying, without sound.

A door opened, and Armand came out, carrying a hockey stick. 'Who's there?'

'Only me,' said Ellie, humping her shopping up the steps, and then turning to give a hand to Mia. 'Orphans of the storm and all that. May we come in for five minutes and use your phone?'

Armand shouted back into the house. 'It's all right, Kate. It's only Ellie. Plus a girl.'

Where Ellie had built a conservatory on to the back of her house, Kate and Armand had constructed a rumpus room in which the family could relax and muck about. At Armand's shout, Kate appeared with a baby in her arms, and a toddler clinging to one leg. Kate took one look at Ellie and said, 'Bubble, bubble, toil and trouble. I'll just finish giving this lot their tea and then you can tell us all about it.'

'Bless you,' said Ellie, dumping all her belongings. 'I'm not here, you understand. You haven't seen me. If I could just use your phone for five minutes, I'll get out of your hair.'

Armand closed and locked the door against the dark night, and pulled down the blinds. He was not as tall as Kate, but he was a bundle of energy with a sharp tongue and a warm heart. He removed a toy rabbit with only one eye from a chair, and pushed it towards Mia. 'Sit before you fall down. Kate, I'll give the babe his bottle while you deal with Madam. Find yourself a seat, Ellie, and Tell All.'

'Can't,' said Ellie. 'The less you know the better.'

Armand started throwing toys into a large cardboard box with his usual forcefulness. Reaching past Mia, who was still standing by the door, he put his hand on her arm to nudge her in the direction of the chair. He hardly touched her, but Mia opened her mouth and

183

screamed. With eyes fast closed, she gulped and screamed again. And went on screaming.

Armand was shocked. 'What did I do?'

Alarmed, the toddler started to cry. Kate pushed the baby into Armand's arms, and soothed the toddler out of the room. 'No need to cry, little one. The lady's poorly and I'm going to help make her better, all right? Now you go off with Daddy to eat up all your soldiers, there's a good girl. Armand, can you finish giving them their tea?'

Ellie took Mia in her arms. 'There, there.'

Armand took the children off into the kitchen while Kate pushed a chair behind Mia's knees. Between Kate and Ellie, they got the girl seated. Over Mia's head, Kate murmured, 'She's been beaten up. And raped?'

Also speaking softly, Ellie said, 'I suspect it, yes, but I don't know. I need to get her seen by a doctor, privately.'

'What about the police?'

'I'm not sure she's in any state to give a coherent statement.'

Kate took in Mia's damaged face, frowned, and shook her head. 'But wouldn't her family—?'

'They're involved. Or some of them are.'

'Ouch. Her father?'

'Not sure. Maybe. Definitely her stepbrother.'

'Still, the police should be notified.'

'Her disappearance was reported to the police. They interviewed the parents who said the girl had been sleeping around till she'd gone off with some riff-raff or other. They said it was good riddance to bad rubbish. The parents have clout in the community and the police have closed the case. Now, the parents may not care what happens to Mia, but her stepbrother is actively looking for her. What I think is that she should be admitted to a private clinic some- where until she's in a fit state to go to the police. I'll pay, but I don't know how private medicine works. I was going to phone round, see if I could find someone who might know.' She rocked Mia to and fro. 'There, there.'

Kate stood straight and tall, biting her lip. Frowning. 'Tell me the name of the family.'

'Prior. Big developers. As far as the police are concerned, their word counts.'

Kate swallowed. 'Prior? As in the people who've put up that expensive block of flats on the North Circular? The ones who want Roy to mortgage his future to invest in it? I've heard rumours about the way Mr Prior does business. They say that if you want to sup with the devil, you'd better bring a long spoon.' She made up her mind with a decisive nod. 'I'll phone around, ask if anyone knows a doctor who'll see Mia out of hours. I have a client who might know.'

'I don't want you involved.'

'Too late.' Kate whisked herself off into the house.

Mia made a convulsive movement in Ellie's arms, sobbing and shaking so hard it was all Ellie could do to hold her. Now and again she seemed to be trying to speak, but didn't make it. At last she grew quiet, and Ellie was able to pull up another chair to sit down, while still keeping an arm around the girl. Two mugs of tea appeared at Ellie's elbow. Armand, doing his bit.

Ellie tried to get Mia to drink, but the girl turned her head away. Ellie sipped tea and tried to think, and failed. Tried to pray. Didn't get any further than, *Dear Lord, what do I do now? I don't want Kate and Armand drawn into this. I am so stupid. I ought to have been able to think of something else. Don't let them get hurt.*

There were reassuring noises from the kitchen. Children being fed and watered. Armand coaxing the toddler and burping the baby. Kate talking on the phone. There was a small television on the big all-purpose table in the rumpus room. It had been on a children's programme when Ellie arrived, and no one had bothered to switch it off. Mia slumped down in her chair, eyes closed, relaxed except for a faint quiver now and then.

Ellie was stiff from sitting in an awkward position. She inched herself to her feet, rubbing her lower back. Mia didn't move, so Ellie went into the kitchen, where Armand was tidying up after the children's tea.

Kate came out of the hall, shutting off her own iPhone. 'All fixed. Mr Abrahams will see Mia in two hours' time at his consulting rooms in Harley Street, discretion guaranteed. Here's his name and address.' She gave Ellie a piece of paper with the details. 'Mr Abrahams's receptionist assures me that he can get her a room in a private clinic tonight, if he considers it warranted. I'll drive you there, of course.'

'I'm very grateful,' said Ellie, 'but no way are you getting involved. I took a risk coming here but that's where it stops. Mia's stepbrother has threatened to kill her, and I believe he means it. There's been one death in her group of friends already, and I'm not exposing you to him in any way whatsoever. If you can help me get Mia out the back way and across the Green, I'll pick up a black cab there.'

'Mummy, look at me!' The toddler had balanced a spoon on her upper lip.

Kate looked and applauded, while the baby obligingly brought up his wind.

'In this weather?' said Armand, as sleet hit the window. 'Don't be so stupid, Ellie. As if we'd let you.'

Kate picked the toddler up, and gave her a cuddle. 'We've got an hour or so before we need to make a move. Let's put these two to bed and have some supper, while you tell us all about it. Ellie, do you want to phone Thomas and tell him you're going to be late?'

Ellie held up both hands. 'I've only got a silly iPhone and I don't know how to use it. May I use your landline?'

Kate was amused. 'Have my old mobile. It's easy to use. As you can see, Father Christmas brought me the latest iPhone, so I don't need the old one.'

Ellie accepted with pleasure, and indeed,

Kate's old mobile was easy to use. She got through to the house only to find that Thomas hadn't returned yet, so she left a message with Rose to say she was having supper with friends and was that all right?

Ellie could just hear Rose's voice over the noise of her television, which had been turned up high. 'Of course it's all right, and what I say is, it does you good to get out and about a bit, after you've had the flu. Mr Roy has been ringing and popping round to see if you're in, but I told him you'd see him when you were good and ready and he should attend to his own business.'

Ellie grimaced. She'd forgotten about contacting Roy. Well, he could jolly well wait.

'There's only one other thing, some strange woman keeps ringing up asking for you, she's rung twice already, a Miss or Ms Wood-some-thing, most insistent that you call her. I did tell her you might not be back till supper, so she said it was about some tickets for a matinee that you might like to go to with her which, seeing as if you were going to the theatre you'd go with Thomas, I didn't think you'd want to be bothered with. Not that I told her that.'

Ms Woodyates. Oh well, Pat had warned Ellie about Grace Woodyates, hadn't she? 'Thank you, Rose. If she rings again, say I'm out for the evening but will get back to her tomorrow.'

Ellie went to check on Mia, who was still asleep in her chair. Kate came downstairs, having put the babes to bed. She switched the baby

188

monitor on as Armand said, 'Pasta up!' They ate a lot of pasta and vegetables in that household. Armand ladled it out, saying that they must eat first, and hear Ellie's tale after.

So they ate in the kitchen and over coffee Ellie talked. She began with Ursula's challenge to her, and went on from there. Every now and then Ellie leaned back in her chair to check on Mia, but it wasn't till the end of her narration that the girl stirred and opened her eyes. Ellie rose as the girl wobbled to her feet, desperately trying to speak.

As Ellie reached her side, Mia finally made it. 'Tell Ursula, she mustn't!'

'Mia, you can speak to her yourself in a minute. You need to drink something, and to eat. It'll help you to speak. When you've done that, I'll get her on the phone.'

Mia seemed to understand, for when Kate got her a glass of milk and coaxed her to drink, she managed a few mouthfuls. She still shivered now and then, and kept on the far side of the table from Armand, but she did finish the milk, though she refused all offers of food.

Ellie used Kate's phone, which of course had Ellie's old mobile number on it. 'Is that you, Ursula? Good news. I've found Mia. She'd run away from home and was staying with friends. She's been through a bad time, and I'm taking her to see a doctor tonight to get her checked over, but she's safe and wants to speak to you. I'll hand her over to you now.'

Mia grasped the phone in a hand that shook.

'Ursula ... Ursula, are you all right? Anthony is ... I mustn't say, or he'll kill me. But you won't, will you? Promise me you won't. I can't tell you what happened, I mustn't. Understand?'

Ellie put her arm around Mia, as the girl's knees gave way. Mia was frantic, thrusting the phone back at Ellie, whispering, 'Tell her, tell her. Don't come back.'

Ellie took the phone from Mia. Ursula was alarmed. 'What's happened? Mia, are you all right?'

'Ellie here. No, she's not all right,' said Ellie, letting Kate take the girl from her. 'She's been beaten up by someone, possibly her stepbrother. She's been desperate to speak to you, but can hardly talk at the moment. Anthony's been trying to find her, but I got to her first.'

Ursula was keeping her head, but her voice shook. 'You think she saw something? Something to do with Lloyd's death? And he's trying to make sure she won't talk?'

'Something like that,' said Ellie, who didn't want to speak of rape until she was sure of the facts. 'She's safe now. All right?'

'But where has she been? Why hasn't she rung me? I've been half out of my mind, telling myself I was worrying unnecessarily, and trying to get on with my life. Why didn't she come to me when she ran away, or ring me to say she was safe?'

'A long story, Ursula. She hasn't got a mobile any more. Look, I'll ring you again when I have some news. All right?'

She shut off the phone. Mia was crying on Kate's shoulder. Ellie looked at the clock. 'It's time to go.'

Armand and Kate had been talking to one another in low voices. Now Armand reached for his car coat. 'It's all settled. I'm driving you.'

'It's too dangerous. Anthony is persistent; went up and down the shops in the Avenue, till he traced her to where she worked. It won't take him long to find the flat in which she was sheltering, and one of the girls there will need no urging to tell him that I took her off in a cab. They even have the number I used to call the cab firm. I tried to leave a false trail by asking the cab to go to the police station, and then countermanding the order and asking him to take us to my old house, but it won't take him long to discover where I actually did go.

'Once he locates my house next door he'll be round here, probably tomorrow morning. If the decorators are still there, and I think they haven't quite finished, he'll ask them if they've seen me and Mia, and they'll happily say that yes, they saw us this evening and left us in the house when they knocked off for the night. Then he'll ask the neighbours and they'll refer him to you two because we're known to be such close friends, and I'm not having you lot placed in danger. Think of the children.'

'We've thought,' said Kate. 'I'm taking them to stay with a friend for a few days. If he comes here, he'll find both houses empty.'

'Except for Armand—'

'He'll be at school all day and will bring a colleague – a man who used to be a rugby player and who weighs half a ton – back with him after school for some supper.'

Armand looked fierce. 'I've no intention of backing down to a bully. I see enough of that at school. Give in to them once, and they think they can always get away with it. If he starts threatening me then I'll threaten back, with a hockey stick. Besides which, I'll deny everything. I can say, "Yes, I took my car out last night, but that's to play squash at the club, which I often do. Yes, the wife and kids are away for a few days; so what? Get lost, Mr Whatever-your-name-is."'

'Prior,' said Ellie. 'Anthony Prior. He has a number of friends he might call on to help him. I don't like it.'

'Neither do I,' said Armand. 'But I couldn't sleep easy, thinking of you wandering around on your own, afraid of being beaten up by some overgrown louts. Besides, it's only going to be necessary to hide Mia's whereabouts till she's in a safe place where he can't get at her. Two days, max.'

Ellie looked at Mia and thought it was going to take more than a couple of days before the girl was fit to talk.

Armand stuck out his chin. 'It's all settled. My car's in the drive. I'll put your bits and pieces of shopping and Mia's case into it now, with my gym bag. I'll drive off nonchalantly, waving to any neighbour who happens to be around, making sure they see I've no passengers. Meanwhile, Kate here kits Mia out with a long, dark coat and you walk her across the Green to the bus stop. I like that part of your plan. I stop by and pick you up from the bus stop and take you on to the doc's. Understood?'

He looked so fierce that Ellie could only say, 'Thank you, Armand,' and help Mia into the long, black coat which Kate produced for her. 'Mia, do you understand what we're going to do?'

'Don't leave me,' whispered Mia. 'Please!'

'I won't leave you,' said Ellie, wondering how late she was going to be getting home. Well, it couldn't be helped. Mia was in no state to be left by herself.

It was still raining and very cold as Ellie helped Mia down the garden, into the alley and across the Green. The girl tottered along, leaning on Ellie. 'Not long now, Mia. Just a few more steps and we'll be safe.'

They got to the bus stop. No sign of Armand. Ellie turned Mia into her shoulder, and put her arms about her. It was like holding a child, keeping her safe from harm.

The harm, of course, had already been done.

Ellie's feet were so cold she could hardly feel them. She tried wriggling her toes, fidgeting from foot to foot. What was keeping Armand? Had he been detained by some emergency with the children? Had he forgotten that Ellie and Mia were waiting for him? Had she enough money on her to hail a passing cab? Not that she'd seen any pass by in this awful weather. Anyway, she certainly hadn't enough money on her to get her into Central London.

Armand drove up at last, full of apologies, helping them both into the back of the car, the stereo thumping out Vivaldi, the heater working overtime. 'Sorry to keep you. Spotted a neighbour, exchanged a few words about the weather as I got in. She could see there was no one else in the car as I drove off. Kate heated up a cup of soup in the microwave and put it in a Thermos, which is on the back seat. See if you can get Mia to drink it.'

Trust Kate to have a good idea like that. Only, Mia wouldn't drink. Ellie began to wonder if the girl was, perhaps not intentionally, going to starve herself to death.

It was a nightmare journey into Central London. Mia whimpered every now and then, cowering from the bright lights of street lamps. The traffic was dense, even though the rush hour was theoretically over. Ellie began to wonder if they'd be late for their appointment, in which case the doctor might well have left and they'd be stranded without anywhere to go.

'Tim here. Just checking. You know where the place is? On the Avenue. There's a light over the front door. Best knock that out before you ring the bell.'

'We done the light already. She's out for the evening. She left a sidelight on in the front

194

room, but there's a gap in the curtains we can see through.'

'You wait for her, then. Got your masks?'

'You got our money?'

'Sure. Remember, you can take her mobile, her cards and money and duff the place up a bit, but leave the landline phone in working order. Understand? A pity you couldn't get one of the usual crowd along. Will the young one be up to it?'

'Sure. He's been out with me before. See you, right?'

ELEVEN

Wednesday evening

Armand finally deposited them before an imposing doorway in Harley Street. He said he'd find somewhere to park and get back to them. Ellie coaxed and gently pulled Mia up the steps and propped her against the portal while she attacked the speaker phone. Finally they were indoors, where decor and receptionist announced that here ruled Peace and Quiet. Ellie gave her name and confirmed she'd pay all the bills for Mia's treatment.

They sat down to wait but within a few minutes the receptionist said she was so sorry but there would be a further delay, an emergency, and she hoped they'd understand.

They waited. Mia wouldn't release Ellie's hand. Ellie thought longingly of her own home; of Thomas coming back tired from his day out, and Rose waiting to cook for them. She put the thoughts out of her mind, using the last of her paper tissues on which to blow her nose. Armand came to join her. The receptionist offered tea or coffee. Ellie accepted; Mia refused, drifting away into a doze, relaxing her hold on Ellie's hand.

They waited.

Mia started awake, looking around, eyes wide with fear. 'Where...?'

'At the doctor's. You're quite safe.'

Mia repeated the word 'safe' under her breath, but clearly did not believe it. She hunched forward, her eyes restless, her breathing rapid.

Ellie tried to pray. *Dear Lord, dear Lord. Be with Mia, and all of us. Give us courage. Protect us. Keep my loved ones safe.*

Mia looked on the verge of passing out. How long would the doctor be? Was there anything Ellie could do in the meantime? Mia might or might not want to die, but she'd perked up no end when she'd thought about Ursula, had even managed to speak to her on the phone. If Mia wouldn't eat or drink for her own sake, perhaps she would for Ursula's?

Ellie tried it. 'Mia, we need you to help us, so that we can keep Ursula safe. Could you manage to drink some soup, to give you strength?

And then you can give us a better idea of what to say to her if you think she's in danger.'

For a long moment Ellie thought Mia was too far gone to respond, but eventually she reached for the cup of soup, and managed to take a sip ... and then two. She'd drunk the whole cup by the time Ellie and Mia were called in to see the doctor, and though wobbly, the girl managed to walk into his room unaided.

The doctor was dark-eyed and comfortable-looking. He reminded Ellie of Thomas, and she trusted him on sight.

'Tell me all about it, eh?' he said.

Mia looked at Ellie. The doctor looked at Ellie. Ellie obliged with a report on what she knew, cutting her story as short as she could. Mia's friend Ursula had been worried when Mia disappeared, her parents weren't worried, Ellie had gone looking, had found her a couple of hours since, and learned there was someone else hunting for Mia, of whom the girl seemed afraid. In Ellie's opinion, Mia was in a bad way, and not yet up to giving a statement to the police. What did the doctor think?

The doctor had switched his attention to Mia early on in Ellie's recital, at one time bending forward to take her hand in his, and stroke it. Whether it was his healing touch that persuaded Mia he could be trusted, or his quiet strength, the result was a breakthrough.

Mia tried to smile at the doctor. A poor attempt, but recognizable. She even tried to talk. 'Will you help me?'

Ellie was banished to the waiting room while the doctor and his nurse examined Mia. Armand had had the forethought to bring some homework with him to mark. Seeing Ellie sit with idle hands, he offered his book of Sudoku puzzles to do, which she declined. Sudoku was beyond her.

Eventually the nurse beckoned Ellie into the consulting room. Mia was sitting in a chair, looking so frail it was a wonder she still breathed, but she tried to smile, and managed to half whisper, half murmur a message.

'Tell Ursula ... warn her ... stay away? Tell her, I'm safe now. Thank you, Ellie. Thank Armand, and Kate.'

The nurse put her arm round Mia, and helped her to stand. 'Come along now, my dear,' she said, and led the girl away.

The doctor put Ellie in the picture. Ellie shuddered. It was worse than she'd thought. He concluded, 'When you ring for information, refer to my patient as "Flavia", and leave a number where you can be contacted at the desk on your way out. I am not going to tell you where my patient will be staying. It's better that way, don't you think?'

Feeling as if she'd been hit over the head, Ellie went out to give Armand the doctor's verdict.

'It's bad, Armand. She's been raped and beaten many times and over a period of maybe ten days, or two weeks. He can tell that from the way some bruises have faded over time, while others are fairly fresh. There's been some damage below, which ought to have been attended to at the time, but what's more there are bites which have turned septic. She'll need antibiotics, possibly something the doctor called "tidying-up", which I don't like to think about. He's taken photographs of everything for a possible prosecution case at a later date. At some point the police will have to be involved, but she won't be well enough to talk to them for some time.'

'Bites?' said Armand, horrified.

She gulped. 'And she's pregnant. I'd hoped against hope that she wasn't, but it did occur to me as the worst possible scenario, and it's true.'

Armand said something under his breath.

'I agree. The doctor's admitting her to a private clinic under an assumed name, and they'll do what they can for her. He says we won't be able to contact her, nobody will, until she's fit to answer questions, but that I can phone him for news once a day. He says we should take the threats against her seriously and I agree. The problem is that until Mia's well enough to make a statement, the police aren't going to listen to anything I say.'

He put his papers away, his mouth tight. 'Who's the father?'

'She doesn't know.' Ellie got to her feet thinking, pregnant, can they abort? Should they? Who was the father? What a can of worms.

Armand insisted on dropping Ellie back to her

house, though she wasn't sure he ought to do so. She said, 'Can you concoct an alibi for yourself?'

'I'll go on to the club. It's open till half ten. Talk to one or two people. Phone Kate to tell her what's happened.' He was quiet for a while. Sighed. 'Pregnant, you said? What's going on in that house? Locked doors, beatings, threats. The parents must have known.'

Ellie nodded.

'What will you tell Ursula?'

'Enough to stop her flying back to be with Mia.'

'Will you tell the police that you've found the girl?'

'I'm not sure. They're not looking for her. Her parents aren't, either. Perhaps, I don't know, we wait till Mia can speak to the police herself?'

Armand ground his teeth and said several words under his breath about animals as compared to supposed human beings. Ellie agreed.

As she clambered out of his car in her driveway, she counted the bags she'd been toting around all day. Her handbag, Thomas's book, her shoes from the menders, the tartlets from the baker. No birthday card? Ah, she'd not bought it in the end, had she?

She let herself into the house as Armand drove off, only to realize she'd lost the chops and sausages she'd bought from the butchers. Had she left them in Armand's car? The lights of his car were disappearing round the corner. Too late, too late!

She shut the door heavily, only to be pounced upon by a sprite in a flurry of perfume, trailing scarves and an over-bright green silk suit.

'There she is at last, the naughty little girl, staying out so late without permission! What are we to do with her, Thomas?'

Ellie gaped.

'Naughty, naughty!' said Ms Woodyates. 'Here we've been, waiting up for you for hours and hours, and dear Thomas has had to entertain me all this time. What a bad little girl it is!'

Ellie continued to gape.

Thomas appeared at Grace's shoulder, looking anxious. He, at least, had taken on board the fact that Ellie was way beyond light repartee.

He said, 'There now, Grace. You see she's returned safe and sound. Let me take those things from you, Ellie. You look worn out. Grace was kind enough to bring you round a ticket for a matinée, and decided to stay as she was anxious to hear if you'd some news about the missing girl.'

Ellie blinked.

'Oh, tra la!' sparkled Ms Woodyates, clasping her hands to her chin in a girlish fashion. 'Don't tell me you've forgotten all about our little black sheep, when you were so anxious to discover something about her only this morning.'

Was it only that morning? Ellie allowed Thomas to take her coat away from her. 'So sorry,' she managed to say. 'Visiting a friend. Very poorly. Couldn't get away.'

'Cancer?' Grace jumped to conclusions and

Ellie was happy to let her. No way was she going to tell this chatterbox that she'd found Mia. 'My poor mother died of it, and then my younger sister – who was the real beauty of the family, you know – and then a cousin and two of my oldest friends. But we must look ever onwards and upwards, mustn't we?'

Ellie nodded.

Thomas was holding up an overcoat for Grace to get into. 'Now you've seen she's safely back home, shall I phone for a cab for you, or did you come in your car?'

'I have my trusty steed outside.' Grace had accepted that she was being thrown out in the nicest possible way, but wasn't giving up yet. 'Dear Ellie, I can see you're not exactly "with it" at the moment. I'll call round tomorrow morning, shall I? I know we're going to be the greatest of friends, and I'm looking forward to having a nice, long chat with you.'

Thomas eased Grace out of the door as Rose appeared in the kitchen doorway, also looking anxious. Rose was in her dressing-gown. Was it that late? Yes, it was. Oh dear.

Rose spoke to Thomas and not to Ellie. 'There, now. Miss Quicke was only saying to me yesterday that it looked as if Ellie were on the trail of some bad people once again, and that we must take extra good care of her.'

Ellie blinked again. *What* was that Rose had said?

Thomas said, 'You're absolutely right, Rose. A large hot drink and a couple of small sandwiches, don't you think? Have you eaten at all, Ellie?'

Ellie nodded. Rose disappeared into the kitchen, muttering, and Ellie disintegrated. 'Oh, Thomas, your chops for supper. And some Cumberland sausages, four for you and two each of ordinary for Rose and me. I've lost them somewhere and they won't be much good by morning, will they? I'll have to throw them away. But they may be in Armand's car, of course. Only, I don't think I left them there.'

Thomas put her in a hall chair, and proceeded to take off her heavy winter shoes, and rub her feet in his warm hands.

She'd finished her paper tissues. She sought for a hankie, and didn't find one. Her nose was running. He put a hankie in her hand and she blew, hard.

'I bought them for your supper but then I had something to eat with Kate and Armand, but you mustn't tell anyone because I don't want to put them in danger, and Mia's all right really, at least, she will be – I hope – though she's been terribly badly treated and she's pregnant and you mustn't ask me where I've put her because I don't know.'

'My dear love.'

He half carried her into the sitting room, installed her in the big armchair by the fire and wound a rug around her cold feet, putting them up on a stool. 'Thank God you found Mia, and that you're safe.'

'You've been praying for us?'

'Pretty well non-stop since early afternoon. I got so fidgety in my meeting, I couldn't have got through it without prayer.'

She was still crying, and still blowing her nose. 'But I lost your lamb chops!'

'You retrieved the lost lamb. You wonderful woman. Here am I, a simple scribe, idling away my time in a meeting discussing a moot point in theology, while you go out and fight the powers of darkness.'

'Oh, don't be silly. It wasn't that bad.'

'Wasn't it?' His eyes always saw more than most.

She didn't reply. Yes, it had been bad, but it was the threats to Mia and the relentless hunt after her which frightened her really, not what she'd actually seen. Except that, come to think of it, Mia's bruises had been a testimony in themselves. The doctor had said there'd been bites, which needed antibiotics. Where were the bites? Don't think about it. And then the pregnancy.

Thomas held both her hands in his. 'Can you tell me?'

At that moment, Rose brought in a Thermos of hot soup and sandwiches. Chicken soup and ham sandwiches. With her husband and her friend seated one on either side of her, Ellie told them what had happened.

'...And I'm so afraid I've left a trail which they may be able to follow and, if the worst comes to the worst, they may come here for Mia. I've tried to protect Armand and Kate, and it may never happen, but I get the shivers when I think of what they might do to everyone I love. They know my name, you see, and I left my phone number here with ever so many people.'

'Fear,' said Thomas. 'It makes us give in, even before a finger has been laid on us. Put it in proportion, Ellie. They – whoever they are – are not going to go round beating up ordinary citizens because, if they do, the police will be called in to deal with them.'

Ellie tried to calm down. 'I don't think Anthony cares, so long as he gets his own way. You didn't see what he did to Mia. At least I assume it was him, because it's him that's trying to find her. Whoever did that is looking at a long prison sentence, and it looks as if the family have closed ranks, because they told the police she slept around, which is a lie. We mustn't forget that Ursula believes Lloyd's death was murder. Perhaps Mia saw something, could witness to it? She's too confused, too ill at the moment to make a statement, but when she's recovered her strength she could explode the Prior family reputation and send at least one of them to jail.'

'One thing's for sure.' Rose, sitting on the other side of the fireplace, seemed to have taken on the mantle of Miss Quicke herself. 'You won't let them get away with it. And if any bully boy shows his fists around here, I'll set about him with the frying pan.'

Ellie tried to laugh, but couldn't quite make it.

Thomas poured out some more soup for her. 'We will pray for protection, and take a few precautions. Giving in to an aggressor only makes things worse. Now I've been thinking; all this is hearsay, and we need to check some facts. What do we really know? The girls in the flat pointed the finger at the stepbrother, but he might be protecting someone else, a friend of his, for instance, and that's why he's trying to find her.'

'She was locked in her room,' said Ellie, pushing the emptied tray aside. 'Her mobile phone was smashed. She needed help to get away.'

'We have only heard about that through the girls in the flat, who got it from Malgosia, whom you haven't spoken to at all.'

'Why would Malgosia make it up?'

'A good point. And we mustn't forget Ursula's brush with Anthony and her smashed mobile. Hmm. I think on the whole we're justified in getting involved. You should tell the police what's happened.'

'I tried that.' Ellie got to her feet, moving stiffly. 'They didn't want to know. And until Mia is able to give a coherent account of what happened to her, I'm not sure they'll change their mind. After all, her parents have given her a shocking reputation.' She looked at the clock. 'If you don't mind, I think I'd better go to bed.'

She grumbled her way up the stairs, telling herself that she really ought to have made sure that Rose was all right before she went, though really Rose looked a lot more lively than Ellie felt tonight. As for Thomas, he hadn't seen Mia's injuries. Thomas was a big, strong man and didn't understand that normal people felt fear when they were threatened. Thomas wasn't taking the matter seriously enough.

Midge the cat was nowhere to be seen. Just as well. If he'd come winding round her legs at that moment, she'd have shoved him out of the way.

She shed her clothes and stomped into the bathroom to have a good long shower in hot water, and it didn't lift her black mood at all. When she came out, Thomas was switching on the electric blanket. And so he jolly well ought!

Thomas said, 'You're overtired.'

'Is that so surprising?' Her voice rose. 'Here I've been, going round trying to solve everyone else's problems, and when I get home I find Little Miss Stick Insect all over you.'

'Ellie, don't tell me you're jealous?' He made the mistake of laughing.

Ellie lunged at him with both fists. 'I hate you!'

Thomas drew her close to him. 'There, there.'

She despised women who burst into tears and took refuge from the world in a man's arms. 'She's size six and anorexic—'

'Yes, yes.'

'And stinks of perfume and someone ought to take those trailing scarves and strangle her—'

She could feel him laughing. 'You *are* jealous!'

207

'First Diana, and then that bundle of bones–'

He picked her up and deposited her on the bed, lying down beside her. 'I do love you, Ellie Quicke. Here, have a tissue.'

Ellie sniffed, took a tissue and blew, eyeing him sideways. 'I've been making a fool of myself, haven't I?'

'Mm. Delightfully. I enjoyed it.'

'I don't normally make scenes. Do I?'

'You're allowed one every time you save someone's life. And I promise to fend off all the women currently vying for my favours. Is that a bargain?'

She sniffed, and blew again. 'How's your cold coming on?'

'An early night with some hot honey and lemon should see it off. How about you?'

Wednesday late evening

'Are you there? Can you talk? Yes, I'm still at the dinner, but I'm in the foyer. I wanted to be sure—'

'Yes, the boys came down to the pub after, and I paid them off in the Gents. No, no one saw. They said it went off all right, although I think they were a bit heavy-handed. I told them to throw a scare into her, but I gather they spilt the red stuff.'

'What do you mean? Wine?'

'Blood. But she's all right. I mean, they phoned for an ambulance for her when they left. She got the message all right.'

Anthony laughed, and cut off the call.

Thursday morning early

Ellie was on her way downstairs next morning when the phone rang. She squinted at the grandfather clock in the hall, which said five to eight. She scooped up the newspapers from the mat on her way to the phone, wondering if Rose had been able to get herself to bed last night. She felt bad about having walked out on her like that.

'Mrs Quicke? Is that you?' An unfamiliar woman's voice, commanding but woolly, as if the speaker was talking through a mouthful of food. 'Mrs Belton here, Ursula's mother. I need to contact her, urgently. She told me you'd given her your mobile. Only...' A break in the voice. Almost a wobble. 'Only, she can't work out what the number is on the phone you've given her.'

'Oh, how stupid of me. I forgot to give it her. Hang on. I'll get it for you. It must be somewhere in my address book.' Ellie dropped the newspapers, trying to open the address book.

'The thing is ... the thing is...' Was that a sob?

Ellie abandoned her search in the phone book. 'What is it, Mrs Belton? Is something the matter?'

'I'm afraid, yes. I'm at the hospital, you see. Been there all night, ever since ... but they've stitched me up and I'll only have to wear a sling for a couple of days. I'm sure I'm perfectly all right to go home and they need the beds, don't they?'

'What's happened?'

Mrs Belton tried to laugh. 'Oh, nothing out of the ordinary, just a mugging on my own doorstep. I should have known better, shouldn't I, at my age? Two of them wearing masks, would you believe? And the police don't seem able to stop them. The worst of it is that ... so sorry–' her voice thickened – 'I'm afraid I can't talk properly at the moment.'

'That's dreadful.' DI Willis had spoken about some mask-wearing yobs, hadn't she? 'You want me to phone Ursula for you, to tell her what's happened?'

'I'm using the phone at the hospital, waiting for a taxi. At least, I was till I realized they'd taken my handbag with all my money and cards in it, as well as my keys and my mobile. And what they got up to inside the flat, I daren't think. So now I haven't any money to pay a taxi, and I'll have to wait for an ambulance to take me back.'

'The police know?'

'I suppose so. I wasn't conscious when they brought me in. The nurse said someone would be coming to see me from the police, but they haven't turned up yet and I'm desperate to get back home, to see what damage they've done.'

Thomas came galloping down the stairs, pulling on an outsize navy blue sweater which made him look more like a seafaring man than ever. Ellie held up a hand to check his progress while Rose appeared from the kitchen, hair awry but decently dressed. Rose was holding a

210

box of eggs. 'Two boiled, or scrambled with bacon?'

Ellie said, 'Hold on a minute, Rose. Mrs Belton, I'll ring Ursula straight away. Stay where you are. I'll be round to collect you in half an hour, maybe three quarters.'

Putting the phone down, Ellie told Thomas and Rose what had happened. 'So I'd better ring Ursula straight away.' She stopped. 'I've just had a thought. It's as if Mia was standing beside me and shaking her head. She was desperate that Ursula shouldn't come back. Do you think this could be related to...? No, it couldn't possibly. Could it?'

Thomas stroked his beard. 'There's no point alarming Ursula at this hour of the morning. Let's see what the damage is first, shall we? If it was just a bit of rough-housing by a couple of yobs then Ursula will have to know, but there's no need to drag her back. What could she do that her mother's friends couldn't do better?'

'Not sure she's got many friends. I'll get a minicab and fetch her; settle her back at home. I must have some breakfast first, though.'

Thomas followed her into the kitchen. 'She'll be in shock, and if she's lost her cards and her money, she'll need help to get sorted. I'll drive you both.'

'Have you time? What are you supposed to be doing today?'

For a moment his face reflected panic. Obviously he had something important on. But then he smiled. 'I'll make time. This is more

211

important.'

Rose crashed plates on to the table. 'Whatever is the world coming to? You'll both have eggs and bacon, with mushrooms and tomatoes. You'll need it. Fortify yourselves for the day ahead. My mother always used to say, if you start the day with a good breakfast, you can cope with most things.'

TWELVE

Thursday mid-morning

Mrs Belton agonized all the way home from the hospital about how she was to get into her flat without a door key. Of course Ursula had a key, but she wouldn't make it back to London for hours, would she?

Ellie didn't say that she hadn't phoned Ursula yet.

Thomas suggested, 'Has a neighbour got a spare key?'

'Most certainly not.'

Ellie remembered Mrs Belton saying that she was not on speaking terms with her neighbour. Oh dear. Did this mean a call to the locksmith? Ellie was sorry for Mrs Belton because the woman had been through a tough time. Her neat clothing was blotchy with blood, her right arm in a sling, and her face a patchwork of cuts and

212

bruises. One of her shoes was missing and her tights were torn. And she sniffed, perpetually, although she declared she didn't want a handkerchief, or tissues. Ellie tried hard to make allowances but had to admit the woman irritated her profoundly.

'Steady does it,' said Thomas, helping Mrs Belton out of the car. The front door of the flats was closed. Ellie scanned the facade with its carefully netted windows, but not a curtain twitched.

'What's that?' Mrs Belton pointed into the flower bed beside the path. A good quality handbag, rain-soaked and gaping, but recognizable. Before Ellie could say anything about fingerprints, Mrs Belton swooped on it, and with a cry of relief produced a bunch of keys, which she handed to Thomas.

'Thank goodness, my keys! They've left me my diary too. Oh, but my purse is empty, the cards gone. Even my library ticket! And my mobile!'

Ellie stifled the comment *what did you expect?* as she helped the woman over the step into the hall. 'Left hand flat, Thomas.'

Thomas opened the door, and stood back to let Mrs Belton enter.

'Oh, no!' Chaos and destruction ruled. Mrs Belton dropped her handbag, making little gasps of distress. 'What have they done? Oh, how could they! Look at ... Ursula's pictures! Oh, it's too much!'

She would have sunk to the floor, but that

Thomas managed to lift her into an upright chair with a broken back. The vandalism had been thorough. No pictures had been left on the walls, no item of furniture left upright. Books and smashed china lay higgledy-piggledy around. The television screen had been kicked in. The landline phone had been placed, with precision, on top of a settee that no longer offered comfortable seating.

Mrs Belton rocked to and fro. 'Oh, I can't bear it. All my lovely things.'

Ellie darted into the kitchen. Untouched. The bedrooms? Also untouched. Now what did that mean? Presumably the gang had been after money and valuables, but they'd already taken Mrs Belton's purse and cards, so why bother wrecking the flat? Were they looking for things to sell, but if so, why hadn't they searched the bedrooms for jewellery, clocks, watches?

Thomas had his mobile out and was calling the police.

Ellie put her arm around Mrs Belton's shoulders. 'There, there. It's only things, and things can be replaced. I know, because I lost my old home to fire and it was horrible at the time, such a shock. You are insured?'

'Yes, of course. I ... all my papers are...' she pointed to an old-fashioned wooden desk, which was now lying on its side and lacked its sloping lid. The papers that had been inside were in a heap beside it. A cheque book amongst them.

'Oh!' Mrs Belton struggled to her feet. 'My

214

laptop's gone! All my work schedules, my reports!'

'Are you sure it's not here?'

'I left it open on my desk there when I went out last night. It was connected to the mains. You can see they've unplugged it and taken it! Oh, what am I going to do?'

Thomas tried to calm her. 'Do you back up regularly?'

'Yes, of course, I ... a girl at work nearly got the sack when she forgot to, so I always back up.' She scrabbled in her handbag, taking out a plastic make-up bag. Opening that up, she produced a memory stick. 'At least I've got this.' She started to shake.

The doorbell rang, announcing the arrival of a policewoman who said she'd expected to see Mrs Belton at the hospital. She gave her name, but Ellie failed to catch it. Milford, or Milbrook, something like it. She seemed capable and made the right sort of noises to Mrs Belton, while Ellie made cups of hot, sweetened tea all round. Mrs Belton, getting paler by the minute, tried to tell the policewoman what she knew.

'I'd been out to a lecture at the Town Hall by the Historical Society. I was offered a lift back, but it would have been quicker by bus as it happened, because they had to drop two other people off first. Anyway, I suppose it was about half past ten when I got back. It was very dark. I remember thinking the light bulb must have gone again over the front door. I walked up the path, taking out my keys to open the front door, and then someone – someone tall, wearing a horrible mask, I only caught a glimpse but I think it was a Dracula mask – leaped on me from nowhere and hit me on my cheekbone – here. Someone else grabbed at the strap of my bag from behind. I had it across my body, and I went over backwards. I must have hit my head as I fell.'

She touched the back of her head. 'And then, it's all a blur. They used me as a punchbag. And laughed!'

'There were just two of them? Both masked?'

Mrs Belton shuddered. 'Yes, two of them, but I don't know what the other mask was. Something white with a big, gaping, red mouth, I think. I seem to remember being dragged into the hall, but then nothing till I came to at the hospital.'

'How did you manage to phone for an ambulance?'

'I didn't do it. I suppose someone passing by must have done so. I was out like a light. It was chaos at the hospital,' she said, tears forming in her eyes from weakness. 'Some drunken louts in a car had rammed another car and there were six or more of them, all still drunk, reeling around, bleeding over everything. Disgraceful! It was hours before they came to attend to me. Then I had to wait for an X-ray for my wrist, and they said it was lucky it wasn't broken, though what's lucky about what happened to me, I do not know.'

The policewoman said, 'A neighbour must

216

have heard the fight and phoned for an ambulance.'

'Her? She wouldn't give me the time of day. She's—' Mrs Belton tapped her forehead – 'Alzheimer's. Carers three times a day. She's in bed by seven every night.'

'Can you remember anything else about the two who attacked you? What they were wearing?'

Mrs Belton was sinking lower in her seat. 'Dark clothes. I don't know. They were big and strong.'

'Accents? Local? Did they say anything?'

Mrs Belton looked puzzled. 'I don't think so.' She put her hand to her head. 'I ache all over. My head's pounding.'

'Did they steal much?'

'My laptop, money and cards. Mobile phone. I don't know what else.' She looked around at the debris of her belongings. Some daffodils had been trodden into the carpet, and this jogged her memory. 'Those daffodils were in a blue vase. It had a small chip on the top, but I still use it. It was Bristol glass, you know? That intense blue. My mother gave me two pieces, and I can't see them. I can't cope. When my daughter comes...' She dissolved into tears.

Thomas and Ellie exchanged glances. Ellie said, 'Ursula can't be here for a while. Suppose we pack a bag for you, Mrs Belton, and you come home with us, have a bath and go to bed with some aspirin. You'll feel better after a good rest.'

'No, no.' She wavered to her feet. 'Things to do. I must just go to the bathroom and then I must let the insurance people know, cancel my cards. I'm with the Sentinel people. One call and they cancel everything for me. The folder should be in the desk, but...'

Thomas took charge. 'Let me see if I can find the paperwork, while you tell Ellie what you'd like her to pack for you for a few days away.' He raised his brows at the policewoman. 'If that's all right with you?'

The policewoman stowed her notebook away. 'This is the worst case yet. They've always been content just to steal handbags and laptops before. But this–' she indicated the mess – 'it's escalating, I'm afraid. Give me an address where I can reach Mrs Belton. I'll ask the neighbours upstairs; find out if they saw or heard anything.'

Ellie gently steered Mrs Belton into the bathroom and closed the door behind her. As she came back into the sitting room, she heard the front door of the flat slam behind the policewoman. Thomas grovelled on the floor, sifting through paperwork. 'A rum do, Ellie. What do you think?'

'Very odd.'

The landline rang. Mrs Belton called out from the bathroom, 'Will you get it?'

Ellie was nearest and picked up the receiver.

A man's voice. Educated. Forceful. 'Well, is Ursula back yet? Tell her to ring me.'

'What?'

The call was cut off. Ellie stared at the receiver, then replaced it on top of the damaged settee. She thought: they left the phone in full sight, where we'd be bound to see it. They didn't trash it, as they trashed everything else in the room. Therefore the men who trashed the room wanted Mrs Belton to be able to accept phone calls.

The man on the phone had expected Ursula to come running back to London when she heard what had happened. It couldn't be a chance call from an old friend, wanting to get back together, could it? No, it couldn't. The wording was specific. 'Is Ursula back yet?' He must know what had been happening to phrase it like that. And he wanted Ursula to ring him.

Which meant that he knew all about the trashing. Which meant that there was a connection between him and the vandals in masks, wasn't there?

Ellie felt quite dizzy. What was going on? Why was it so important for Ursula to return to London?

Mrs Belton limped out of the bathroom, blowing her nose with tender care. 'So sorry, I seem to have gone all to pieces. I've just realized, I can't leave. Ursula will be expecting me to be here when she returns.'

Ellie helped her into her bedroom. 'Don't worry. We'll tell Ursula where you're to be found. Just concentrate on what you'd like me to pack up for you.'

Thomas held up a file. 'Eureka. The insurance

details. And the number for Sentinel.' He lifted his voice. 'Mrs Belton, have you a camera by any chance? I could take some photos for the insurance people.'

'In the right hand drawer of the table in the hall. Or rather, that's where it ought to be.'

Luckily, the vandals hadn't touched that table. While Ellie helped Mrs Belton to change and pack for a few days away, Thomas found the camera and took pictures of the damage. He also asked permission to take photos of Mrs Belton's ruined face when she was ready to depart.

'Leave everything to us,' he said, helping her into his car. 'We'll cancel the cards and inform the insurance company. All you have to do is relax and get better.'

'I daren't think what Ursula will say. Her pictures—'

'We'll ring and explain.'

Thursday midday
Ellie administered aspirins, tucked Mrs Belton up in bed in their spare room, and went downstairs to join Thomas, only to find him on the phone to the insurance people.

Rose came into sight and hovered. 'Mr Roy...' she began, and twitched a smile as Ellie clapped her hands to her forehead. 'Well,' said Rose, 'I did promise to tell you he'd called as soon as you came in, and so I have. I also told him that other people have their troubles, too, and he shouldn't expect you to have a hankie ready every time he gets a runny nose.'

'Er, no.' Ellie subdued a desire to giggle.

'He really is a very silly little boy,' said Rose. 'At least, that's what Miss Quicke says.'

'Er, yes.' Ellie wondered at Rose's use of the present tense, but decided that now was not the time to ask about it. 'Rose, I'm sorry to impose a guest on you, but Mrs Belton's been mugged and her flat wrecked. We simply couldn't leave her there, could we?'

'We shall rise above it. Which reminds me that that funny Ms Woodyates popped round again this morning and said she'd wait for you, but I told her you'd gone out for the day, which I hope was what you wanted me to say.'

'Cards cancelled, insurance informed,' said Thomas, putting the phone down. 'The insurance people will send someone round to the flat to check in due course, but promised to let us know beforehand. Now, Rose: what's for lunch?'

'Ant, where are you? I've got a small problem.'

'You've got a problem? What about me? And you'll have to get off the phone sharpish as I'm waiting for Ursula to call. It can't take her that long to get back from Portsmouth. In the meantime I'm chasing my tail, trying to find Mia. I thought I'd be able to pick her up at the bakery where she's been working, but she's left there and the manageress wouldn't talk, but I got a lead on her by asking where the immigrants worked locally. The blonde at the café parted

with the information for a tenner. It seems Mia went AWOL yesterday in the company of an old woman, a Mrs Quicke. Mean anything to you?'

'Never heard of her. Do we really need to get Mia back? I mean, she's family, sort of, and not exactly a threat, is she? Why not let her go?'

'That's what I thought at first, but that was before we knew how much we need Ursula on our side. If Mia meets up with Ursula now, do you really think she'll keep quiet? Of course not. The whole story will come out and then we'll be in the shit. No, Mia has got to be found and dealt with.'

'Not another accident!'

'Of course not. I've got someone who'll take her off our hands.'

'But if she's gone off with an older woman—'

'The blonde didn't have an address, but Mrs Quicke's in the phone book and I plan to pay her a visit this afternoon. So what's your problem? Run out of condoms?'

'You know I paid the boys off last night? As agreed, I let them keep her mobile and the stuff from her purse, and they assured me they'd left the landline alone ... but they've taken her laptop as well.'

'So?'

'It's not exactly an up-to-date model, but it's got all her work stuff on it. So I thought I'd give them fifty for it as it might come in useful. I mean, she must be in trouble without it. We could tell Ursula we'd discovered it somewhere and she could have it back for her mother when *she met up with us. Right?'*

'Sometimes, little brother, you amaze me. Very well. Another fifty it is.'

Thursday early afternoon
The phone rang under Thomas's hand. He picked it up, only to hand it to Ellie.

It was nice, fat Jackie from the bakery. 'Mrs Quicke, sorry to be ringing you so soon, but that man came again to the bakery today. I said nothing. But now I hear that he frighten one of my friends who is also working in the Avenue, and she say Mia was with us but is now gone. I am sorry, but she say to him that Mrs Quicke has got her. Only, she is not knowing your address or phone number, so that she could not say.'

'Thank you for warning me. It was good of you.'

'Is Mia all right?'

'Not really. I took her to see a doctor, and he has admitted her to hospital.'

'That is good. I thought of doctor, but Mia say, "No, no, he will find me."'

'He won't find her where she is now, I assure you.'

'That is good. Have a nice day.'

Ellie put the phone down, and tried to smile. 'Well, he's a fast worker, I must say. All my precautions, taking Mia round by Armand and Kate's, have turned out to be fruitless. He knows I took Mia, so I suppose we can expect him at any minute.'

223

Thomas eyed the hatstand in the hall, which contained a number of stout walking sticks and large, old-fashioned umbrellas. 'We'll keep front and back doors locked and bolted. If anyone tries to force an entry we ring the police, right? Now, let's have something to eat, and decide what to say to Ursula.'

At that moment Roy burst into the hall from the kitchen, closely followed by the Stick Insect.

'Ellie, I saw you were back so I've given you a few minutes before—'

'Dear Ellie!' Grace was wearing another green outfit, with what looked suspiciously like a mink collar over a neckline far too low for what she had to offer in the way of bosom. 'Dear, dear Ellie! And dear Thomas, too! How fortunate to catch you both in. I saw this dear man go into the house by the side entrance, and thought I'd take you both by surprise.'

Roy and Thomas imitated startled horses, which made Ellie grin. Thomas looked at his watch and said, 'I've just remembered an important phone call.' He almost ran down the corridor to his office.

Roy fidgeted, eyeing Grace with distrust. 'I'm sure that ... I'm sorry, but I have a most urgent matter to discuss with my cousin.'

'Oh, don't mind little old me,' fluted the Stick Insect, tucking her arm inside Roy's and making him flinch. 'Ellie and I are such good friends, I'm sure you won't mind my sitting in on your confabulations. My friend always used to say I have an extraordinary ability to get straight to the heart of the matter. Are we in here?' She led the way into the sitting room, towing a reluctant Roy along with her.

Ellie folded her arms across her chest, stifling an impulse to roar with laughter. Then, meeting the distress in Rose's eyes, Ellie sobered up.

'Rose, it's all right. I'll deal with her. Meanwhile, could you see that the kitchen door is locked and bolted? Just in case.'

'You haven't eaten yet.'

'Soup and sandwiches for me and Thomas? Nothing for the others, or they'll be here for hours.'

She marched into the sitting room to find Grace still with her arm firmly locked around Roy's as they looked out on the wintry garden.

'Grace, I'm so sorry, but I'm afraid this con-versation I'm going to have with Roy is private, family business. I know you'll understand. It was good of you to call. And yes, we must make a date to meet up some time soon.'

Grace's mouth turned down, but she absorbed the rebuff with a smile that didn't look too strained. 'Oh, what a pity. I had been so looking forward to a nice visit. It's just like you, always thinking about other people, but you must take some time for your dearest friends, don't you think?'

'Indeed,' said Ellie, lying through her teeth. She escorted Grace to the hall and out of the front door, promising to ring as soon as she had a free moment. Grace took her by surprise,

225

bending to kiss Ellie on both cheeks in farewell. 'Till we meet again, *chère amie.*'

Ellie double-locked the door behind Grace and shot home the bolts. Now for Roy, who was pacing up and down, biting his lower lip.

'Roy, before you start, I need something to eat. Come into the kitchen with me.'

'We can't discuss this in front of Rose.'

'Why not? I know exactly how this conversation is going to go: you're going to ask me to buy your flats so that you can buy into Prior's Place, and I'm going to say "no".'

'I can show you the figures that prove—'

'There is no way *I'd* ever want to do business with the Priors.'

Roy gaped. 'Why ever not? They're one of the soundest, best respected—'

'I've been hearing another side of things. Roy, you were at his party in the new year. Did you like the way your wife was being fondled by one of the other guests? Didn't you see the way that the young people were being used in the same way to soften up potential buyers? And then there's the mystery of the boy who jumped; what part did the Priors play in that tragedy?'

'But that's nothing to do with ... Ellie, I've promised!'

'Not in writing, I trust.'

'Just a scribbled note. He needed that to show the bank.'

'Who will come down hard on him unless he can sell the flats fast? And in this difficult time, do you honestly think he's going to manage that? Roy, I'm ashamed of you. What would your mother have said? You know she didn't want to put any money into that project.'

'Ellie, don't be like that. It's not my fault.'

Ellie sighed. No, it probably wasn't. He'd been born terminally stupid about money. His mother had decided against leaving him a lot of money for that very reason. Instead, she'd given him a block of flats which she'd hoped would provide him with a secure income for life. 'So, what steps have you taken?'

He revived at her softer tone. 'Well, naturally, I tried to sell my flats first, but no one's biting at the moment. Then I asked around to see if I could get a mortgage on them, but that's difficult too.'

'Why not be satisfied with what you've got? You're a brilliant architect, but no financial brain. Don't you think you'd be better off without any assets other than what you earn?'

'That's what Felicity says. It's all right for her, with a financial genius for a father and all the money her first husband left her. I want to provide for her myself, and let's face it, someone stands to make a mint with Prior's Place.'

Ellie rehearsed such phrases as: *You must be joking!* And: *The Priors saw you coming!* She could see that manly pride was kicking in. Roy didn't like to think he couldn't match his wife's money. No wonder Felicity was alarmed; Felicity understood her husband better than most wives did.

Ellie took Roy's arm, and sat him down on the settee beside her. 'Dear Roy, you are the kindest, sweetest and most loving of husbands and fathers. Felicity loves you for yourself, and not for your money. You have a real talent for your work, which is something that I don't have, nor Felicity, nor Kate, nor anyone else I know. You are brilliantly creative, which we are not. We can only admire. To each his own. Handling money is another matter. Yes, it is,' she said, as he would have protested.

'But—'

'So wouldn't it be best if you let other people deal with that side of things for you? I can't handle big money either and I know it, which is why I let other people do it for me. Now, how would it be if I asked one of them to look at this project for you, and give you an idea of how profitable it is likely to be?'

He grasped at the olive branch. 'You think you can find a financier to back me?'

'It's always possible,' said Ellie, not at all sure she meant it. 'The great thing is to use the right key in the lock. Architects are creative builders. Financiers move money around. I think you should stick to what you do best, and leave the boring bits to other people.'

He nodded, absorbing the idea. 'You're right, Ellie. This finance business has been getting to me. It's not my line at all, and I'm going to leave it in your hands to deal with. I'll tell Prior so, and get him off my back.'

Ellie almost patted him on the head and said

Good Boy. But managed to smile and urge him to his feet instead. 'It will put Felicity's mind at rest to know that you're leaving all that side of things to the experts.' She soothed him out of the front door, and made sure the door was safely bolted against the outside world. What next? Food, she hoped. But first she'd better check with Thomas.

Her beloved was scoffing an enormous wodge of sandwich, grunting to someone on the phone and, at the same time, tapping on his keyboard. When he saw her he held up one finger, gave a final grunt into the phone, and dropped it back on its rest. 'Save the mark! Don't they teach children nowadays to read a calendar? This chap said he didn't think I meant it when I told him copy date was January seventh. Have you eaten?'

'I will in a minute. Thomas, how much do we tell Ursula, and how can we prevent her rushing back to London?'

He took another huge bite, chewed, and swallowed. Ellie's mouth watered, but she made herself wait.

'Be devious. Let her think she's pulling the strings. Ask her opinion about everything. I agree she should keep away. We can provide the help her mother needs, don't you think?'

'Agreed. I'll phone her in a minute. Must eat first.'

As she returned through the hall the landline rang, and she answered it while looking at her watch. The afternoon was wearing on, and she was so hungry she felt hollow.

'Mother, is that you? Are you there?'

'Diana?' Was something wrong with her daughter's voice?

'Can you come? I need ... I don't know what to do. I'm at the old house.'

'What? No, I'm just going to have my lunch.'

'I wouldn't ask if it weren't urgent.' Was that a sob?

'Diana? Are you all right?'

'No, not really. I rang the police and they want me to go to hospital, but I can't, not with people coming to look round the house. Stewart rescued me, but he can't stay long. You will come, won't you?'

THIRTEEN

Thursday afternoon

Ellie stared at the receiver. Diana in trouble? Whatever next! Had she really mentioned police? Hospital? No, no. There must be some mistake. It was Mrs Belton who had needed the police and been taken to hospital.

Stewart rescued Diana? Oh, come on! Ridiculous notion. Ellie was not going to run to Diana's side without good reason. Diana had pulled tricks like this before and anyway, she had to eat something or she'd fall down. And,

230

she had to phone Ursula.

Didn't she?

Well, Mrs Belton was fast asleep upstairs, and it wouldn't do any harm to postpone the call to Ursula. As for Diana ... wait a minute. Had Diana said she was at Ellie's old house? If she'd got into trouble there, twisted her ankle or whatever ... well, she could jolly well wait till Ellie had eaten. How dare she try to summon her mother to her side for such a trivial matter! But, how typical!

Police? Hospital? Ellie shrugged. She was going to eat before she did anything else, and only after she'd eaten would she take a cab over there. She would not disturb Thomas again; he had more than enough to do and needed to catch up on what he ought to have been doing that morning. She must remember to take the keys to the old house with her. Now where had she put them? In a safe place. But which safe place?

Rose had gone off for her afternoon nap, leaving soup on the stove and a pile of sandwiches on the side. Good.

It was nearly three when Ellie got out of the minicab at her old house. The sky was leaden, but it was not raining for once. The house looked bright and shining, lights were on in every room, and the garden was still in need of attention. The 2Ds notice board was still up. Because it had got dark so early, there were lights on in most of the surrounding houses, though none at Kate and Armand's next door.

Ellie rang the bell and used her key to let herself in. The house echoed to her call of 'Hello!' There was no response. No workmen lurked. There was a pronounced smell of new paint and freshly cut wood, and the central heating had been left to tick over. No Diana. What was going on? And then she saw the remains of a mobile phone on the floor, and drew in her breath. Oh, no. Not again!

Footsteps came down the drive, and Diana appeared. 'I was sitting in my car with the doors locked, waiting for you. What took you so long?'

Diana's face was puffy with newly created bruises, there was a cut on her mouth and her nose looked twice its normal size. The fake fur on the collar of her black winter coat had been partially torn away, and she'd lost an earring. Her voice was shaky, and so were her hands.

Ellie thought: no, it can't be him again! Why should he attack Diana? 'What happened to you?'

'I was showing some prospective tenants round and, as I walked them back to their car, a man came up behind me and asked if I were Mrs Quicke. I said I was Ms Quicke, yes, and he followed me back into the house, slammed the front door and started slapping me around, asking me what I'd done with his sister! I tried to say I didn't know what he was talking about, I asked him to leave, but he didn't stop, not for a minute. I got out my mobile to ring for the police; he wrenched it off me and stamped on it.

'It was a nightmare. When I fell down, he picked me up and started all over again. And then Stewart let himself in – he'd come to check up on something the workmen had done – and this man threw me across the hall and squared up to Stewart. I thought there was going to be a fight, for Stewart's as big as him, if not bigger. But he pushed past Stewart and ran out of the front door. I don't understand. Did he think I was you? And if so, why?'

Ellie said, 'Oh, dear. How awful!' and didn't know how to begin to explain.

Diana held her forefinger under her nose. 'Is my nose bleeding again? I ran the cold water tap and bathed it, and I thought it had stopped, but...' She was almost in tears.

Ellie wanted to put her arm round her daughter, but didn't quite dare. Diana was not one to encourage familiarity.

Diana dabbed at her nose, sniffing. 'Stewart rang the police for me, because I wasn't sure which way up I was. They sent some stupid berk of a constable round who seemed to think I'd been asking for it, taking prospective tenants around by myself, and laying myself open to every nutter that passed by. He even asked if it were Stewart who'd attacked me! I ask you!'

'What was his name? The policeman.'

'How should I know? Maybe Stewart remembers, for I don't. After he'd gone, I sat in Stewart's car while he went to see if Kate were in so that she could look after me for a bit, but she wasn't there. Then he locked me in, and went to the Avenue to get me some sweetened tea and some biscuits, because I'm such a sight I couldn't go anywhere.

'The tea made me feel better, but I didn't know what to do about the next client that was due, because Denis can't leave the office if I'm out on the job. I rang him and told him what had happened and he took the same line as the police, that I'd asked for it! Can you believe it? In the end Stewart agreed to show my clients round for me while I sat in his car. It was decent of him, I suppose. I said, "Won't you get in trouble with my mother?" and he said you'd understand, but he couldn't stay long as he had another appointment to go to.

'That's when I rang you. Since then I've been sitting in my own car with the doors locked. I don't understand anything, and I don't know what to do next.' With a wail, she finally gave way to tears.

Ellie managed to put her arm round her daughter's shoulders. Diana was taller than her, but for once she didn't reject the offer of comfort. 'There, there.'

Diana gulped and sniffed. 'That man said he'd not finished with me. He said he knew where I lived, that he'd traced me through the phone book.'

Ah. So that's how he'd arrived at this address. And, seeing Diana here, showing people around, he'd leaped to the conclusion that she was Mrs Quicke. He'd never seen Ellie, and when Diana said she was Ms Quicke, he'd thought he'd got the right person. The phone book entries were only changed once a year, and the phone for this house was still listed in Ellie's name. She'd only moved to the big house when her aunt was dying, and Miss Quicke's number had been ex-directory. So he wasn't going to trace Ellie by that means, which was a comfort, sort of.

'He's after me, not you,' said Ellie.

'What! But who is he, and what does he want with you?'

Ellie took the photos out of her handbag. 'Is that the man who attacked you?'

'How should I know? He wore a mask. A wolf's head.'

'You mean that you let a man wearing a mask into the house?'

'No, no. He didn't have a mask on when he came through the door, I'd have noticed that. He was putting it on as I came back into the house. I know I'm going to have nightmares. Who is the man in the photo, anyway? And why should he want to attack me?'

'If I'm right and it's the same man, his name is Anthony Prior and he beat up his stepsister so badly that she ran away. I took her to a place of safety and now he's trying to track her down. I dread to think what he might do if he found her.'

'He can't just go around assaulting people. What are the police doing about it?'

'Her family say she ran away because they

objected to her sleeping around, so the police aren't interested. If they could only see her now ... but the girl was so badly beaten, she's in no condition to make a statement to the police yet. Anthony wants her back before she can do so. He knows I took charge of her, and he mistook you for me. There is a local gang who wear masks and go round terrorizing householders at night. Everyone's heard about them, and I suppose he thought that wearing a mask would be an elementary precaution against being recognized.'

'Gracious me!' Diana tried to laugh and cry, both at once. She shook off her mother's arm. 'Well, well. It seems you owe me, mother.'

'Yes.' Ellie looked around at the newly-decorated house. 'I was so angry when I saw that you'd put the house up for rent instead of living in it for yourself, that I told Stewart to rent it out for me instead. But I was wrong. A gift is a gift and what you choose to do with this house now is your concern, not mine. I hope you found a tenant for it today. Did you?'

'Stewart did. The clients that he took round for me want to take it.' She tried on a laugh and it came out as near hysteria. 'There's a funny thing; he's working for you, but he found me a tenant.'

'Where are you living now?'

'Nowhere. I put my bits and pieces in store and spent last night at the office on the daybed. You'll let me stay with you now though, won't you?'

Ellie grimaced. 'Of course. Rose's bedroom is vacant.'

'What? Surely I can have the guest room.'

'I've someone in it already. Another victim of the Priors. At least, I think the two cases are connected, although when I come to think of it, I'd have a hard job proving it. And before you throw another wobbly, the other person is in a far worse state than you, so be grateful for small mercies. Now, are you fit to drive us both home?'

'Ant, what's up? Has Ursula phoned yet?'

'I wish. There's no sign of her at her mother's place. No sign of the mother, either. I don't understand it. Will you check back with the boys, see if they overdid the damages bit? She can't still be in hospital, can she? I tried the neighbour, but she's not in this world, totally out of it.'

'But you've found Mia?'

'I traced Mrs Quicke to her house; it's empty and to let but she was there, showing people around. I had words but she's a tough nut, wouldn't even admit to knowing Mia. Unfortunately we were interrupted before I could really get down to it, and then she called the police, so I had to leave.'

'Don't tell me the perfect Anthony failed!'

'A setback, that's all. I'm going back to the Quicke woman's house now, to see if I can get something out of the neighbours. And I've got another address for her, so I'll get her soon. I

237

want you to go to Ursula's when you finish work and wait for her. Right?'

'I don't like this. Suppose the Quicke woman took Mia to the police?'

'We'd have heard if she had. And until she does, we're safe, right?'

Thursday early evening

Diana's driving was usually excellent, but this evening she was not herself. She took corners either too wide or too close, and stalled at the traffic lights. Ellie was relieved when they eventually crawled into the driveway of the big house, even if they did only just miss one of the cars already parked there. Ellie identified the cars: Thomas's and Stewart's.

Diana took no notice of either, but staggered to the front door and waited to be let in. 'I could murder a gin.'

As Ellie let them into the hall, doors opened and people popped out of them; Stewart from the sitting room, Rose from the kitchen, and Thomas from his office. Also, Mrs Belton, inching her way down the stairs with an expression of suffering on her face.

All four opened their mouths to speak but Ellie forestalled them, shedding coat and handbag. 'Let the wounded soldier through first. Diana, up the stairs to Rose's old bedroom. You can get yourself cleaned up in her bathroom and have a rest, or come down to join us when you feel like it.'

Diana did not know Mrs Belton from Adam,

238

but recognized at once that this was the rival to her occupation of the spare room. Assuming the mantle of the Tragedy Queen and developing a worse limp even than her rival, she winced her way up the first few steps, holding on to the banister. 'It's an insult that I, who will inherit this house one day, am sent to sleep in the servant's quarters.'

Mrs Belton saw no reason to put up with this. 'If you'd been driven out of house and home—'

'I'm homeless,' said Diana, nearing the top of the stairs. 'Can you say the same?' She expected Mrs Belton to move over for her but Mrs Belton, with one arm in a sling and the other hand clutching the banister, was made of sterner stuff and stood her ground.

To her audience's fascination – which woman would give way first? – Diana had to edge around Mrs Belton. But Diana was not beaten yet. She said, 'Oh, and Stewart, I've left my overnight bag in my car. Bring it up for me, will you?' She dropped her keys over the banister and, without waiting to see if Stewart would obey her, went through the door on the landing that led to Rose's old quarters.

Stewart threw up his arms, but collected the keys. He was grinning. So was Thomas. Mrs Belton, having won that battle, sailed down the rest of the stairs without limping.

Rose, however, was not amused. 'Is Diana staying for supper, too? I can't produce meals out of thin air, you know. Oh, and that Grace person – "Disgrace" I call her – has been here again, but I told her you were out for the day and she went away.'

Ellie rubbed her cold hands together. 'Diana got beaten up in mistake for me. I think she met up with the same person as Mia and Mrs Belton. How are you feeling now, Mrs Belton? Do go through into the sitting room and find yourself a comfortable seat. Thomas, Rose: Diana's homeless. I'll find her somewhere else to live tomorrow.'

Rose said, 'Humph!' and stalked off back to the kitchen.

Mrs Belton inclined her head graciously to Ellie. 'Thank you for asking. I've had a nice nap, but could do with some paracetamol and a hot drink. Do you know when Ursula will be arriving, and may I ask where she is to sleep?'

'I'll get you some painkillers in a minute, Mrs Belton,' said Ellie, 'but I must see to my daughter first.'

Stewart bumped back into the hall, carrying the large suitcase which was Diana's idea of an overnight bag. 'Upstairs?' he said.

'I'll come up with you,' said Ellie, mounting the stairs. 'Rose's bed was stripped. I'll have to find some bedding, and clean towels.' She leaned over the banisters to talk to her husband. 'Thomas, you want to speak to me. Is it urgent?'

'When you've got a minute. I'll see to Mrs Belton, shall I?'

Stewart mounted the stairs at Ellie's side.

240

'You'll want to know what happened. I went to your old house to check on the skirting board in the master bedroom that the workmen were supposed to replace and hadn't, and walked in on some comic book villain attacking Diana. I was so surprised I didn't think quickly enough. I ought to have tackled him, but he pushed past me and fled. Diana was in a bad way. I called the police and they took our statements, but I didn't know what to do next. Diana had some clients due to look over the house, but she wasn't fit to show them round, so I did it for her. They said they'd take it. Only, afterwards I thought you'd be justified in sacking me for doing that. I would have phoned you, but I don't have your new mobile phone number.'

'You did the right thing, Stewart. I've changed my mind. I said I'd let her have the house, and so I will. She can do what she likes with it. What did you make of her assailant?'

'The police asked me that, but it all happened so quickly, I only got the most fleeting impression. He was wearing an animal mask.' He humped the suitcase into Rose's room. From the noise of running water, they gathered Diana was in the bathroom next door.

Ellie saw that the room – though of a decent size – was hardly fit to house anyone at the moment, as they'd pulled furniture this way and that, clearing Rose's things out. First she drew the curtains. Now, where was that summer weight duvet?

Stewart said, 'What can I do to help? I'm

pretty handy around the house nowadays.'

'Top of the wardrobe, spare duvet in a plastic bag. There should be a pillow or two there as well. I'll fetch linen from the cupboard on the landing.' She retrieved clean towels, duvet cover, sheets and pillowcases, and admired the deftness with which Stewart helped her make up the bed.

She said, 'Tell me what else you remember about the man.'

'Nothing much. He slammed the front door in my face and, by the time I'd got it open, he'd reached the road and was taking off his mask. He was running away so fast, I can hardly say.' He frowned. 'Fair hair, I think. And I think, yes ... I think he was wearing a suit. Grey, pin-striped.'

He looked puzzled. 'I've only just remember-ed that. When the police came, they seemed to think the masked gang were youngsters larking around. Although what youngsters would think they were doing, attacking a woman showing clients around a house, I don't know.' A sudden thought. 'He wasn't that young. I'd say late twenties. You know how thin most teenagers are. They can be big-boned, but they haven't filled out yet. This man was as tall as me, and had filled out.'

'Gracious!' said Diana, making an entrance, wearing only bra and pants. 'Aren't you mother's little helpmeet! She'll be asking you to put on a frilly apron and use a feather duster in a minute.'

Stewart flushed, but managed to keep his mouth shut.

Ellie said, 'You wear me out, Diana. Either keep a civil tongue in your head, or find yourself a B. & B. somewhere. Understand? And you can apologize to Stewart. You should be on your knees thanking him for saving you today, instead of being rude to him.'

Stewart shook his head. 'It's all right, Ellie. After all, if we'd left it to Diana to make the bed, she'd be sleeping on the mattress.'

'I'd have asked Rose to make it up for me,' said Diana, smiling sweetly. 'After all, that's her job, isn't it? Or isn't she up to doing even that, nowadays?'

Ellie pushed the last pillow into place, and realigned the telly so that Diana could watch it in bed. 'You leave Rose alone. And now I'd better go down and see about supper.'

'Which,' said Diana, 'Rose should be doing, right?'

Ellie ignored her. 'Stewart, I've got some photos I'd like to show you. See if anyone in them rings a bell.'

Once downstairs, she showed him the photos and he hovered over the one featuring Anthony Prior. 'It might be him. The same build. But, of course, I didn't see his face. Who is he?'

'Anthony Prior. Son of the developer. But I can't be sure, of course.' Ellie explained how she'd come to tangle with the Prior family, and Stewart nodded.

He said, 'You think this man tracked you

down to your old house by the entry in the phone book? So he might pay a visit to Denis at Diana's flat next?'

This struck both Ellie and Stewart as a beautiful thought. Stewart rubbed a hand over his mouth to stifle a grin. 'Dear me.' Not meaning it.

Ellie didn't bother to hide her amusement. 'I'll tell Diana to warn him.'

Stewart put his arm around Ellie and gave her a hug. 'I love you, mother-in-law.'

She went on tiptoe to kiss his cheek. 'Call me Ellie, please, son-in-law. It was a good day for us when Diana brought you into the family. Give my love to your darling wife Maria. Now, would it be best if you kept little Frank with you this weekend? I hardly think Diana's going to be able to look after him.'

She let him out into the winter evening, double-locked the door, and shot home the bolts.

What next? Supper for five. In the old days Rose would have thought nothing of rustling up a meal for five, but she might not be up to organizing it now. Ellie's instinct was correct. Thomas was in the kitchen, throwing together the ingredients for the main course, while Rose sifted something in a bowl. Pastry or crumble topping?

'Mrs Belton's vegetarian,' said Thomas, layering lasagne at speed. 'So I'm making two lots, one veg and one not.'

Rose looked as fierce as her mild countenance

allowed. 'She says she's used to a bath sheet, not a fiddly little towel, and would I find her something more suitable. People nowadays don't ever say "thank you", do they? I was always taught to say "thank you" for everything I received, and she never even thanked Thomas for getting her a hot drink and some aspirin.'

'Have you put the cheese in the sauce yet, Rose?' said Thomas. 'Is there enough for both dishes? Ellie, go and do your phoning. The number's on my phone pad in the office. I'll cope here. Lasagne to start with; apple crumble for afters. And there's some cheese, too, though perhaps not enough.'

Rose ladled sauce. 'They should be grateful for what they're going to get. Not that I've ever known Diana say "thank you" for anything.'

Ellie clapped her hands to her head. 'Of course. I must phone Ursula—'

'You'd better phone Mr Abrahams first. That's the doctor who's looking after Mia, isn't it? He rang earlier, but wouldn't tell me what it was about.'

Ellie went through the hall, ignoring a plaintive cry from Mrs Belton that she'd appreciate someone turning on the television set for her, as she went. Ellie was beginning to share Rose's opinion about both their unexpected guests.

Ellie got out the telephone number Mr Abrahams had given her to phone for news of Mia. It matched the one Thomas had taken down on his pad. She knew it was going to be disturbing news, even before she reached him. 'You asked me to ring you about...' She tried to remember the name he'd given her to use. 'About Flavia.'

'I'm so sorry, Mrs Quicke, but bed rest and antibiotics didn't do the trick. Flavia started to bleed heavily early this morning, and miscarried at noon. We will have to do a D. & C. to make sure everything's come away. She's heavily sedated at the moment, and I don't think she realizes what's happened yet. I hope the news will be a relief to her when she comes round, but it may not be. I would welcome some input on this. Do you know how she felt about being pregnant? I couldn't make out what her feelings were when I told her last night.'

'I know what you mean. She seemed fatalistic and terrified by turns. Everyone I've spoken to says she was a nice girl, definitely not the sort to sleep around. I've not heard of her having a serious boyfriend, so I suspect the pregnancy was down to rape. But if she had realized she was pregnant, she might have felt she should carry the child to term. You will arrange some counselling for her?'

'Of course. How is the manhunt going?'

Ellie grimaced. 'Getting nearer. I've got two more victims of vicious attacks under my roof at the moment, though neither is in need of your services, I'm happy to say. Do you think ... do you have a fax machine there? Would it be possible for you to fax through some photos of Flavia's injuries? I need something, anything, to take to the police.'

'I'll do that.'

The pictures came through within ten minutes, but alas, it was too late to find DI Willis at the police station, though Ellie tried and left a message for the woman to ring her.

Then she squared her shoulders, flexed her neck, and put in a spot of praying. *Dear Lord, this is me again, asking you to help me say the right things to Ursula. She did ask for help – in her own fashion – by going to church for a sit-in. You know far more about this affair than I do. Tell me what to say to her.*

She wasn't sure that He'd got the message, but lifted the phone and got through to Ursula.

'Ursula, where are you? Are you with friends?'

Ursula gasped. 'Is the news that bad?'

'No, but it is disturbing.'

'I'm at the house, which I share with five others. Three of my friends are in the kitchen, but I've had my supper, was just settling down to some work. Somebody's died? Not Mia?'

'Nobody's died.' Except the foetus. 'Ursula, you drew us into this business, but I don't think you were entirely straight with us. You presented it to us as if it were some kind of puzzle to be solved. You talked of a broken engagement, but you got me to take your ring back. A disappearance, you said, and I agree that you really were worried about Mia. But when you spoke of a murder, you didn't tell us why you thought it wasn't an accident, and you weren't afraid to tackle the man you thought responsible.'

Ursula caught her breath. 'Was I right?'

'I think so. It's time to grow up, Ursula. Stop playing games, because everyone else has.'

'What's happened? Tell me!'

'Your mother was mugged on her doorstep last night, and spent the night in hospital. She's all right, apart from cuts and bruises on her face and a sprained wrist, but she had her money, cards and mobile phone stolen from her handbag by two lads in animal masks—'

'Oh, no!'

'And her living room was wrecked. Every piece of furniture turned over, every ornament and every picture smashed.'

'What! Oh, no! I don't believe it! She's all right? I must get back, I don't know how late the trains run, but—'

'Use your head, Ursula. Isn't that what he wants?'

'What? You mean...? No, no! He couldn't possibly—'

'Your mother phoned me to fetch her from the hospital and when we got to her flat I took a phone call meant for her, which said that Ursula should contact him immediately.'

An indrawn breath. 'You mean, he'd go to all those lengths to get me back?'

'Why, Ursula? Why is it so important to him that you return to London?'

'I ... don't know. I'll have to think.'

'All right, you do some thinking, but while you're thinking, he's still trying to find Mia. He knows I took her away, he knows my name, and now he's trying to find me, in order to recover Mia. He beat up my daughter today because he thought she was me. The police were contacted for your mother's assault, and also for that of my daughter, but they don't seem to be tying these two incidents to Mia's disappearance. Are they right, or wrong?'

'You did say Mia was all right, though. She is, isn't she?'

'Define "all right". She's shattered. She's been beaten up, raped, and bitten. Some of the bites were going septic. She was also pregnant.'

Ursula dropped the phone with a wail.

'Ursula! Pick up!'

Ellie waited. Eventually Ursula picked up the phone. She was crying. 'Mrs Quicke, don't go on at me, please! I had no idea! I've got to think. I need to speak to my mother.'

'She's staying with me. I'll get her to ring you in a little while, after she's had supper. Now, don't worry too much about Mia. She's in a private nursing home and being well cared for. She'll stay there until she's well enough to make a statement to the police. She lost the baby, by the way.'

Ursula was crying hard.

Ellie put the phone down and sat back in Thomas's chair, feeling worn out. At some point Thomas had come in and seated himself opposite her. Listening.

Ellie pressed her hands against her eyelids. 'Was I too hard on the girl? I don't know what came over me.'

Thomas shook his head. 'She hasn't been totally honest with us. She was naive, not realizing what a dangerous game she was playing.'

'Thomas, I'm so sorry. I ought to have phoned you before I brought Diana back here, but I couldn't think what else to do at short notice. So much is happening, so quickly. I'll find her somewhere else to live tomorrow.'

'Ah, that reminds me. A couple of phone calls: Armand rang to say Kate's gone off with the littlies to stay with a friend. He says he found your sausages and chops in his car and proposes to eat them this evening with a friend of his from school. He hopes you don't mind.'

'So he did find them. Good.'

'Then Mrs Belton's been asking for her daughter. I told her you were trying to contact Ursula this very minute. Meanwhile, we've a nice little comedy playing out in the kitchen. Come and see.'

'Ant, where are you? I've been sitting outside Ursula's place for hours and there's still no sign of her or her mother.'

'That's ridiculous. She left hospital this morning. I checked. The Man's going frantic. If we don't deliver Ursula on time, he's going to cut his throat.'

'Not really?'

'No, of course not really. But, as usual, it's left to us to do the dirty work. I've been chasing around all day ... well, never mind that. Why

are you ringing? More bad news?'

'I know you don't think I've much in the way of brains, but I've been working on the problem. Daniel's been keeping me company this afternoon. He's as anxious as we are to see Ursula. He's reached the stage of being so angry with her that he'd like to do her an injury. We can work on that, can't we? He says his mum's got the Quicke woman's phone number, so what I suggest is this...'

FOURTEEN

Thursday evening

As they entered the kitchen, they heard Diana complain, 'I really don't see why we have to eat in the kitchen. What's the matter with the dining room, may I ask?'

Diana and Mrs Belton were standing side by side, with identical expressions of distaste upon what could be seen of their faces through their cuts and bruises.

Rose was bending down to take hot plates out of the oven, and what could be seen of *her* face was pink with indignation. 'I can't be expected to traipse food all the way across the hall into the dining room.'

Ellie rushed into the fray. 'It's nice to eat in here in the winter, when the food comes hot to

251

the table. Mrs Belton, would you care to sit here, and Diana beside you?'

Mrs Belton groaned artistically as she seated herself. 'I do hope the food isn't too rich. I'm a martyr to my stomach.'

Diana snapped out, 'I could eat a horse.'

Thomas served Mrs Belton as Rose drained vegetables. 'Can you manage with one hand, Mrs Belton?'

Diana stared at Rose. 'Have you laid a place for yourself, Rose? You aren't expecting to eat with us, are you?'

Rose quivered with indignation, then drew herself up to her full five foot. 'If you'll excuse me, Ellie, I'll take my supper next door where I can watch my television programme in peace.'

Ellie gasped, 'Rose, no! Diana, how dare you! Apologize at once.'

Rose tossed her head. 'It would curdle my digestion to eat at the same table as her.' She slammed her plate on to a tray and left the room.

Thomas had his stone face on. He served Ellie and himself without speaking.

Silence ensued. Then Rose turned her television on next door, and everyone jumped. Rose liked to hear everything properly. Rose liked action films with lots of gunfire and explosions. Loud.

Ellie said, 'I trust no one's going to ask Rose to turn the sound down, after that display of bad manners. Mrs Belton, a glass of apple juice?'

'Nothing stronger?' asked Diana.

252

'It is most unwise,' said Mrs Belton, 'to drink anything strong when you're on painkillers.'

'I can take it,' said Diana, being flippant.

'Well, you didn't have to spend the night in hospital, as I did.'

'I expect that, as I'm younger than you, I shall recover more quickly.'

Mrs Belton bridled. 'I understand you were only attacked by one man, whereas I had two assaulting me.'

'Mine was something of a gorilla—'

'One of mine moved like an eel—'

'Ladies,' said Thomas, 'could you manage a trifle more food?'

Both declined.

Ellie was puzzled. She'd thought both women had been attacked by the same man, but there seemed to be a discrepancy here. 'Diana, Stewart said your man was as tall as him and well built, probably in his late twenties. Well dressed.'

Diana nodded. 'And strong.'

'Mine were strong, too,' said Mrs Belton, not willing to be outdone. 'The one who clasped me from behind, I shudder just to think about it. His breath stank. I don't know when he visited the dentist last. I can still feel his greasy leather jacket across my throat. I shall have nightmares, I know I will.'

'Leather jacket?' said Diana. 'Mine was wearing ... oh, I don't know. A good quality suit, I think. Definitely not leather. But his mask...' She pushed her plate away. 'Ugh. A wolf's head

253

with a horrible sort of mane.'

'A skeleton,' insisted Mrs Belton, 'and a Dracula's head. As if I could forget!'

Ellie collected dirty plates and put them into the dishwasher, while Thomas dished up apple crumble and got some cream out of the fridge. As Ellie returned to her seat, she took a good look at the two women, sitting side by side. Mrs Belton's face bore the most damage on her right side. Diana's on her left.

Ellie asked Diana, 'Was your man left-handed?'

'Of course not.'

'Mine was,' said Mrs Belton. 'I don't know about the man who held me from behind, but the man who hit me was definitely left-handed. Odd how much one remembers, isn't it? Oh, dear—' with a hand to the side of her face – 'I have a horrid feeling that he's jolted one of my crowns loose.'

Diana arched her eyebrows. 'I'm happy to say that my teeth are all my own.'

'Give it time,' said Mrs Belton, grimly.

Ellie avoided Thomas's eye, lest she laugh out loud. What a duel! Who'd have thought Diana could be bested by words. She remembered something she'd meant to do earlier. 'Diana, you'd better use the landline here to phone Denis; warn him that he might get a visit at your flat.'

'I don't need advice from you,' said Diana, causing everyone else in the room to grit their teeth.

254

Mrs Belton waved away the offer of a pudding. 'I really must speak to my daughter. I expected her to be here long before now. You have children, Ms Quicke?'

'A son. Too young to help.'

'I'm more fortunate than you, there. My daughter is always ready to help.'

Before Diana could have a fit, Ellie ushered Mrs Belton out of the kitchen. 'I'll show you where there's a phone you can use in private. Press the Redial button and you'll get through to her.'

Ellie left Mrs Belton and returned to the kitchen, where Thomas was clearing the table. There was no sign of Diana.

Thomas said, 'Diana wants some coffee taken up to her room. I agreed, to keep the peace. I checked on Rose, and she's OK. What did you make of the two women's stories?'

'I don't understand. I thought there was just one attacker, and that he was Anthony Prior, but there seem to be three. Do you agree?'

'Diana's attacker is different from the other two. Mrs Belton's assailants were probably younger, from the way she says they moved. One moved like an eel, remember? Of her two, one was left-handed and the other had bad breath and wore a leather jacket. But, they all wore masks.'

'Masks are the trademark of the youngsters who've been creating mayhem locally – supposedly a teenage gang. Now where did I get that idea from? Not sure it's even right – but

Anthony Prior isn't a yob, is he? I'm bewilder-ed. I thought the attacks were all tied up with someone looking for Mia, and now I don't know what's going on.'

'I think you're right, and they are.'

'I wish I knew what to do next; apart from getting rid of Diana, that is.'

'My love.' He kissed the tip of her nose. 'Your instincts are infallible. How do you propose to do it?'

She couldn't help grinning. 'I'm rather hop-ing that Anthony – or whoever it is in the wolf mask – is about to pay Denis a visit. With any luck, our most unfavourite estate agent will end up in hospital, and Diana can get her flat back.'

'What a reprehensible thought,' said Thomas. 'Thoroughly endorsed, on my part. Now, will you take coffee up to Diana, or shall I?'

Mrs Belton was on the phone to Ursula for some time, but Ellie refused to fret about her phone bill. This was an emergency, and in an emergency you broke all the usual rules about not spending time on phone calls to mobiles – especially when the mobile was still in her name.

Midge the cat came down from the top of one of the bookcases, but was restless, declined to sit on Ellie's lap. He disliked Diana, could smell that she was in the house, and refused to settle. Ellie and Thomas turned on the tele-vision, but couldn't concentrate, either.

Eventually Mrs Belton came in, looking worn

out. No wonder, thought Ellie; the woman spent last night in hospital. She needs painkillers and an early night.

'Thank you for the use of your phone. My daughter and I had a good chat. She wants me to go and stay with a friend for a while. She thinks it will do me good to get away and my friend's delighted to have me. I'll phone the office tomorrow and tell them what's happened.'

'An excellent idea,' said Ellie.

'As for the mess at the flat—' Mrs Belton shrugged – 'my insurance policy is New for Old, and I'm looking forward to replacing everything with new furniture. I could do with some new clothes, too, and I can get them in the sales. As for my laptop, I can now get a brand new one. As Ursula says, it's an ill wind.'

'Indeed it is,' said Ellie, thinking that Ursula knew exactly how to present the situation to her mother. Good for Ursula.

'There are one or two things I shall miss. My Bristol glass, for instance. And Ursula's art. But she says there are lots of antique shops where I'm going, and I can have all the fun of hunting for something nice there.'

'Excellent idea,' Thomas agreed.

'The only thing is,' said Mrs Belton, 'Ursula would like to talk to you, Mrs Quicke. She says she has something to tell you. She wants us to meet up at Waterloo Station tomorrow morning for a coffee. I must say I can't see the point of it, but she insists on coming up to meet me.'

'That's a good idea,' said Ellie. 'She's making sure you are properly looked after all the way. I'll take you to Waterloo by minicab, and we can all have a coffee together before you go wherever it is you're going. It's best if you don't tell me where that is, right?'

'That's what Ursula said too. I'll leave you the keys to the flat so that you can let the insurance people in, if you will. I'll ring Ursula every night from my friend's house, so you can always get a message to me if anything comes up, but you don't need to take me to the station. I'll take the bus and the tube.'

'We won't hear of it. Much too tiring for you. Besides, I'd like a word with Ursula myself.'

The phone rang at Thomas's side. He listened to the excited voice at the other end, laughed, and passed the receiver over to Ellie. As she identified her caller, Thomas urged Mrs Belton out of the room, saying he'd get a hot drink for her to go to bed on.

It was Armand. 'Hey, there! We've just had a visit from some dude who thinks he's James Bond and guess what, his nose bleeds just like everyone else's.'

'Calm down, Armand. Was it Anthony Prior?'

'Dunno his name. Tall, well-set-up guy in a good suit. Good-looking in a macho sort of way, but if he were a boy in my class at school, I'd suspect him of bullying. Used to getting his own way. Very pressing to know your whereabouts. I'd got my friend the rugby player here for supper and he'd brought a six pack and well, you know how it is, I don't usually, but when the cat's away—'

'Kate and the children are safe?'

'She rang me this evening. She's fine. The babe's teething and she's worried about me, but she needn't have been, eh?'

'Your visitor knew we were friends?'

'He wanted your address and I shook my head, all sorrowful, and said yes, we used to be really good friends, but you'd gone all up-market when you moved away and didn't want to know us now. He saw the kids' toys and said maybe my wife knew where you were, and I said we'd had a bit of a disagreement and she'd gone back to her mother's in Liverpool for a bit. I said I didn't really care if she came back or not.' He belched. 'Do you think I'll get detention for telling lies?'

Ellie tried to sound censorious. 'Armand, I never asked you to lie for me.'

'It was fun, though. It nearly worked too. Only my stupid mate had to give the game away by laughing. That's when my laddo tried to barge past me into the house, to see for himself who might be lurking within, so I popped one over his guard and caught him on the nose. Splat! Amazing how much blood can spray out of one nose. Some got on the wallpaper. Kate'll have my hide for that. Anyway, he limped off. Well, I might have planted a kick on his backside as he withdrew. He's driving a Jag, by the way. Want the number? I wrote it down on the wallpaper just inside the hall. Oops, Kate'll have me for that too.' He reeled off a number and Ellie wrote it down.

'Armand, you're a treasure beyond compare!'

'X-factor, that's me. Ta-ra, now. Got one more beer to drink before we doss down for the night.'

Thomas returned in time to find Ellie still laughing. She told him what had happened, and he smiled too. 'Better take a black cab tomorrow, rather than use your usual minicabs. Harder to trace.'

On that solemn note, they made sure the house was locked up tight, and went up to bed.

'Ant? You sound funny. What's the matter with you?'

'Oh, one thing after another. The Quicke neighbours were a washout. I had to wait till they came home from school. They're teachers. One was just a little squirt, but the other was the size of a barn. Drinking beer and eating sausages. The little one said they'd lost contact with Mrs Quicke when she moved away and hadn't bothered to leave them her address, but I didn't believe him. I could have taken him, but not the two of them together. I'll try that one last address tomorrow.'

'Why not tonight?'

'I'm ... feeling a little tired.'

Friday morning
Waterloo Station. Hustle and bustle and anxiety. Which platform? Where's the Underground?

Where did she say we'd meet up? Under the clock?

'Here I am,' said Ursula, materializing at their elbows. Something had happened to Ursula. She was wearing a knitted black beret over her hair, a black jacket and jeans. There were dark lines at forty- five degrees under her eyes; she looked as if she hadn't slept much, and yet she was more stylish than ever. She'd lost all pretensions to being pretty, but she was now a very striking young woman. Perhaps 'handsome' was the right word.

She kissed her mother's cheek, took Mrs Belton's suitcase from Ellie, and whisked them to a quietish coffee bar above the concourse.

'Time for elevenses,' she said. 'I'm paying.'

'No, you're not,' said Ellie, taking out her purse, 'and I'm buying your mother's train ticket as well.'

'You've done more than enough,' said Ursula, but Mrs Belton accepted the notes thrust upon her, with a nod of thanks.

'The thing is,' said Ursula, over croissants and cappuccinos, 'that you can get into situations without realizing exactly what's really going on, and then it's too late to back out.' She put a hand on her mother's arm. 'It's not your fault. It's mine. What happened to Mia is partly down to me.'

Mrs Belton wasn't having this. 'Oh, come now, Ursula—'

'Yes, it is. You don't know the half of it. Let me try to explain what happened. It started in the school holidays. I was going out with Dan and he knew the Priors because the younger brother – Timothy, the one they call Dumbo because of his big ears – was friends with him from the early days. Dan and I didn't have much money, but the Priors invited us into their set and naturally we were flattered. We paid our way, sort of. Dan coached them for free on the tennis courts, and I'm a good listener.

'Also, I hit it off with Mia, who was on the fringe of their circle, so to speak. Mr Prior had adopted her when he married Mia's mother, but she didn't fit in. She didn't even look like the rest of the family, being so dark while they're all so fair. And having been brought up without much money, she wasn't used to their wild ways.'

'What wild ways?' said Mrs Belton. 'You never mentioned—'

'I knew you wouldn't approve. They would get paralytic and spew up, have casual sex with the girls who hung around with them. There were plenty of young girls who would do anything to be noticed by the Priors. They drove fast cars rather dangerously, they threw litter around, and bad-mouthed anyone who remonstrated.'

She swallowed, braced herself. 'At Christmas time it became a point of honour for each of us to steal something from the shops to give as presents. We pooled the lot, gave a prize to whoever stole the most valuable item. I won twice.'

Mrs Belton looked shattered. 'How could you!'

'And they used drugs,' said Ellie, making it a statement.

Ursula gave her a straight look. 'Yes, some of them did. I didn't, nor did Dan or Mia. Lloyd didn't either.'

'How did they get the drugs?'

'Through one of the boys, nicknamed Bullseye.' Ursula shivered. 'I never liked him. He got the nickname because he said he always scored when he wanted a girl. I wondered for ages how he managed it, because I thought he was repulsive.'

'He used the date rape drug, Rohypnol?'

'I don't know,' said Ursula, a little wildly. 'Tim warned Mia and me never to touch a drink that he'd handled but, as to proof, I don't know. None of us four were into sex. I didn't because my periods have always been all over the place, I couldn't settle on the Pill, and I daren't risk it. Mia didn't because she hadn't found anyone who turned her on that way yet. Lloyd didn't, from principle. Dan was unsure of himself. If I'd encouraged him ... but I didn't. So he didn't.

'We thought ourselves a cut above the others because we didn't indulge in casual sex and drink ourselves silly every weekend. Stupid, stupid! It never occurred to me that I might be targeted as a pair of legs, because I was with Dan, and Dan was Timothy's friend. Naturally, I thought the gang would respect that, and that they'd respect Mia because she was a Prior. I didn't see the price tag until too late.'

Mrs Belton allowed a frown to crease her forehead. 'My mother always said nice girls sing for their supper. Wasn't that enough?'

'Not in their circle, but I didn't realize it for ages. At first the price tag wasn't too high. They wanted Dan to wangle them some tickets for the tennis club dance for free. He was doing some coaching for the club, so it was easy for him to pinch some. It was ridiculous, because of course they could have afforded to pay, but it amused them to get something for nothing. I wasn't too happy when I heard about it, but Dan said the Priors had promised him a job at the new Health Centre when it opened, so it was all in the family, like. He was dead keen on getting that job, and doing them a favour here or there seemed, well, not a problem.

'Anthony was the leader of the group. Last year he started to pay me more attention, flattering me, asking me to help outsiders feel at ease at their parties. The first time it was some decrepit old man whose wife had recently died. He had goggly eyes and all the while I was dancing with him, I was making fun of him behind his back. That was not very nice of me, particularly since he was pathetically grateful for my company. I didn't realize what I was doing, then.

'The next time they had a party at their house, Anthony asked me to pretty up to a stupid-looking rich boy straight from school: all sweaty hands, obviously way out of his depth. I was sorry for the poor creature, and spent most of the evening with him. He was nice.' Tears stood out on her cheeks. 'Only, later on I heard they'd got him into a poker game after I left, and taken thousands off him. They laughed, said he could afford it and that I'd done a good job, but I began to feel ... dirty. Used. I told Dan I wasn't going to play that game any more. I said I wasn't one of their groupies, jumping through hoops for money. Dan was worried, said we had to be careful not to get on the wrong side of the Priors. That was when I decided to accept my father's invitation to go to New York in the new year.

'Dan said I'd have to put in an appearance at the Grand Opening, even if it was only for a few hours before I flew out, and of course I agreed. He gave me a wonderful designer dress for Christmas. It was a bit short, but I wore it to please him. Only, when we got there, Anthony said he wanted me to "look after" one of the guests, some rich Middle Eastern princeling. He said that was my job for the night. He complimented me on the dress, which he said he'd told Dan to put on his account at the shop. I felt like tearing it off there and then, but of course I didn't. I told Dan how I felt, and he said it didn't matter if I cosied up to this chap because I was due to fly out in the early hours of the next morning.

'So I did as Anthony asked and flirted with the man, only to discover he thought I was his for the night. Not just the evening. I was

265

furious. I ran off to find Anthony and told him I didn't play those sort of games, and anyway, didn't he know I was going to America that night? He was livid, because he hadn't known. He said I owed him. Even the dress I had on...!

'I fled to the ladies and found Mia there, in tears. She said Anthony had fixed her up for the night with one of the councillors, and he'd had his paws all over her, and she couldn't bear it. Anthony had said she should pull her weight for once, that the Priors needed some contract or other from the council, and her "friend" was going to fix it for them if Mia were *nice* to him.

'I couldn't think what to do. I mean, I was getting out of there, resolving never to have anything to do with the Priors ever again, but Mia ... she suggested coming to see me off at Heathrow just to get away from the party, and I agreed. We stayed in the ladies till it was time for me to go. Only, when we came out, Anthony was waiting for us. And Dan. To do him justice, Dan put his arm around me, told Anthony that I was off limits and that he was taking me out to Heathrow that minute. Anthony didn't like it. He glowered at me. Said he'd catch up with me on my return.

'He got Mia to stay by saying the councillor had already gone home, very annoyed that she'd disappointed him. He said some of the gang were moving upstairs for a private party, and he'd see she got home safely afterwards. She looked at me, hoping I'd ask her to come away with us, but Dan whispered in my ear that it was our last evening together, and I refused to take the hint. If only I'd known!'

'How dare Anthony!' Mrs Belton was indignant.

'Easily,' said Ursula. 'He'd paid for me, you see. In advance. With patronage, with parties and lifts in fast cars, and with a stunning dress. Only, I hadn't read the price tag.'

Ellie nodded. 'Corruption. Little by little. But you got away.'

'Oh yes, I got away and did a lot of thinking. I realized how nearly I'd become one of the good-time party girls that I despised. I worried that Dan was allowing it to happen. He came to the airport to meet me on my return, and that's when he told me about Lloyd's accidental death. I couldn't believe my ears. The way Dan told it to me – he hadn't been there when it happened, of course – but he seemed uneasy about it himself, saying he was sure there was nothing wrong really. He, well, he protested too much. At one point he blurted out that Timothy had been involved in some way, but then retracted what he'd said. You remember Dan and Timothy had been friends for ever?

'I asked Dan what Mia had said about it, because she and Lloyd had been good friends; not lovers, but friends. I told him I'd been trying to reach Mia for days but she wouldn't answer her phone, and that's when Dan said that Mia had been disowned by her family because she'd been sleeping around. There was no way I could go along with that. Mia wasn't like that, she wasn't! I was so upset, I let fly at him, and he ... he said I was being stupid and ungrateful, and couldn't see which side my bread was buttered.'

She swiped her hands across her cheeks to get rid of her tears. 'We quarrelled, and I saw what I'd known for ever, but never acknowledged before: that Dan was not as strong as me, and that I couldn't rely on him when the chips were down. That was such a terrible moment, I couldn't think what to do or say. My future had been all laid out for me for years and if I broke with Dan I knew I'd be so lonely, so alone. Dan seemed to think I'd given in, that I'd "seen sense and would behave myself" in future. In other words, go along with Anthony's little plans. I didn't disabuse him.

'The next day I caught up with Anthony at the club, surrounded by some of his pals. I challenged him about Mia. He repeated the slander. I told him he was a liar, and that he could count me out in future. He got his mates to hold me while he assaulted me, pulled up my skirts and ... no, mother, he didn't rape me. Worse, in a way. He tickled me till I was helpless, and then, when at least one of his pals was getting red in the face, he said, "Hold back, men, I've got other plans for her". And he let me go.

'I couldn't confide in you, Mother, because you were really poorly, and I didn't want to worry you when there was nothing you could do about the situation. I rang Mia's home, and got nowhere. I went to the police, ditto. I knew

I couldn't go through with the engagement to Dan, but I couldn't face seeing him again. I've been so fond of him for so long, I thought I might break down and go back to him. That's when I decided to spend a day in a church where I knew no one would look for me. I needed to get everything straight in my mind, and then go back to uni early. And that, Mrs Quicke, is how I came to meet you and ask for your help. I do apologize for dragging you into this mess, but if I hadn't, Mother would have been left in a terrible state, so I'm thankful that I did.'

'Yes,' said Ellie, thinking through what the girl had said. 'I'm glad too. So you think Anthony wants you back, in order to sleep with his client? And Mia? Do you have a theory about what happened to her, and why Lloyd died?'

'I think ... I don't know. I didn't dare imagine, it's so horrible. But if Mia was being raped at the party upstairs, then Lloyd would have tried to stop it. Perhaps he was dealt with because of what he'd seen? Perhaps Mia knows something? I suspect that if I wander back into Anthony's orbit now, I'll end up like Mia.'

Mrs Belton opened her mouth to express her horror at what she'd heard, but Ursula forestalled her.

'I know, Mother. Your little girl has been extremely stupid, and foolish, and I'm responsible for getting the flat wrecked, and I'm very, very sorry.'

'Talking of the attack on your mother,' said Ellie, 'Have you ever known Anthony wear a

Halloween-type mask?'

'Why? Yes, of course. Tim bought a whole lot of masks for their last Halloween party and they went out with the invitations: Draculas, skeletons and animal heads, you name it. As it happened, we didn't go to the party. Lloyd hates – hated – Halloween, so he got the four of us tickets to see *The Lion King*. It was great.'

'So there were plenty of masks going spare after Halloween?'

'Sure.'

'Do you know of any group of youngsters who might have got hold of the masks, and hide behind them to commit acts of antisocial behaviour?'

Ursula's eyes went blank. She hesitated. Looked down and away. 'No, I don't.' She looked at her watch. 'Mother, we ought to be going. Ten minutes to catch the train. Mrs Quicke, you've been so kind. May I ring you now and again to catch up on the news? And you won't look to see which train we catch, will you?'

She'd lied, thought Ellie. Ursula did know something about the masked gang, but didn't want to say. Why not? We–ell, it could just be that Daniel was involved, and she would still want to protect him, even now. Or, was there another explanation?

FIFTEEN

Friday late morning

Ellie rang Thomas from the railway station. 'They've just gone, and I'm on my way back. I'm going to call in at the police station on the way. Everything all right at your end?'

'That Grace woman rang; wants you to go to the cinema with her this afternoon. I made your apologies. Pat's gone down with a sore throat again, so I told her to take the day off. Nothing much in the post, but young Daniel Collins has been on the phone twice. Says he's recovered Mrs Belton's laptop and wants to know where he can find her to give it back. Alternatively, should he come over and give it to you. I know he's supposed to be on the side of the angels—'

'Possibly not as angelic as we'd thought.'

'Ah. Reason?'

'I'm not sure. Something to do with those masks. Oh, it's probably nothing.'

'Well, we'd been so careful so far that I decided against giving him your address. I said you were up in town and returning by way of the police station and he got quite agitated. Said he must see you before you do anything silly.'

'He thinks it would be silly to go to the police?'

'That's what he said. I suggest that if you do meet him, it's in a public place. A coffee shop, perhaps?'

'Before or after I visit the police station? We have a fair amount of new information to give them—'

'But no proof. Have we?'

Ellie sighed. 'I love you, Thomas. Give me Dan's phone number and I'll meet him in Ealing Broadway to hear what he has to say. It's too cold for a salad. I'll stop there to have something to eat before I come on home.'

Ellie watched Daniel enter the upstairs lounge of the café and look around for her. She wondered if he would have changed as much as Ursula had since they first met, and thought that yes, he looked grimmer, and darker around the chin. He was carrying a worn laptop.

She pushed her empty plate aside, and beckoned him over. He put the laptop on the table before her, and seated himself. Nervous? Mm. Yes. There was a nick on his cheek where he'd cut himself shaving. His clothes were a black Puffa jacket over jeans. No leather jacket; not that she believed he'd been one of the lads who'd attacked Mrs Belton.

'Thanks for meeting me,' he said. 'I've been so worried. Nobody's heard anything from Ursula or Mrs Belton. Do you know where they are?'

'Not precisely, no. I understand they've gone off on a short holiday together somewhere. Very distressed by what's been happening.'

He reddened. 'It's been a total shambles. Everyone's buzzing around like anything. We really need her back.'

Ellie nodded, put sugar in her coffee and stirred. 'Are you eating? Having a coffee?'

He shook his head, impatient. Pulled his chair closer to the table. 'The thing is, I really need to speak to her. You can arrange it, can't you?' He was putting on the little boy lost act. Quite well done.

Ellie shook her head. 'I really don't know where she's gone. She says she needs some "space", is that the right word?'

'But you know how to contact her? I don't know what I'll do if I can't get hold of her soon.' Did his eyes fill with tears? Was this helplessness the thing that Ursula had feared might work on her, might undo all her resolutions to avoid him in future?

Ellie sipped coffee and put the cup down. 'Is that Mrs Belton's laptop? Where on earth did you find it?'

'Offered a reward for it, of course.'

'How did you know where to offer a reward?'

'Oh, at the pub.' A lie. 'I knew she had all her work on it. I thought if only I could get it back for her, she'd put a word in for me with Ursula.'

'No, no. Mrs Belton has all her work on a memory stick. It's a pity you got it back, because she was looking forward to getting a more up to date model.'

He leaned forward. 'Well, I'm sure I could arrange that for her. How much do you think we should offer her?'

Ellie sighed. 'Who would you get the money from, Dan?'

'Why, from Ursula's friends.'

'The ones who abused, raped and beat up Mia? And left her pregnant?'

His face went slack with shock.

Ellie pulled out the photographs of Mia's ruined face and laid them on the table. 'Do you really want to bring Ursula back, to suffer the same fate?'

He ran the back of his hand across his mouth. 'That's not Mia. She's dark, not blonde.'

'That's Mia. She cut off her hair and dyed it, in an attempt to disguise herself. Anthony wants her back. Can you think why?'

He stumbled over the words. 'She's his half-sister.'

'I don't think that stopped him from acting as her pimp. She wasn't a willing whore, was she?'

He pushed back his chair, half stood, looking wildly around. Then sank back into it again. 'Where is she? What have you done with her?'

'I? Nothing.'

'But Anthony said you took her away. He can't know about this. He couldn't have done this, not to Mia!'

Ellie was silent, letting him think it through.

His eyes went from side to side. He frowned;

held his lower lip between his teeth. His hand went to his pocket to bring out a mobile, and then shoved it back again. Was he weighing his loyalty to Anthony against his horror at what had been done to Mia? Which side would he come down on? It was a toss-up, wasn't it?

He lost all colour in his face. His eyes seemed darker, his mouth firmer. 'I've got to get her back.'

'Who? Ursula, or Mia?'

He groaned. 'Ursula. We've got to get her back or we lose everything. My job, everything.'

'Your job is worth reducing the girl you love to a battered piece of meat?'

'No, of course not. It isn't like that. She'll be well paid. You don't understand.'

'I rather think I do. And so does Ursula.'

'Look, I only need to talk to her for a few minutes and—'

'And what would you say to her? "Come into my parlour, said the spider to the fly?"'

'What?' He didn't know the saying. 'No, I ... Look, this is too important for us to play games. Let's put this on a business footing. You get a cut too. Right?'

'Daniel, go home and tell your mother what's been going on.'

'A thousand pounds.'

Ellie gathered her belongings together. 'Is that all that Ursula's worth to you? My answer is still no. Besides, you haven't got a thousand pounds, Daniel.'

'I can get it. Easily.'

'I daresay. Now, if you'll just let me get out, I'm on my way to the police station to hand in these photographs of Mia.'

He picked them up and ripped them into small pieces.

She shrugged. There were plenty more at home. She'd just have to stop off there on the way to the police station to collect them, that's all. She walked away from him, hesitated, and went back for the laptop.

He said, 'If you leave that here, she can get a new one.'

That was how it worked. One small step into a grey area, telling yourself it didn't matter if you cheated an insurance company, because nobody was hurt by it. And the next day it would seem natural to go one step further and put in a false application, and so on. Step by step down the primrose path. And if she left the laptop, she'd be in Dan's power.

Ellie picked up the laptop, and left. Once down at street level, she summoned a passing black cab. She thought he might try to follow her, but the lights changed at exactly the right moment to let her cab pass through before turning red.

'Dumbo, where are you?'

'Organizing stuff. I should be getting the Quicke woman's address any minute now. She met Daniel at a café, spent some time with him and left in a taxi. I've got one of the lads

following her on his bike, and I'm following behind him in the car. We're in touch by mobile in case I lose them at the traffic lights.'

'Don't be stupid. I'm on my way to her place now. She lives in a block of flats over on the Argyle Road. I'm hoping to pick up Mia from there and take her to a safe place.'

'What sort of safe place?'

'What do you think? I have someone prepared to look after her, so long as she behaves herself.'

'That doesn't sound very nice. You mean—'

'She'll be a working girl, yes. But what else is there for her? The parents don't want her back, and she's no use to us any more, is she? But enough of that. I've been thinking. The only way to get Ursula back is to go and fetch her. Now I can't do it – too much on at work. But tomorrow I want you to go down to Portsmouth, you and Dan. And Bullseye.'

'What? Not Bullseye!'

'How else are we to make sure she behaves herself? Dan knows where she lives down in Portsmouth. He'll get her to meet him some-where. Gives her a drink, or gets her into the car, and Bullseye does the rest. She'll be out for the count till you can get her safely back home, and after that it'll be plain sailing. Any ques-tions as to why you're toting around a sleepy girl with you, you say she's drunk. Right?'

'I don't like it.'

'I daresay. But she's left us no choice, has she? Dan will play, won't he? We can always let

277

him have first go after the client's finished with her. You too, if you like. But nobody touches her till she's been with the prince, right? The Man's going spare, calling in favours from everyone, but it's not working. Ursula's our last hope.'

Friday afternoon

Ellie got the taxi to drop her round the corner from her house – just in case she'd been followed. She didn't think she had been, but there was no point in risking it.

A cyclist whizzed past her and turned into a neighbour's drive. She wondered who might be visiting there; as far as she knew, the house was occupied by an elderly couple who rarely went out.

Well, it was no business of hers. She hoisted up Mrs Belton's laptop and made her way up her own driveway. Two cars were there: Thomas's and Diana's. Oh dear, what was she to do about Diana? There were lights on in Thomas's office, and in Rose's old bedroom – which was now Diana's – upstairs. Outside Roy's office were three more cars: his and his right-hand man's, and their office manager's. The firm was doing so well now that soon they'd need to spread upstairs into the flat above, which was let out at present.

A car she knew well crept into the drive behind her, and Kate got out. She hadn't brought her children. She narrowed her eyes and nodded to Ellie, indicating that she had information to impart. Ellie decided not to go through the front door because it would alert Diana to the fact that she'd returned, and she had no answers for her at the moment.

Instead, she led Kate through the side gate and in through the kitchen door. It was mid-afternoon. Rose was dozing in her room, and Ellie could talk to Kate undisturbed.

'Trouble?' Ellie disposed of laptop and outer clothing. 'What have you done with the children?'

'Dumped on friends for an hour. I can't stay long, but I've some information you might like. Mr Prior's going down the tubes. Overextended in all directions; desperately trying to rid himself of some of his properties. Without success. I talked to three people I know in the City, and they all said not to touch his projects with the proverbial. Roy should keep well out of his way.'

'You've told Felicity?'

Kate nodded.

Ellie made the connection. 'You stayed with Felicity last night?'

'I did. Roy was gracious but really doesn't like wailing babies, and the little one is teething. I wanted to check with you if it's safe to go back home tonight. Armand's been boasting about having repelled boarders, but somehow I'm not convinced. Won't the Priors try again?'

'They might. Armand got a bodyguard to stay with him last night. Could he make a similar arrangement tonight?'

'He might. But for how long? For the weekend? Next week?'

'The police must act! But, until Mia is well enough to make a statement, I'm not sure we've got enough to make them take action.' She gave Kate a rapid run-down of what had been happening, trusting to her friend's incisive judgment to sort out what was and what was not feasible.

Kate held up one finger. 'One: you can't use Ursula's story because it's hearsay and therefore useless. Two: the photographs of what has been done to Mia are also useless until she can testify as to how she got her injuries. The doctor can testify to the fact that she was injured, but he can't prove who did it.'

Kate held up a third finger. 'Diana can testify to an attack by a masked intruder and Stewart can testify to his presence, but neither of them are able to make a positive identification.' A fourth finger went up. 'Mrs Belton has told the police about masked intruders, but can't make any identification either.'

A thumb. 'You could have Armand's testimony but, since he admits damaging the intruder, and hasn't yet made an identification, I'm not sure...' She pondered. 'Ah, what you have got is the registration number of the car in which Armand's attacker disappeared. He could testify to that, and the police can trace the driver. Otherwise, all you've got is a lot of circumstantial evidence concerning masked attackers. Didn't you say that DI Willis was interested in them?'

Ellie took in a deep breath. 'Yes, Kate. You're right. That's the angle to take. Can you drop me off at the police station in a minute? I'll collect some more photos of Mia, and we'll be off.'

Kate looked at her watch. 'I left the kiddies with Felicity and her friend Caroline, whose husband works at the Town Hall. You remember her? She had some interesting gossip about Mr Prior, if you've time to listen. Called him Posy Prior. I suspect the nickname is ironic, but I didn't have time to enquire.'

Ellie was rummaging around in the freezer. 'Sure, if I've got time after I've been to the police. I wonder if Diana's going to stay for supper. I wanted to get rid of her today, but haven't done anything about it yet. Ah, these venison steaks will do nicely. Now for DI Willis.'

It was easier said than done to talk to DI Willis. Ellie sat in the foyer of the station and waited, watching the clock tick forward, and worrying. The DI was in a meeting. The DI had gone out. Was the DI avoiding Ellie? Possibly, even though Ellie had told the desk sergeant that she had some information about the masked men.

Eventually a woman detective constable came out of the inner sanctum and beckoned to Ellie. The girl looked familiar. Ah, this was the DC who'd interviewed Mrs Belton at her flat the previous day. Was it only yesterday? What was the girl's name? Mil-something. Milstone, Milford, Milbrook? Milburn.

281

'You have some new information?' The usual interview room, rather chilly. An overhead light buzzed. Flickered.

'Tea?' Ellie erring on the side of hopefulness.

The DC was unresponsive. She had a flat face with a broad nose, but her eyes were bright. Not exactly podgy but no sylph. Her legs and thighs were substantial.

'You have some information for us, Mrs Quicke?'

'I have a tale to tell that bears on the problem of the masked gang. I suggest you record it, rather than take notes, because so much has been happening.'

The DC's eyebrows shot up.

'I'm not wasting your time,' said Ellie, holding on to her temper. 'You've been looking at isolated instances of what appears to be juvenile, antisocial behaviour. I've been drawn into something larger and nastier, which includes the activities of masked men. Will you hear me out?'

Once the tape was running, Ellie began her story. She kept it as neat and tidy as she could, but it was still over an hour before she finished.

'So, you see, the masks keep cropping up everywhere. Not just on the juveniles, who presumably were the ones who trashed Mrs Belton's place and stole her laptop ... which I've brought with me, by the way. You may be able to get fingerprints from it. A mask also crops up on a much older man, who is going around frightening people, using his fists, trying to find

Mia through me. My next-door neighbour that was says he'd know the man anywhere, and can supply the registration number of the car he was using when he tried to threaten him. That's it.' She laid a card on the table with the number of the car Armand had given her.

'And this–' Ellie laid the photos of Mia's injuries on the table – 'this is the evidence of what's been done to the missing girl.'

The DC looked at the photographs again, studying each one with care. 'Who does she say did this to her?'

'She's not well enough to make a statement yet. I don't know exactly who did this to her, but it's her stepbrother who's trying to find her. I showed his photograph to the girls in the flat and they agree that it was he who was looking for her.'

'Produce the girl. Or, tell me where I can interview her.'

'I can't. Not yet.'

The policewoman had an unreadable face. She excused herself and left the room, only to return with a folder, which she placed on the table. DC Milburn settled herself. 'Mr Prior is a long-standing and generous benefactor for many charities, including the police ones.'

'We're not talking about Mr Prior. We're talking about his son, Anthony.'

The girl produced a faint smile, which looked painful. 'Do you know the family at all?'

'No.'

'Can you give me one reason why a much-respected man like Mr Prior would countenance boy gangs committing antisocial behaviour?'

Ellie had had only one idea in that direction, and didn't like it much. Ursula had lied when asked about boy gangs. Ursula hadn't been a member – not her style – but she had known, or guessed, something about them. Ellie, following that line of thought, had remembered Dan Collins's mother and her household of students. Hard-up students. Young men who might have had access to the joke masks through Dan, who was part of the Prior circle. Or perhaps might just have got the idea of using masks from that last Halloween party?

Might these same hard-up students have been pointed in the direction of Mrs Belton and told to rough her up, in order to entice Ursula back home? It was only too easy to set youngsters off on a path to destruction; more difficult to stop them.

Fact: a lad in a mask had taken Mrs Belton's laptop. Fact: Dan had returned it. He must have had at least an inkling of where to look for the laptop, in order to be able to retrieve it so quickly. Ellie understood why Ursula had been reluctant to point the finger in that direction, but she herself had no such compunction in doing so.

'What I think is that the community is composed of individuals who move in different circles but can, and do, interact, sometimes in surprising ways. I mean, a councillor's son might know all sorts of young people whom his father has never met or even heard of. Students, for instance. Someone in student-type accommodation might move in two quite different circles, knowing some much younger lads who will do anything for a laugh, while also being friends with men he might have met at private school.

'No, I don't think the councillor is behind the boy gangs, but I think that the councillor's son knows some of the people behind these attacks. Else how would I have come by the stolen laptop?'

'We don't even know that this is Mrs Belton's laptop.'

'Boot it up, and see. Give it to the technical bods. They'll tell you whose it is.'

'Daniel Collins must have told you how he got it.'

'He said he offered a reward in a pub. I don't believe him. I think he has some connection to the lads with the masks. As for why he gave it to me, he's trying to use it as a weapon in order to tempt Ursula back to town. I hate to think what for.'

'Spell it out.'

'To sleep with a man who might help Mr Prior out of his financial problems.'

The DC was not impressed. 'Pimping? Mr Prior? Really?'

'I'm not sure that he knows exactly what's been going on.'

'I should think not, indeed. And you think this girl Ursula will happily lie down and spread her legs for a client of Mr Prior's?'

Ellie pushed the photos of Mia towards the policewoman. 'No, I don't. She's safely out of their reach at the moment, but I think she'll end up looking like this if they manage to get her back to London.'

The DC looked undecided. 'This is complicated. Most of it is hearsay. You must admit that. You've told me an interesting story, but you haven't brought me anything to substantiate it. I'll have to take your story to the DI, and she's out at the moment. No doubt she'll get in touch with you, if she decides to take the matter further.' She stood to show the interview was at an end.

Ellie also got to her feet, admitting defeat.

All of a sudden, the DC whirled round and slammed the file on to the table. Her face was red. 'I've tried to keep my mouth shut, but really! You've no idea what sort of man you're talking about. I'll tell you what sort of man Mr Prior is. I have a younger sister who is handicapped, but she does voluntary work at a day centre, and he's been so good to her, helping her to get a better wheelchair. He's always popping in there, helping to sort out problems. How dare you go around spreading rumours, and trying to smirch the reputation of a man who's next door to being a saint!'

With an effort she pulled herself back under control, picked up the file and stalked out.

Ellie checked to see whether her jaw was still attached to her head. Had she really heard a testimonial for Mr Prior, painting him as whiter than white?

She left the police station in a daze, wondering whether by some chance she'd misunderstood everything she'd been led to believe. Was Mr Prior really a saint?

Well, probably not a saint. Saints don't crop up every day, and most people were a mix of good and bad, grey instead of black or white.

'Posy Prior'. That was the nickname which Kate had used. Kate had got it from Caroline, whose husband worked at the Council. Ellie dithered. She ought to go home and start supper, check on Rose, and arrange for Diana to leave. She hailed a passing taxi, and directed the driver to Felicity's. It wouldn't take long to check out the Prior reputation, would it?

SIXTEEN

There were only four children at Felicity's, but they seemed to be everywhere: under chairs and tables, sitting on people's knees, playing with bricks and books and biscuits. It was a toss-up whether the bricks or the biscuits made their way into mouths, but it didn't seem to matter much. Some adult would pick up the child and cope.

Ellie accepted a child on to her lap, without being too sure what sex it might be, or whose child it was. The child crooned to her, and she crooned back. Caroline, dark and a little fierce, spooned mashed banana into the nearest child, and dished the dirt on the Priors.

'He's called "Posy" because he always comes up smelling of roses, but someone with a keen nose might detect another odour.'

'Corruption?' Ellie found her little finger being guided into a child's mouth, and felt tiny teeth breaking through the gum as he or she chewed away.

'Not exactly,' said Caroline, accepting a cake from Felicity, who was busy baking. Felicity always baked when she was stressed. Caroline bit into the cake and said, 'Yum. Whatever Mr Prior wants, he always seems to get. He calls it luck, but some people think his run of good fortune is too good to be true. His detractors mutter about bribery, but I don't think it's that. I mean, no one's suddenly acquired a small fortune and retired to the Bahamas. However, people who oppose his plans do suddenly die, or emigrate, or have an unexpected change of heart. My husband says it's voodoo; joking, of course.'

'If it isn't just favourable coincidence, then how do you think it works?'

Caroline wrinkled her nose. 'Having been to a couple of his shindigs, my guess is that he puts long legs and blonde hair to work on the middle-aged men whose wives understand them all too well. I suppose he uses an escort agency to get the girls. My husband thinks they're briefed to get the men into incriminating situations, someone takes photos and ... whifft. The opposition melts away. But that's just gossip. No one's ever put in a formal complaint, but then nobody who's been caught that way is going to complain about it, are they?'

Kate picked up a toddler, and gave it a cuddle. 'That's slander, Caroline. Be careful.'

'Mm. That's what my husband says. He says there was a woman councillor who was opposing Prior on some pet project of his, and he went to the police with some trumped-up charge against her. She had to drop the case and resign from the council to avoid prosecution, not because she was guilty as charged – which no one thinks she was because it just wasn't her scene – but because mud sticks and he was talking about a nasty, smelly type of mud that the tabloids would have loved. He's got the police in his pocket and it's easy to see why. Every year he gives them a nice round sum for their social club on top of what he dispenses to local charities. They love him.'

Ellie was thoughtful. 'So I gathered. He goes in for a lot of high profile publicity?'

Caroline nodded. 'Anything that might get his photo in the papers. He's in the Gazette almost every week. He's a first class, fully paid-up member of the baby-kisser brigade, with a lovely head of white hair. They say politicians get on much better if they have a full head of hair. And he smiles, oh how he smiles! He looks like Santa Claus. Without the beard, of course.'

Kate said, '"A man can smile and smile, and be a villain." That's a quote from somewhere. Shakespeare, I expect.'

'His wife, now.' Caroline became even more animated. 'She's gross! Yuk! Tight blonde curls, diamonds flashing all over, a bosom that sticks right out, and massive hips. A superb complexion, hardly needing the aid of cosmetics. She's got a wonderful dentist, I'll give her that; blindingly white teeth that may or may not be her own. I expect she was a real blonde bombshell when she was young. But now, well, I'm not sure that she's an asset to him any longer. I saw her last at the opening of Mr Prior's latest – you were there, weren't you, Felicity? – and the word "whale" came into my mind.'

Felicity took tins from the oven, used a palette knife to turn out a couple of Victoria sandwiches and put them on a wire tray to cool. 'I thought her formidable. Her eyes were everywhere. It was she who was really in charge that night. She directed the waiters and saw that people were properly looked after.' Felicity could be very sharp at times.

A phone rang and everyone looked around, juggling children. Not Felicity's landline. Not Kate's mobile.

Ellie's. Kate took the infant Ellie had been cuddling, and Ellie managed to find her mobile and answer it.

'Ellie?' It was Thomas. 'Where are you?'

'At Felicity's.'

'Diana says she's going over to rescue Denis and bring him back here to our place. I said had she asked your permission, and she said she didn't need it. Thought you'd like to know.'

'The nerve of her.'

'Quite. Perhaps you can have a word with her?'

He cut off the call. Ellie explained to the others what he'd said, and Kate offered to drive her over. 'I need to pop back home anyway, get some clean clothes.'

Ellie was alarmed. 'You aren't thinking of going back yet, are you?'

All three women looked at Ellie, but it was Felicity who broke the silence. 'Don't get me wrong. I like having Kate here, and Roy can jolly well put up with it for a couple of nights, but how long is this going on for?'

Caroline was anxious. 'Anyone who opposes the Priors has to back down, sooner or later. My husband says it's best to tread carefully around them. Perhaps I have been a little indiscreet this morning, but it won't go any further, will it?'

Kate said, 'We've too many hostages to fortune. I'm not sure what I'd do if he threatened my children.' She frowned, heavy-browed. 'I can't quite see how to stop him. If it *is* him. We don't know that it is.'

Ellie was thoughtful. 'If we can't attack him personally, there may be another way to stop him. I might have an idea about that, but I need to talk to Thomas about it first. Meanwhile, Kate, I won't put you in any more danger by accepting a lift. I'll take a cab.'

Diana had bought and turned a large house into flats some years ago, keeping the best one for herself on the ground floor. As Ellie's cab drew up at the kerb, she spotted not only Diana's car, but also a police car and an ambulance.

'Some sort of carry-on?' commented the cab-driver. 'Want me to hang around for you, missus?'

'No, thanks. This will be fine.'

Ellie walked into the foyer, found the door to Diana's ground floor flat wide open, and far too many people crammed into the small living room.

Working backwards from the doorway were two police officers, one male, one female, who had evidently just arrived. The woman officer had her hands raised trying to calm Diana, in nose to nose confrontation. Diana was screaming with rage. The male officer was endeavouring to use his phone: calling for reinforcements?

Beyond Diana, a scene of destruction: chairs overturned, a television on its side, smashed crockery, an occasional table broken, and two men being held apart with some difficulty by a couple of bulky paramedics. The men who were fighting were also shouting.

'I'll sue you to hell and beyond!'

'You should be locked up!'

One of the fighters Ellie identified as Denis, Diana's slightly sinister partner at their estate agency. Blood poured down his face and spattered his clothing, while a nasty bruise was coming up on his chin. A woman paramedic was trying to clean him up, despite his efforts to get at his opponent who was – surprise, surprise! – Anthony Prior, also dishevelled but showing no obvious signs of injury.

Diana plunged between the police officers to grasp Ellie's arm. 'Mother! Thank goodness you've come. Perhaps you can talk some sense into the plods.'

Uh-oh, thought Ellie. Not a good idea to call the police 'plods'. Even if they were. And yes, a quick look informed Ellie that both members of the thin blue line were better equipped with brawn than brain.

'Now, now,' said the larger of the two paramedics to Anthony. 'If you'll just hold steady for a minute!'

Anthony managed to break the hold the paramedic had on him, and kicked Denis where it hurt most. Denis bent over with a yell, one arm covering his tender spot, the other flailing. The flailing arm caught Anthony on his nose, making it bleed. Denis must have caught Anthony in the same place as Armand had done. Diana screamed, naturally. Ellie wanted to laugh, but didn't quite dare.

Heavily breathing, the two men were dragged apart by the sorely tried paramedics, with the slightly tardy aid of the police.

Denis sank to the floor, writhing. Diana tore into the kitchen and came back with a wet cloth to apply to Denis's face, which was not where he was hurting most. Anthony covered his own face with both hands, moaning.

At least they weren't all shouting now.

'Now,' said the male officer, breathing hard. 'Just what's going on here?'

Neither of the fighters seemed capable of talking, so Ellie volunteered an opinion.

'Judging from previous behaviour, I imagine that Mr Prior – that's him with the bloody nose – came to elicit some information from Denis – that's him on the floor. Mr Prior, finding himself met with a refusal, set out to wreck the place, whereupon Denis objected, as one would, wouldn't one?'

'He's broken my arm!' That was Anthony.

'I don't think so,' said his paramedic. 'But let's have a look, eh?'

'He pushed past me,' gasped Denis, still holding on to himself. 'Said I had his sister here.'

Paramedics and police turned to look at Diana, who said, 'Don't be stupid! I'm not his sister. I'm Diana Quicke, and this is my flat!'

Again, Ellie had to subdue a desire to laugh out loud. 'Suppose we all quieten down and let the paramedics do their job?'

The television set, which had been teetering on the brink for some time, now descended to the floor with a crash. Diana burst into tears. 'My beautiful new telly!' She aimed a kick at Anthony, and missed.

Anthony laughed. 'Serves you effing well right.' His eyes were watering, blood was pouring down his chin, and he looked far from the well-groomed young man of the photographs Ellie had been toting around.

'Bastard!' cried Diana, and would have tried to kick him again if she hadn't been pushed back and down into a chair by the woman police officer. Everyone's eyes then went to Diana's bare feet and legs. And then to Denis's bare feet and unbuttoned shirt. And back to Diana's unzipped black skirt. Ellie could almost see the thought balloon over everyone's heads, 'They were at it in the bedroom.'

'Harrumph! Well, now!' said the male officer, notebook to the fore. 'Anyone need to be taken to hospital?' He cocked an eye at the paramedics.

'No great harm done,' said Denis's paramedic. 'Superficial cut to the head, bruise on chin, possible concussion, have to watch it for a few hours.'

Anthony's paramedic had been stemming his nosebleed and moving his arm around. 'A bloody nose and possible sprained elbow for the other.'

'He broke my arm!' insisted Anthony. 'It needs to be X-rayed. I'm going to sue the pants off him and get damages, as well.'

'It's not broken,' said the paramedic, packing up to go.

Anthony turned to the police. 'I insist you arrest this man. He assaulted me and broke my arm. You all saw it.'

'No, we didn't,' said the woman police officer.

'My father,' said Anthony, 'knows your chief constable well. You'll lose your badge for this.'

'Your father,' said the male police officer, looking wooden, 'may be King Canute for all I know. We can't report what we didn't see. Now, let's have it from the beginning.'

Ellie suggested that everyone sat down, and with the departure of the paramedics, they righted the furniture and found themselves seats.

Diana eased herself closer to Denis. 'I don't know this man from Adam, but the other day I was showing some people round a house I own not far from here and he came to the door and said was I Ms Quicke, which of course I am. He said I was hiding his sister, which of course I wasn't. He was wearing an animal mask, and he really frightened me. When I said I didn't know what he was talking about, he started to hit me. You can still see the marks.'

And indeed, the police could.

Anthony jeered. 'How did you recognize me, when I was wearing a mask?'

'I didn't recognize you then, no. Luckily a friend intervened and you ran away, but—'

'You're quite mad.'

Diana raised her voice. 'I recognized your voice when you came to the door here today and started yelling to be let in.' That stopped him for the moment. Diana continued. 'When you assaulted me the other day, I reported the incident to the police and the case must still be on file. After that, I went to stay with my mother. This flat is mine, but recently I lent it to my partner here. I'd been told that this mad-man – whatever his name is – has been asking around trying to find me, and it occurred to me that he might come here because my name and address is in the phone book. So this morning I came here to talk to Denis about moving out for a while, perhaps coming to stay with me at my mother's.'

Here Diana almost blushed. Meeting Ellie's eye, she said, 'Well, I told Thomas I was going to fetch Denis, and he said he'd speak to you about it, so I thought it would be all right.'

Ellie ground her teeth. The effrontery of the girl! She could twist facts for England!

'But when I got here we, well, got side-tracked.'

To their credit, the police didn't even snigger.

Diana continued, 'When this man started thumping at the door and ringing the doorbell, we were a little slow to answer it, I suppose. I got to the door first and looked through the spyhole. I saw this man, a complete stranger. He was yelling that he knew I was in here and had his sister, and I realized I'd heard him say those words before. I'd already had a taste of his fists, so I rang the police.

'Denis didn't understand what the man was like. He thought he could reason with him – show him around, prove to him that we didn't have his sister in here. I told him not to, but he opened the door, and got knocked down! Can you believe it? This man walked straight in and threw a punch, and Denis went over, just like that! I was so frightened. I ran out into the road in my bare feet, and grabbed the first person who was passing, and got them to phone for an ambulance.

'I didn't go back into the flat till the paramedics came and they got here long before the police, and by that time my beautiful flat was wrecked, and this man was trying to slap Denis back to consciousness, and then they started fighting. Why don't you arrest him and take him away and lock him up and make him see a shrink because I don't know where his sister is, and I don't care, either!'

'I can't believe it!' mumbled Denis. He didn't look his usual well-polished self either, but his cold, grey eyes burned as he focused on Anthony. Holding one hand to his jaw, he waved the other arm at the destruction around him. 'Criminal damage. Assault. Throw the book at him.'

Anthony said, 'My father's solicitor will tear you to pieces. The police can bear witness you assaulted me; broke my arm and my nose.'

'A householder has the right to self-defence,' said Denis, valiantly trying to rise from the floor, and falling back again.

'You did the damage yourself,' said Anthony, very sure of himself. He added an insult designed to hurt. 'Old man!' Next he turned on Ellie, eyes narrowed. 'So you are the original Mrs Quicke, are you? It's you I have to thank for wasting so much of my time?'

'Yes, it's me,' said Ellie. 'And if we're going to play childish games, my husband's bigger than you and I know where the bodies are buried, which is more than you do.'

He made a convulsive movement as if to attack her, but Ellie merely smiled. 'Oh, please do hit me. I'd love that. So would the police. That would give them all the evidence they need to haul you off down to the police station and charge you with grievous bodily harm.'

'We're doing that, anyway,' said the policewoman.

Anthony flushed. 'What? You daren't lay a finger on me! My father would—'

'Whoever he is, your father is not above the law, and neither are you,' said her colleague. 'We'll get the police surgeon to look at your arm at the same time. So let's be going, shall we?' He turned to Diana and Denis. 'We'd like you both to come down to the station with us now, to file a complaint. Are you prepared to do that?'

'When we've got some shoes on,' said Diana. 'Oh, and mother, it's all right if Denis stays with us tonight, isn't it? I mean, he can hardly stay here in this mess.'

Ellie told herself that she could bear it, if she had to. And obviously she did have to. 'Of course, dear. He can have Mrs Belton's room.'

Anthony simply couldn't believe that he was being hauled to his feet by two police officers. 'What? You, you fellow! Let go of me! It's me that's going to swear out a complaint against these two. And ... what was that you said, woman? Mrs Belton's been staying with you?'

Ellie said, 'She's moved on, now. I'm afraid I don't know where so it's no good you trying to batter the truth out of me. Mia is out of your reach too.'

He spat at her.

'Now, now!' said the woman police officer. Her colleague gave Anthony a shake, and thrust him towards the door.

Ellie murmured to their departing backs, 'Have a nice day.' She reflected that some policemen and women were all the better for being 'plods' because they knew black and white when they saw it, and never bothered about shades of grey. She wondered how long they'd hold Anthony. Overnight, perhaps?

Time for a council of war.

'Dumbo, you've got to get me out of this. They're keeping me down at the police station on some ridiculous charge. Father's out and so is she. I need you to get hold of a solicitor and ... yes, I know what time it is, just do it! I'm not spending the night in here with the winos.'

'Ant, what you done now?'

'I was finding Mrs Quicke, that's what.'

'You should have asked me. I got her address hours ago.'

'What!'

'Sure. Followed her from the Broadway. Big place, locked up tight. Servants, some sort of business being run in the coach house at the

300

side. Lots of people around; cars coming and going. She must be well off.'

'Well, don't do anything till I get home. Right? Now, get me out of here!'

Friday evening

Back at home, Ellie threw together some sort of meal between making and receiving phone calls – one of which left her feeling disorientated, and inclined to retire to bed to weep. But she couldn't do that, not with a houseful of people. Besides, she wasn't made of paper, was she? Once she'd calmed down, she'd be able to think of a way through this horror.

Thomas was distracted, trying to drag his attention away long enough from his conference on the morrow to listen to what Ellie was saying, but not succeeding terribly well. After all, it was a really important event in his life. Ellie told herself she mustn't be selfish, demanding his attention all the time.

Denis and Diana were all over one another. Yuk!

Rose sniffed at regular intervals, driving everyone crazy.

They ate round the kitchen table, but at Ellie's suggestion, took their coffee into the big sitting room at the back of the house. The front doorbell rang now and then, ushering more people in for the council of war. Denis received a phone call on his mobile and was last to join them, looking furious and muttering to Diana.

Finally, all were seated. Even Rose, who Ellie

insisted should be included.

Thomas gathered everyone's attention. 'It's been a terrible time for all of us. We're going to need cool heads and courage to get through what's coming, so before we start, I'm going to ask you all to join with me in a couple of minutes of silent prayer, asking God for protection, and for the courage to outwit evil.'

No one objected. Not even Denis, who Ellie thought was probably an atheist if he was anything.

A moment of calm followed, which was much needed. Ellie even managed an arrow prayer herself: *Dear Lord, save us. Please.*

Thomas came out of his moment of prayer with a smile. 'Over to you, Ellie.'

'Aren't you going to chair the meeting, Thomas?'

'No, no,' he said, settling back comfortably. 'You have all the information at your fingertips, so bring us up to date. Start with the phone call you had this evening which upset you so much.'

Of course he'd noticed. She looked round at the anxious faces of her friends and family. 'I suppose you could say we're all under attack, one way or another. I know I am. Yes, Diana? What is it?'

'Someone knows we're here. Denis had a phone call on his mobile just now.' She was controlling herself with an effort. Denis slumped forward, holding an ice pack to his chin. Ellie had never seen him anything but totally in command of himself and the situation, but now he seemed shrunken. Humiliation at being knocked out in front of Diana? His eyes still burned with fury, but it was a banked-down fire.

Diana said, 'Denis and I laid a formal complaint against Anthony Prior this afternoon at the police station. He, in turn, laid one against us. The police were very polite to him. More so than they were to us. A solicitor arrived at the station to represent Anthony before we left, and now–' she swallowed but continued – 'they've traced us here. I don't understand how they seem to know our every move. How did they know how to contact us?'

'I expect that now Anthony's sorted out that you are estate agents, he's tried the agency phone. That gives Denis's mobile number if you're out of the office, doesn't it? It's no magic that he tried it and got you here.'

'Oh. Well, yes. I suppose that's it. Denis, you tell them what he said.'

Denis's chin was swollen, and he spoke with difficulty. 'Whoever it was – and it wasn't Anthony – didn't give his name. It was a deep voice, not one I recognize, saying that if I knew what was good for the agency, we would withdraw all charges against Anthony. Otherwise, the speaker couldn't be responsible for what might happen to any properties we had on our books. There was some mention of–' he blenched but continued – 'arson. That any property on our books might go up in flames.'

Diana moaned softly. 'We'll have to withdraw

the charges. We can't risk it.'

Roy could hardly sit still. 'These threats! Why don't the police take them seriously? I was just about to leave work when I got a phone call from Prior. He asked how I was getting on with raising the money to buy into the new block. I said I was having to back out, shortage of cash, terribly sorry and all that. He said he was sorry to hear it, that he'd give me twenty-four hours to rethink. I went home and...' his voice broke.

He took control of himself with an effort. 'There was another phone call, not from Prior. A deeper voice. Saying that people who broke promises shouldn't live in glass houses and that there was a lot of glass in my house, and what a pity if it got into my little girl's eyes, or my wife's.

'I was so jittery I could hardly hold the phone, but I managed to get through to the police to tell them what had happened. I had to admit I didn't recognize the voice. They said they'd log the call but it was probably just a joke. A joke! I didn't want to alarm Felicity, but she saw I was distressed. Kate was there too. Kate said I must tell you, Ellie, and you said we were having this meeting, so that's why I'm here.'

He got to his feet, started to tramp around the room. 'I'll have to sell everything I've got, everything. I don't know how, at the moment. Kate says I mustn't give in, but I'm not risking my family's eyesight.'

Thomas guided him back to his seat. 'Calm down, Roy. We're here to find a way out of this, and that's what we're going to do.'

There was an indrawn breath from Armand, who put up his hand to speak next. 'I had a call rather like that when I got home from school. A deep voice. I don't know this Mr Prior, have never spoken to him to my knowledge, so can't say who it was. The voice said I'd been very foolish to suggest Anthony had made threats—'

'What?' said Ellie. 'Wait a minute. You didn't report Anthony's visit to your house to the police, did you? Now, I only told the police about it this afternoon. I said you thought you'd know the man again, and had the licence number of his car.'

'Which means,' said Armand, 'that what you said to the police this afternoon went straight back to Mr Prior.'

Thomas lifted a finger in a warning gesture. 'Let's be accurate. The deep voice doesn't necessarily belong to Mr Prior himself. It might be someone acting for him.'

'Either way,' said Armand, 'when I got the call, I started laughing because it sounded so ridiculous. After a little while, I realized that it was serious, and I got angry. How dare he! So I rang Kate to see if she were all right, and she said I should ring Ellie. And that's why I'm here.'

Diana looked bewildered. 'Did Armand get a visit from Anthony too? Why?'

Ellie explained. 'Yes, he did. Anthony visited him in an attempt to discover where I might be.

Anthony came off worst in that encounter, which must have hurt his pride. Armand's wife and children have been staying with Felicity and Roy ever since, but as Kate has pointed out, this can't go on indefinitely.'

Ellie looked at Thomas for a lead, but he signed for her to proceed.

She said, 'I, too, have had a phone call from Mr Prior. It definitely was him. A lightish voice, with a slight Midlands twang. I've never to my knowledge met him, but I have no doubt that it was the man in person. He said that he'd been informed that I was slandering him, that he felt his reputation was under threat. That, as he was so much in the public eye, he could not afford to let the matter pass. With sorrow, he was therefore instructing his solicitors to sue me. He said he was sure to win the case, as I hadn't a shred of evidence against him.

'He went on to say that if I made a public apology at a drinks party he's giving tomorrow night, and brought Ursula, he would forget the matter except for the small matter of damages. I am supposed to send him a cheque for a million pounds to the charity of his choice. With those conditions met, he would be prepared to forget the matter.'

'What!' Armand jumped up from his chair. 'A million pounds? And I suppose we can guess which will be the charity of his choice! Himself! Or, I suppose, he'll distribute some to his favourite charities. You won't pay, of course.'

Thomas said, 'Didn't he ask for Mia, as

well?'

'No, he didn't. I'm not sure why. Perhaps he knows she's no longer marketable. As for paying him off, certainly not! I don't have that sort of money. All my worldly wealth goes into my charitable foundations, and I couldn't possibly persuade the trustees to let me have any for blackmailers. And I wouldn't dream of asking.'

'Bravo!' Thomas clapped.

SEVENTEEN

Thomas's praise made Ellie go pink with pleasure. 'Well, now we've put all the pieces together, we can see how he works,' said Ellie. 'As soon as he's opposed, he uses threats both in his own name, and also through someone we can call Deep Throat for ease of reference. He follows up the threats by getting others to take physical action: wrecking Mrs Belton's flat, and so on.'

'Agreed.'

'Yes.'

Diana said, 'Anthony's Deep Throat, isn't he?'

Ellie hesitated. 'I don't think so. Anthony's voice is rather like his father's, wouldn't you agree? A light, well-educated, public school voice. Does that chime with what everyone has heard of the phone threats?'

A general shaking of heads. 'A deep voice. Very masculine.'

Ellie continued, 'I agree that Anthony does seem to have done some of the rough work, including today's visit to you, Diana, and his visit to Armand. But Mrs Belton described two quite different people: younger, thinner, not so well groomed, so well spoken or even so well washed.'

Roy was puzzled. 'How many people are there working for Prior?'

'I'm not sure that they are all working for him, precisely. I think that there's a chain of command, with Mr Prior at the top. He maintains a front of solid respectability, and sues anyone who dares to murmur that he's not perfect. Then there's the Deep Throat person, who acts for him. Deep Throat is the enforcer, making sure that opposition vanishes wherever it raises its head. Perhaps it's Mr Prior's solicitor? I really have no idea. Also acting in his father's interests is Anthony Prior, who has – don't let's forget – a number of bright young things of both sexes prepared to go along with his slightest whim.'

'So the people who attacked Mrs Belton are in Anthony's group of friends?'

'N–no. Anthony's friends are all much of a muchness, as you can see from these photos that Dan threw away. Young, well dressed, slender of body, educated. See?' Ellie passed round the photos. 'On the fringe of his group,

Anthony also has access to a number of pretty young girls who are used by his father to attract and amuse businessmen with whom Mr Prior had dealings.'

Armand threw the photos down in disgust. 'Not a thick-necked thug among them. Are we looking for bouncers from a nightclub, perhaps?'

Ellie shook her head. 'No, I don't think so. It's horrid, but I'm afraid the link is through Anthony's younger brother, Timothy, and his friendship with Dan, Ursula's ex-fiancé. Tim and Dan have always been close. Dan has no money; is desperate for a job, which he's been promised by the Priors. Dan lives at home in a boarding house for students run by his divorced mother. Their lodgers are all hard up, young and hungry. The Priors held a Halloween party last year and had lots of masks for their guests. Dan and Ursula didn't go, but I wonder if it gave the students the idea that they could behave as badly as they liked, if they wore masks.'

'Supposition,' said Thomas.

'Yes, but I saw a Halloween mask on one of the student's doors in that house, and I'm thinking that one of the Prior brothers asked Dan to find some lads willing to do a job for them. Dan certainly knows more than he's let on. He knew where the stolen laptop could be found, didn't he, and how to retrieve it? Which means he had contact with those who stole it.

'We mustn't forget that Ursula believes

Lloyd's death was murder, not an accident. Now, she wasn't there. Dan wasn't there. She didn't have contact with Anthony and his lot afterwards, except for a confrontation that ended badly for her. Dan, on the other hand, continued to see his old friends. I'm thinking Dan learned something about Lloyd's death afterwards, something that he doesn't want to take to the police, possibly something that proved Tim was involved? Whether she's picked up a hint from Dan, or whether she's just acting on her knowledge of the people involved, Ursula refused to go along with the official cover-up – which is why we're all here today.'

Thomas said, 'More supposition, but it does feel right. It seems to me that Ursula is the key to unlock the cabinet of mysteries. She's no shrinking violet, but a player of some strength. Is it a good idea to keep her out of the action?'

'She's also vulnerable,' said Ellie. 'The Priors want her to help them snare another rich businessman. Remember what happened to Mia. Should Ursula risk the same fate? She knows the group has access to drugs through someone called "Bullseye", so-called because he always scores with women first time. Is "Bullseye" using Rohypnol, the date rape drug, to make sure he always scores with women?'

'You think that he might have used the date rape drug on Mia—'

'I fear so. Let's consider the following scenario. We know that some councillor or other wanted Mia's company at the Grand Opening, and that she was a virgin at that point. We know that Anthony got her to go upstairs only because he said the councillor had left the party. Suppose he hadn't? Suppose she was drugged, and raped, and that after that others took their turn to ... oh, it doesn't bear thinking about. Is this what's in store for Ursula if she returns?'

'I'm not suggesting that Ursula walks into the Priors' net,' said Thomas. 'But it occurs to me that she may not be safe from predators, just because she's in Portsmouth. How long did it take for her to come up to London the other day?'

Silence. Reluctant nods.

Ellie was worried. 'You think she's actually safer up here with us?'

Roy was twisting his hands. 'For how long? How long is this going to go on for? I've got twenty-four hours to find the money – which I can't do – and after that, I'd not be able to leave Felicity alone for a minute.'

Thomas reminded them, 'If fear is faced, it can be dealt with.'

'Precisely,' said Ellie, though her heart was beating far too fast. 'Now, let's take a good long look at these threats. If any of us are taken to court, well, I can afford as good a solicitor as Mr Prior. Probably better. Threats to sue are merely that: threats. We can deal with those in the courts in the usual way. As a matter of fact, I don't suppose it would ever come to court, because then everyone would hear what we thought about the Priors and their reputation would be called into question.'

'But the very real threats to our wives and children!' said Roy.

'Oh, them. Well,' said Ellie, 'I think I know how to neutralize the boys who think they can get away with murder in masks. They're only students, after all.'

Armand said, 'Hah! Students! I know students all right. Half flash and half foolish. Have any of them been through my hands? Give me some names.'

'Ursula Belton, Daniel Collins.'

'Belton. Hah! Intelligent. Could have become an academic, but decided to be artistic instead. Collins: brains of an ox, and muscles to match. Into team sports; captain of this and that. Not one of mine. Never been in trouble that I know of. But, Collins, Collins? Is there a younger brother?'

'Yes, there is,' said Ellie. 'You know him?'

'Average brain. Bit of a tearaway. Exclusion for setting off fireworks? By the name of Kyle. That the one?'

'Sounds like him,' said Ellie. 'I know there's a younger brother still at school. I do hope he's not involved, but if he is ... oh dear, poor Mrs Collins.'

Thomas had his diary out. 'If we pay the Collins household a visit first thing in the morning, I could still make the eleven ten train. It's a trifle early for students to be out of bed, but—'

Ellie shook her head. 'Thomas, I wouldn't hear of it. That's an important conference you're going to, and you'll miss the first session if you don't catch the nine o'clock.'

'I'll go with you, Ellie,' said Armand, cracking his knuckles. 'Students! Hah! Do I know students! The earlier the better; rout them out of bed, bring the might of the law down on them. They'll crack all right. You and I, Ellie. We could take on the world and win.'

'Yes, but I thought Roy or Denis...' She looked at Roy, and then at Diana and Denis. All three looked away.

Roy said, 'Nobody better than you for dealing with things, Ellie. A great relief. Let me know how you get on, right?'

'That's it,' said Diana, her arm tightly through Denis's. 'I'm not letting Denis risk life and limb again.'

But, thought Ellie, you're quite prepared to let someone smaller, frailer and much older confront the baddies for you. Armand's a shrimp compared to Roy and Denis. On the other hand, come to think of it, I'd rather have Armand on my side in a fight than anyone else. Except Thomas, of course.

Goodnights were said. Roy and Armand went out together. Denis and Diana drifted up the stairs, also together. Ellie called out after them, 'I haven't had time to change the sheets on Mrs Belton's bed, Diana. I hope Denis won't mind?'

They disappeared, still locked together. Ellie shrugged. She didn't like the idea of their sleeping together under her roof, but if they did, well, it was just too late for her to do anything about it.

Thomas was looking worried. 'I really ought to be with you tomorrow. Should I cancel?'

'Certainly not. Put in some extra praying for me when you're on the train.'

Ellie shook Rose's shoulder gently. Rose had fallen asleep early on in the discussion, but woke with a smile. 'All settled? That's good. Miss Quicke has been telling me it's about time those boys were sent to the naughty step.' Yawning, she collected used coffee cups and saucers and went off to the kitchen.

When she'd gone, Ellie said, 'Thomas, about Rose.'

He put his arm about her shoulders and gave her a hug. 'I've seen it before, haven't you? Someone so near the end of their lives that they imagine they're really hearing and seeing the one they love who's already gone across. They project what they'd say to one another as if they were both still here. Rose loved your aunt, and your aunt loved Rose. Let's leave it at that. Will you ring Ursula now, or in the morning?'

Ellie was tired, but said she'd ring now. Thomas went to help Rose tidy up in the kitchen. Midge the cat strolled in to wind around Ellie's legs now that Diana had gone upstairs. He looked well fed. Perhaps he would settle on her lap, even if Diana was still in the house? Ellie sat and he leaped on to her lap as she got through to Ursula.

'Ursula, my dear. There've been some developments that you ought to know about...'

Armand collected Ellie at half past eight next morning. 'Kate says she wants to come home tonight so we'd better get ourselves sorted. I agreed. So let's up and at 'em. First, tell me everything you know about the attack on Mrs B. And I mean *everything*.'

They arrived at the Collinses' house and sat in the car while Ellie cudgelled her memory for everything she'd been told, or had observed. 'We haven't any proof they're involved,' she said, wondering if they were making almighty fools of themselves.

Armand twitched his nose. 'It smells right. When you've been dealing with teenagers as long as I have, you get to sense when they've been up to something. I phoned one of my colleagues last night to get the low-down on this particular piece of dirt, and the verdict is that he's heading for Juvenile Court as fast as he can. So let's go crack the little tyke open, right?'

Ellie allowed him to brush aside her uneasiness, and stood beside him as he hung on the doorbell. Dan's room was to the left of the front door. No lights visible. No lights visible in any of the other windows, either. A glow-worm advanced from the back of the hallway, and Mrs Collins said, 'Yes? Who is it?' in a voice that declared its owner had only just risen from her bed.

Ellie would have gone for a softer approach,

but Armand took over. 'Mrs Collins, this is Kyle's class teacher from school. It's urgent that we speak.'

Both heard Mrs Collins's indrawn breath. Had she been expecting a visit from officialdom? What did she know of her younger son's goings-on? Keys were turned and Mrs Collins let them into the shadowy hall. She was wearing a full-length pink woollen dressing-gown over pyjamas, and bedroom slippers with a bunny face on each of them. There was a twist of pink tulle around the curls on her head.

'What's happened? What has he done now? I'm afraid–' a despairing look up the stairs – 'he's not up yet but, well, you know what teen-agers are, they lie in bed till noon at weekends. Forgive my ... I haven't had time to dress yet, and I haven't had my first cup of coffee. Always so civilizing, don't you think? Coffee. Will you have some?'

Ellie gestured to Dan's closed door. 'Dan not up yet?'

'What? No, he ... I mean, yes. He went off early with some friends, a trip down to the coast, I believe. I think he's hoping to see Ursula.' Still talking, she led the way down the hall to the sunroom in which she lived by day. She switched on lights, revealing the same dis-order and air of faint decay that Ellie had observed earlier.

Armand hung back, looking up the stairs. 'Which is his room? The sooner I can speak with him, the sooner we can sort this out. I'm sure he's been misled by older heads. Maybe we won't have to involve the police—'

Ellie laid a hand on Armand's arm. 'Hold on a minute.' She'd spotted something that hadn't been on the big table on her previous visit. A Bristol blue vase, which she'd last seen in Mrs Belton's flat. It was of an unusual shape, with a chip out of the rim. It now contained a bunch of tulips. 'Mrs Collins, where did you get that vase?'

'Why, Kyle gave it to me. He knows I like pretty things. It's not precisely to my taste but...' She licked her lips, looking from Ellie to Armand and back again. 'What's he done? He hasn't stolen it. No way! He's a good boy, really.'

Armand set off back to the stairs. 'Which room? I don't want to wake the whole household.'

Mrs Collins got in front of him, somehow, a bunch of keys in her hand. 'I'll show you. He'll have locked the door. He always locks his door, but I have a master key, of course. You will be gentle? He's only fifteen, you know.'

'Sixteen,' said Armand. 'I checked. And already known to the police.'

Ellie followed them up the stairs and across the landing. Mrs Collins unlocked the door; Armand flung it open and strode in. A television set flickered at the end of the bed, on which lay a youth, headphones on, music tinnily echoing throughout the room. Green pinpricks of light showed where a computer was on standby. The

317

room stank of stale beer.

Mrs Collins bleated, 'He'll be in a terrible temper if you wake him too quickly!'

'I'm in a worse temper already,' snarled Armand. He pulled the duvet from the sleeping figure, and hauled him upright.

Ellie switched on the lights and closed the door behind them. She stumbled over a couple of empty cans of beer. Two more lay under the bed, together with a half-eaten, cold pizza.

'Whaaat?' said the slack-mouthed but otherwise good-looking youth. At least, he would be good-looking if he'd been washed and shaved and brushed. Wearing boxer shorts only. And the headphones, which Armand removed in one deft swoop.

Kyle cracked open one eye, and then another. He recognized Armand, and cringed.

Armand thrust his face at Kyle. 'You know me, don't you? You little idiot, how do you think we're going to be able to keep you out of the courts now?'

Ellie appreciated Armand's masterly technique. He'd threatened, but at the same time given Kyle hope that somehow or other Armand could get him out of trouble. She looked around. Kyle wasn't one to hang his clothes up at night, was he? A black, fake-leather jacket lay on the floor in a twist of T-shirts. And on the back of a chair hung a skeleton mask.

'Armand, look. That's the jacket he wore when he put Mrs Belton in hospital and wrecked her flat, and there's his mask.'

Kyle tried to pull the duvet up over him, creeping further up the bed till he was jammed against the headboard. 'Whaaat? Who?'

Mrs Collins wailed, hands over her ears. 'Oh, Kyle! No! You didn't, did you?'

'Shut up, you!' But his heart wasn't in it.

Armand gave vent to a great sigh. 'All right. Get some clothes on, and we'll take you down the station. If Mrs Belton pulls through—'

'We didn't hurt her that much! Honest! It was just a bit of fun, like. Only she would struggle, and...' He squinched his eyes shut, realizing what he'd admitted.

Armand shook his head. 'I daresay you didn't mean to hurt her that much, but your mate did a proper job on her, didn't he? And now you'll have to pay for what he did.'

'No, I ... it's not like, I mean, The Man said to give her a fright, but Charlie let her fall and then he said we might as well take...' He wound down with a groan. 'But we did phone for an ambulance before we left, honest we did.'

'Charlie?' said Mrs Collins, in a faint voice. 'I should have known he'd be trouble. Upstairs. Overlooking the front. A student at the University, but hangs around the amusement arcades most of the time. Dan did warn me, months ago, that Charlie didn't seem to care how he got his hands on the money for his new stereo, but I needed his rent. Oh!' She seemed to take in the amount of expensive equipment laying around. 'Kyle, you told me you paid for all this with a win on the scratch cards. Was that true?'

''Course not! Only an idiot would have believed that.'

'Kyle!' said Armand. 'Don't speak to your mother like that. Now, get dressed and let's see what Charlie's got to say for himself. But if he starts laying the blame on you, or another of your friends—'

'Only Jase. He goes out with Charlie, usually, but...' His eyes slid away from them.

'Yes?' said Armand.

Kyle swallowed. 'Charlie's gone down to Portsmouth with Dan, to see Ursula. They asked Jase, but he wouldn't, I don't know why. They didn't ask me, because I'm too young.'

'Not too young to be charged with burglary and assault,' said Armand. 'Let's go see Jase, see what he has to say for himself.'

Jase was roused from sleep, and when confronted with Armand and Kyle, who'd developed verbal diarrhoea, was happy to fill in the gaps. Between them they spilled all the details of what they'd done and when; what they'd stolen and who they'd fenced cards to. Also, how they'd got hold of the masks, which was through a friend of Dan's who often came round. Name?

'"Dumbo" because of the way his ears stuck out. He told Charlie to rough up the old woman. It was his idea, honest.'

'Drugs? No, never. We never took no drugs.'

'But you know someone who...?'

'Yes, well, maybe. Some friend of Dumbo's, called Bullseye.'

320

'Full name?'

'Dunno.'

'Where can he be found?'

'Dunno. At the pub, maybe. Charlie knows him.'

'And Dumbo's real name? Come on, you know him well, don't you?'

'Timothy Prior. He was at school with Dan, yonks ago.'

Mrs Collins wept for a while, then sniffed and made herself some more of her coffee-plus. She said she was going to murder Charlie when he got back, as it was obviously him who'd led her boy astray.

Armand said, 'I expect you're right, but it's a good thing this has all come out now, with the boys happy to cooperate. Suppose you get dressed, and then we can all go down to the police station and see what can be done to reduce the charges. Perhaps the lads will only get probation.'

Ellie went out on to the landing to phone the police station. DI Willis was, predictably, unavailable, so Ellie left a message. 'You asked me to find the masked youths who've been terrorizing the neighbourhood. I'm bringing two of them in to see you in half an hour's time.'

It was another hour and a half before they were free to leave the station. It was DI Willis's day off, and someone Ellie hadn't seen before had taken charge. For once, the name of Prior hadn't reduced a policeman to grovelling servitude. Good. Kyle and Jase were put through the mangle of making statements about everything they'd done and their connection to the Priors, and finally were sent home with a still-tearful Mrs Collins.

As soon as they themselves could leave, Armand settled Ellie in his car, before burying his face in his hands, and then hitting the steering wheel. 'The stupid, dim-brained, incompetent...'

'You really care about these youngsters, don't you?'

'After all these years of dealing with the stupidities of youth, I should be used to it. I am used to it. There's always some climb out of the pit. But there's others, easily led, you can see it coming and you can't stop it.'

'Kyle's got a chance, if you stand by him.'

Armand turned the key in the ignition. 'Not much of one. Where to now, Mrs Q?'

'Home. Armand, can I ask you another favour?'

She told him what she wanted, and he laughed. 'What a lark! Can do. Do you want brains and brawn, or will just brawn do? As for payment, I should think a square meal would do it.'

'Ant, are you there? We got here nice and early, but the bird's flown.'

'What? She must be there. Someone's hiding her.'

'Not here. Dan went in first. Got nowhere. They said she left late last night to visit her

322

mother, but they don't know where her mother is.'

'Idiot! Of course she's there. She's just told them to say she's gone. Go in and check.'

'We have. All three of us. She's not there. We went into every room. There's a couple of other girls in the house, but no Ursula. Then one of the boys called the police so we had to leave. What do we do now?'

Saturday afternoon

Armand dropped Ellie back to her house, which she entered with some trepidation. Who would she find there? What fresh disaster would she have to deal with?

All was quiet when she let herself into the hall, and she relaxed. Of course Diana and Denis would have gone into work as Saturday was the busiest day of the week for them. Roy would likewise be busy in his office next door. Thomas was out, of course. She sent up an arrow prayer that the conference would go well for him.

Kate opened the door to the kitchen, and let her toddler escape into Ellie's arms. Kate was smiling. 'She's here and busy. Come and see.'

Ellie carried the toddler into the kitchen, where the baby was fast asleep in his buggy at one end of the table, while Ursula sat at the other, with all the tools of her trade around her. Ursula looked up from her work when Ellie came in, and smiled. Today she looked serene and strong.

'I didn't go to a hotel last night, as you suggested. I was a trifle short of cash, tell the truth. So I went home to the flat. It wasn't too bad. I expected worse, and I could make a start on clearing it up. Also, I needed my dress and all the other stuff for tonight.'

'So long as no one knew you were there.'

Ursula grinned. 'I've just had a phone call from my house mates down in Portsmouth. The bad boys didn't arrive till after ten this morning. They behaved just as we expected, and the police have been alerted.'

Rose was smiling too. 'I'm making a beef casserole with dumplings, using my biggest pot. We need something warm inside us to keep out the cold, don't we?'

Kate lifted the toddler out of Ellie's arms and set her on the floor. 'Isn't Ursula clever with her hands? I'd never have thought of such a thing. By the way, it occurred to me that it might be a good idea to record all telephone calls in future. You mustn't answer the phone when it rings, but let it record a message. Thomas has already phoned and left a message, but no one else. He's a hoot, isn't he?'

At that very moment the phone in the hall rang. Ellie was halfway there before Kate could grab Ellie's arm, and stop her from picking up the receiver.

Eerily, Mr Prior's lightweight voice filled the hall. Ursula stole out to listen too. 'Mrs Quicke, I'm a patient man, but your persistent attempts to ruin my name are causing me considerable

324

annoyance. May I remind you what is at stake here? My solicitor informs me you are worth a considerable amount, and unless you agree to my terms – my very generous terms – I shall be instructing him to take action on Monday morning, first thing. So I take it that we will see you tonight, six thirty at my place? With Ursula, who I trust will be in the right spirit for a party.'

The phone went dead, but immediately rang again. This time Ellie held on to Kate's arm, as the gruff tones of Deep Throat came through. 'Mrs Quicke, are you there? I fear you have not understood the dangers of the course you have undertaken, and need to be taught a lesson. There is no way you can defeat me.'

The phone line went dead. Ellie told herself to relax, muscle by muscle. Kate, too, was tense.

Ursula rubbed her forehead. 'I've heard that voice before somewhere. But where? It's weird.'

'False?' suggested Kate, attempting to lighten the atmosphere.

'Disguised?' said Ellie. 'Do you think they've discovered that two of their foot soldiers have been rumbled? Jase and Kyle talked their heads off to the police, and were happy to finger Timothy Prior as the one who gave them orders to beat up Mrs Belton. Granted, DI Willis wasn't at the scene, but there seems to be a direct line from the station to the Prior household.'

'Hang about,' said Kate, as the phone rang

again. This time it was Mr Abrahams, who wanted to talk to Ellie. She took the call, but motioned to Ursula to stand by.

The doctor said, 'Is that Mrs Quicke? Can you give me the name of my patient?'

'Flavia,' said Ellie. 'How is she?'

'On antibiotics and painkillers, but improving enough to think of other people. She's desperate to speak to a friend of hers, Ursula Belton. Is there any chance—'

'Ursula's standing right next to me. I'll hand you over, and you can take it from there.'

Ellie and Kate went back into the kitchen, just in time to rescue the toddler from falling off a chair.

Kate said, 'Thomas rang to say he'd met an old friend on the train, who advised him about the laws of slander. He says that if you state an unfavourable opinion, that's slander. If you ask a question, however discreditable the opinion that you offer, then it's not slander.'

'Not? So if I want to get across to people that I think Mr Prior is an evil man, I mustn't say so directly. I must say, "Mr Prior, are you really the evil man people say?" Is that right?'

'Let's practise,' said Kate. 'Oh, and by the way, Roy made it clear I wasn't welcome to stay at his house any longer and Armand won't let me go home, so I'm hoping to sleep here tonight. Is that all right?'

Ellie cuddled the toddler. 'So long as nobody expects me to change bedlinen, that's fine by me. Thomas won't be back till tomorrow afternoon, so you and little madam here can have our bed, the baby can sleep in his pushchair, and I'll sleep in Rose's old bedroom.'

Rose flourished a paring knife. 'How many potatoes shall I peel, do you think?'

'Enough for a small army,' said Ellie. 'I've forgotten exactly how many people we've got coming for supper. Five, not counting Diana and Denis. Can you cope?'

'Of course I can.' Rose seemed to have recovered all her old energy.

EIGHTEEN

Saturday evening
Ellie told herself to breathe deeply. Slowly. She revolved before her pier glass, wishing she'd gone on a diet after Christmas, but more or less satisfied with the midnight-blue velvet gown that Kate had picked out for her to wear. Her mother's cameo brooch had looked right on it to her mind, but Kate had insisted that Ellie wear the gold locket and chain that Thomas had given her.

'When you touch that locket, it will remind you of all the people who love you, and are praying for you,' said Kate.

'You included?'

'I'll try,' said Kate, twitching the gown to lie

327

more gracefully over Ellie's hips. 'Now, with that cream brocade jacket over it, you'll look the bee's knees.'

'I don't feel like it,' grumbled Ellie. 'I don't see why you had to make me dress up like this.'

'You will when you get there. They'll all be in best bib and tucker and you've got to look the part of a millionairess for once. You've got to wear some lipstick too. Not that pale one you sometimes remember to put on, but the deep-red one you got for parties and don't like.'

'Yes, ma'am,' said Ellie, wondering if she knew where that particular lipstick might be. Perhaps in the bottom of her old black handbag, the one she didn't use nowadays?

Kate said, 'Ellie, I'll be thinking of you, every minute. I'd kiss you, but it might disturb your make-up.'

'Bother the make-up,' said Ellie, feeling cross. 'Kiss me and pray for me – for all of us.'

She went down the stairs to meet the others. Ursula was already there, wearing a floor-length hooded cloak of silver tissue. She was so pale her skin looked transparent, and she'd tied her long hair back.

Armand was already there, with two youngish men in evening dress, both openly admiring Ursula.

Armand grinned. 'All present and correct, Mrs Q. Ursula's escorts for the night. Brains, step forward.' A hawk-faced young man bowed to Ellie. 'Civil servant. He plays hockey for the county and so is fairly quick on his pins.'

Civil servants come in many shapes and forms. This one felt like diplomatic corps to Ellie. Not that she actually knew any diplomats, come to think of it.

Armand gestured a heavier-built, youngish man forward. He had a capable air about him. 'Brawn has a black belt in judo, but works as the deputy head of a primary school by day.' In spite of Armand's introduction, the black belt looked as if he had brains as well as brawn. 'Colleagues of mine from university. Both are fit for purpose. Now, are you sure you don't want me to come with you?'

'You look after Kate and Rose for me. We shouldn't be that long.'

'We'll be fine,' said Ursula. It was interesting to see how she dominated the group. With every breath, the silver cloak shimmered under the lights. She was wearing high heels, so she equalled her escorts in height. Recent events had set their mark on her. She had fined down, and the bones of her head had become more prominent. She was not just handsome any more; she was stunning.

'Your carriage awaits,' said the hawk-faced one, opening the front door for them with a flourish. His eyes lingered on Ursula as she passed in front of him, and Ellie thought she could detect a response in the faintest of blushes on the girl's face.

Two cars awaited them. Hawk-face got into the second with Ursula, while the black belt in judo took Ellie in the first.

Judo made sure Ellie's safety belt was fastened. 'Is Ursula currently in a relationship?'

'Not that I know of,' said Ellie, thinking that if she'd read him aright, Hawk-face was going to make a move on the girl that very night. Judo obviously thought so too, for he sighed before asking if Ellie was warm enough, or should he boost the heating.

Ellie was nervous. This sort of thing wasn't her style at all. What, facing down corruption and evil and even – God help her! – a murderer? She kept her hand on Thomas's locket, and tried to pray.

Dear Lord, be with us. Give us the right words to say. Give us wisdom. That was Solomon's plea, wasn't it? But we do need it. So many people, so many children are being threatened. So much damage has been done, so much more threatened. Oh, and do keep an eye on Thomas, won't you? Such an important occasion, such a big opportunity for him – not that he wants fame and fortune, because he doesn't but, oh, well. You know what I mean. Hold my hand tonight. Amen.

The Prior household had floodlighting all the way up the winding drive. What? A winding drive in heavily-built-up Ealing? That must have cost a pretty penny. The house reminded Ellie of a thirties- style liner, all white curves and metal-framed windows. The word 'posh' came into her mind as Judo manoeuvred them into a small space and parked the car. There were quite a few other cars there already. A pre-supper drinks party, right? One of the cars was a stretch limo. The sort that Ellie imagined might possess a cocktail cabinet, and seats that converted into a bed. She'd never been in one, but that was what the sight of it conveyed to her.

Hawk-face had had to park some way back. One strike for Judo, thought Ellie. But if I were Ursula, I'd go for Hawk-face too. That is, if he were free and not married with three children. It occurred to her to ask Judo if Hawk-face were eligible, but she refrained. Just. She applauded herself for her discretion, which was not, she admitted, at all like her. Usually she blurted things out, just as they occurred to her.

'I'm babbling,' she said.

'What?' said Judo, looking in his mirror. 'They're taking their time.'

'She knows what she's doing,' said Ellie, and told herself that Ursula did indeed know what she was doing. Apart from a wobble at the start, Ursula had always known what she was doing, and would be the nemesis of the Prior party. With a spot of help from above.

At last Ellie spotted the shimmer of Ursula's cloak, and signalled to Judo to let her out of the car. More people were arriving behind them. All in good suits and party dresses. Ellie was glad that Kate had insisted on her wearing evening dress.

Ellie led the way into the hall, with Ursula following. Ursula had drawn the hood of her cloak right over her head, while her escorts stood close behind her.

A central chandelier gave a muted light. The party itself spread through double doors – standing open – into a huge sitting room. Everything was white: walls, heavy-looking leather furniture, glass-topped tables, curtains. The floor was waxed pale wood. The pictures on the walls were also muted: pastel swirls, not particularly interesting.

Not particularly interesting altogether, thought Ellie. A wonderful house, decked out by an ordinary mind.

Their host – it must be he, for no one else around looked like Santa Claus without a beard – was receiving guests at the base of a wide curving staircase, but when he saw Ellie, a flash of satisfaction widened his smile.

'So you came!' His lightweight voice penetrated the chatter in the hall with ease. Most people looked around to see who he was referring to. Ellie recognized a councillor or two, various notables whose pictures she saw in the local paper now and then, and a couple she'd met at the Golf Club in the days when her first husband had belonged. A photographer prepared to immortalize the moment for the local newspaper. Also, oh dear, the Stick Insect, wearing heels so high she teetered, and a skirt so short it hardly fulfilled the intentions of the designer, who must have hoped it would be worn by someone with good legs.

Skinny legs, noted Ellie, with satisfaction. She also noted there were three young blonde girls dotted around the place, hanging on to the arms of middle-aged men. Two handsome young men – Anthony and Timothy – had arms around the shoulders of middle-aged women. Arm candy, right? Ursula had taught her to read the room, and now Ellie could see how the Priors worked their guest list.

Dan was there, holding a tray of drinks. Reduced to being a waiter? Ellie had been given descriptions of two other foot soldiers, Charlie and Bullseye, who'd gone down to Portsmouth that morning with Dan in an effort to retrieve Ursula. At first glance she couldn't see either of them.

One interesting and unexpected guest was DI Willis, in an attempt at a party dress that hadn't quite come off; the length being too long, and the maroon of the silk all wrong for her complexion. Also – was that DC Milburn, hanging over a youngish woman in a wheelchair? Ah, the sister to whom Mr Prior had done nothing but good? Ah well. Perhaps he felt the need to surround himself with the signs of his benevolence tonight?

In one corner, with a number of women surrounding him and backed by two middle-aged no-neck type bouncers, was a dark young man in a silk suit. The prince of Araby, or wherever it was he'd come from. The man who'd demanded Ursula be served up to him on a plate. A waiter came through a swinging door, carrying a tray of drinks. He was pock-marked, shaven-headed. Bullseye, dishing out drinks innocuous and lethal.

'Oh, Ellie!' cried the Stick Insect. 'How wonderful to see you. You naughty, naughty thing. Dear Mr Prior has been so distressed by the porky pies you've been telling about him.'

'Lies?' Ellie raised her eyebrows. 'Oh, no. I don't think so.'

Mr Prior lost some of his rubicund joviality, but held on to his smile. He had an excellent dentist. 'Well, well. Now you've come to apologize, and have brought the lovely Ursula with you, all shall be forgiven.'

'I haven't come to apologize,' said Ellie, trying to lift her voice so that everyone could hear. If Mr Prior wanted to stage a scene in public, then she'd give it him in spades. 'How can I apologize for speaking the truth? Why should I apologize when I and my family and friends have been threatened and beaten up? And if you think I'm paying blackmail, then you've got another think coming!'

'What nonsense is this?' He was beginning to lose his temper. A large woman beside him laid a hand on his arm and he turned his head towards her. The woman must be his wife: blonde, statuesque, glittering with diamonds. Yes, Mrs Prior. The woman pointed to the girl standing behind Ellie, and Mr Prior smiled once more and took a step forward.

'Ursula, my dear! Welcome back. We've missed you. Now, let me introduce you to someone who's come specially on your account.'

Ursula still had her hood over her face, concealing all but a red, red mouth. One hand was clenched at her throat, holding something hidden from sight by her hood. Hawk-face and Judo stood one on either side of her, eyes quartering the room.

'I am not a parcel, to be handed over to anyone.' Her voice was slow and rich. It carried a note of menace, which seemed to darken the corners of the room. Ellie felt a thrill crawl up and down her spine.

'I didn't come as a guest. I came to deliver messages from your daughter, Mrs Prior.' She raised her free hand and pointed to the woman. 'From your stepdaughter, Mr Prior.' She pointed to him. 'From your stepsister, Anthony and Timothy. From the girl you raped, Councillor.'

Hawk-face stepped forward to draw the hood a little way back from Ursula's face, revealing a face that was not hers ... a face that bore a life-size photo of the untouched, untroubled Mia. Ursula had enlarged Mia's photograph and pasted it as a mask on to a stick, surrounded by long black curls. The curls were made of black paper, but looked real enough at a distance. There were cut-outs for eyes and mouth. Through the mask, Ursula's eyes glittered.

Everyone jumped as a camera flashed. The local photographer was not going to miss this if he could help it.

A tremor struck the room. Someone laughed, hysterically, and smothered it. A woman standing near Ellie shuddered. The councillor pointed out by Ursula was a weaselly man with a six o'clock shadow. He set down his glass with a click that could be heard by everyone. A stout woman standing nearby frowned at him and opened her mouth to speak, looking bewildered. His wife?

Ellie stepped back into the shadows, allowing Ursula centre stage.

'What?' said Mr Prior. 'How dare you! Who are you?'

'I am the girl you destroyed. Ladies, gentlemen, look around you. See the pretty young men and girls, all working hard to entrap you. Some of them are under age: jail bait. I know what I'm talking about, for I was once one of them. The ploy works, doesn't it? All the little minnows swim into the Prior net and become his puppets. Every now and then a larger fish comes along and then he needs beautiful but educated girls who are harder to come by. His eye alights on Mia, his stepdaughter, and her friend Ursula. Well, why not? They're young, desirable and not yet touched by man.'

Several middle-aged men who'd been cuddling young girls suddenly found they needed both hands to hold their glass. A couple of older women disentangled themselves from the Prior boys.

'Ursula takes fright and runs away, which leaves Mia, poor Mia, who didn't want to stay on at the Grand Opening because a certain councillor was making himself obnoxious to her. She's told he's gone and given a drink by someone she trusts, by her own stepbrother. She falls into a drugged sleep. When she comes round, she's bleeding ... bruised ... bitten. She realizes she's been raped.' She raised her arm and pointed. 'Hasn't she, Councillor?'

All eyes went to the pale-faced, sweating man. 'No, no!'

The stout woman who'd been standing near him whipped her head round to stare first at Ursula, and then at the councillor, who seemed to be shrinking inside his clothes.

'And impregnated. Was it your baby, Councillor?'

'My God! No!'

His wife backhanded him. 'So that's what happened when I had flu and you came home reeking of sex! You swore you'd been with a prostitute!'

He took a step back. 'No, no. That is, yes, I did have her, but I didn't hurt her, I swear I didn't. No, how could I? She was just lying there, and I ... well, anyone would, wouldn't they?' He looked around, and met only averted eyes.

His voice rose to a shout. 'I didn't hurt her! I swear she was all right when I left her.' He swung round on Anthony. 'You were there. You told me she was ready for it. It was you! You hurt her!'

Anthony was smoothness itself. 'No, no. You are mistaken. There were lots of other people there. I took you downstairs and saw you into your car, remember?'

The camera flashed again.

The councillor wiped his hand across his forehead. 'Oh yes, of course you did. I could see ... yes, other men were queuing up to take their turn after me.'

'And this is how you left her!' Ursula reversed the mask in her hand, and now they were faced with the photo of Mia's ruined face: the puffy lips and eyes, the bruised and discoloured skin, the half-healed cuts, the badly-cut and dyed fringe of hair. 'This is what Mia looked like, three days ago. She is now in hospital, being filled up with antibiotics for the wounds inflicted on her, which have gone septic. The DNA will tell us who fathered her child.'

The councillor's wife made as if to hit him again, and he made a run for the door only to be blocked by Hawk-face, who seemed to move slowly, but caught the man in a vice-like grip from which he struggled in vain to release himself. Slowly, he was bent over till his head was touching his knees. Hawk-face released his grip, and the man fell at Ursula's feet. Weeping. 'No, no. Not me. It's a mistake. I'll be ruined ... I beg you...'

Ursula ignored him. The camera flashed.

The councillor's wife seized him by one arm and hauled him to his feet. 'You pitiful little worm!' The camera was right in her face. She spoke to the room at large. 'He'll resign tomorrow.' She towed him after her to the front door, which Hawk-face held open for her.

As it closed behind them the party-goers

shifted, turning to one another, shocked, bewildered. Ellie saw most set down half-empty glasses. A sign that they believed Ursula and were rejecting Mr Prior's hospitality?

The girl in the wheelchair sat with open mouth, stunned. DC Milburn's mouth was also agape. DI Willis sipped her drink, her eyes going round the room, her expression guarded.

Mr Prior tried to regain control. He raised his voice, gathering all eyes to himself. 'I knew nothing of this. In fact, I don't believe a word of it. The girl was a slut who—'

'That's a lie,' said Ursula, dropping her mask, throwing back her cloak and shaking her hair loose. Taller than most people there, she dominated the room, in a short, gold sheath of a dress. 'She was a virgin. You sacrificed her in the hopes of gaining a contract that you would not otherwise have got. After she was raped, she was brought back home to this house, to her own room, and kept here for use by her family and friends.'

There was another gasp from the room. Anthony and Timothy exchanged glances, moved closer together. Daniel set down his tray with care, and rubbed his hand over his mouth. DI Willis half closed her eyes, assessing the situation.

Ursula pointed to Mrs Prior. 'You hated Mia, didn't you? She was more beautiful than you, and kind to everyone. People loved her. You may or may not have known what was going to happen at the party, but once Mia was back in her own home, you chose to ignore what had happened. What's more, you let her be raped again and again. And beaten. Under your own roof.'

Mrs Prior laughed, and shook her head. She stood with feet apart, monumentally sure of herself. Diamonds glittered at her neck and ears and on each of her massive wrists. She hissed, 'Ridiculous!'

Ursula surveyed the room. 'You had her,' she said, pointing to a jolly-looking, corpulent man at Anthony's elbow. 'She used to call you "uncle", didn't she? And her stepbrothers? They took their turn too.' The look of shock and guilt on three faces was enough to convince the most sceptical of onlookers that what she said was true.

Flash! Flash!

Ursula's face twisted. 'I had hoped that Timothy at least ... but Mia says he was one of the most brutal of her visitors. And do you know what this prize family had arranged for Mia's future? When she was no longer of any use to them, they were going to sell her to a pimp in the Midlands.'

'You are bluffing,' said Mrs Prior, in a deep, almost masculine voice. 'You have no proof.' But her hands trembled, making her diamond rings flash.

'I think you'd better leave,' said Mr Prior, pressing a handkerchief to his lips. A strand of white hair fell over his eye. Suddenly he didn't look like Santa Claus at all. 'Your allegations ...

340

ridiculous! As if I would ever have anything to do with such a thing!'

'You took your turn as well, didn't you? Two nights running. I wonder you can sleep at night, after what you've done.'

'Nothing! I've done nothing.'

'I realize you don't actually get your hands dirty yourself, do you? You set up the schemes and, if anything goes wrong, you get your wife to deal with it.' Ursula turned to Mrs Prior. 'I thought I recognized your voice on the phone. It's your job to frighten people into doing what your husband wants, isn't it? First the threats, and then the hard men go in. Anthony was your right-hand man who arranged things for you. He in turn recruited needy young men and gave them their instructions. But your little empire is falling apart because this afternoon a couple of your foot soldiers went to the police and admitted attacking and robbing Mrs Belton.'

Something like a groan went up from the party-goers, who seemed to sway backwards, moving away from their host and hostess. The girl in the wheelchair began to cry, but DC Milburn failed to notice her sister's distress.

DI Willis took out her mobile phone and spoke into it, in a low voice. Checking on what Ursula had said? The man known as Bullseye slid out of the room.

Mr Prior was sweating. 'No! I have never ... Absolutely not!'

'Mia is going to name names as soon as she leaves hospital. You understand?'

'You are pathetic!' But it was he who was pathetic, now. Trembling hands, ageing before their eyes. 'I didn't. At least ... not till ... no, not me!'

'I suppose it would best if you pleaded guilty to rape, rather than face a murder charge.'

A shocked murmur went round the room.

Flash!

Ursula was implacable. 'Yes, murder. Your son Timothy admitted as much to Daniel Collins, my ex-fiancé.'

Daniel's knees gave way, and he sank to the floor, his head bowed. He muttered, 'He was joking. I told you he was joking.'

Flash!

'Anthony killed our friend Lloyd. Worse, he destroyed Lloyd's character, saying he'd got drunk and gone over the balcony. Lloyd hardly drank at all. Timothy told you what really happened, didn't he, Dan? What was it? Did Lloyd see what was happening to Mia and object so strongly that Anthony ordered him to be silenced?'

An indrawn breath. Daniel sobbed, once. 'Yes, yes. I suppose so. Timothy said, hinted ... I wasn't there.'

Everyone looked at Timothy, who passed the back of his hand over his mouth. 'I was drunk. I didn't know what I was doing.'

Flash!

Anthony alone kept his nerve. 'Lloyd should not have made such a fuss.'

'A fuss? Well, that's for the courts to decide.

As for the threats the Priors have been making–' Ursula swept the room with her eyes – 'how many of you would dare to oppose this man, if he said your wife and child would lose their eyesight if you didn't give him what he wanted? That's what a prospective investor was told this afternoon. Or if he threatened to firebomb your premises? That was the word passed to my friend's daughter. We have taped recordings of these same threats.'

A swirl of motion, and somebody crashed across the room, aiming directly for Ursula. Anthony, mad with fury. She didn't flinch.

Judo took one pace to the fore and, bending down, lifted Anthony clear off the floor, deflecting him from Ursula, and sending him skidding across the room. He crashed into a table, and lay there, groaning.

Flash!

Ursula turned to the corner of the room in which her date for the night stood, hardly breathing, his eyes flicking to and fro. 'Your Highness, I regret that I may have given you the wrong impression at the party. I am not for sale.'

He bowed his head. 'I do not regret knowing you, Miss Ursula. It has been an education. Now, it is time for me to leave.' Ursula stood aside as he made for the door, followed by his bodyguards, and disappeared into the night, the door shutting behind him without a sound.

There was a general movement to follow him. No one thanked the Priors for inviting them; no one spoke to their host and hostess, making arrangements to see them again. Anthony's friends, men and girls, left one by one, almost running to get away. Ursula ignored them as they passed in front of her.

No one spoke to Ursula either, as she stood with her bodyguards, one on either side of her. The photographer took one last shot of her, close to. She didn't even blink. He left too.

Daniel got to his feet, and looked across at Ursula, hands outstretched, begging for forgiveness? She looked right through him. He made as if to speak, but decided against it. Shoulders slumped, he, too, went out into the night. He didn't close the door properly, and it blew open again, letting in the cold night air.

Anthony staggered to his feet holding his nose, which this time really was broken. Timothy sank into a chair, head in hands. Each member of the family stared into space, contemplating a bleak future.

DI Willis had been listening even as she talked on her mobile phone. Now she shut it off with a click. DC Milburn's sister asked in a low voice to be taken home, but this was no time for a policewoman to leave. 'I'll get a cab to take you home,' said DC Milburn. She was staying.

DI Willis finished her drink and set down the empty glass with precision. Looking first at Ellie and then at Ursula, she said, 'I promise you this will not be swept under the carpet. I shall need names, statements.'

'Tomorrow,' said Ellie.

Only then did Ursula relax. Hawk-face put his arm around her shoulders and steered her to the door. Judo collected the mask she'd dropped. Ellie led the way out to the cars, making sure to close the front door behind her. No sense in wasting heat on such a cold night.

Judo would have opened his car door for her, but she shook her head.

'Ursula will break down in a minute. I'd better go with her.' She climbed into the back of Hawk-face's car, and accepted the girl into her arms. Ursula hardly seemed to be breathing. And she was cold, so cold.

Ellie chafed Ursula's hands, murmuring 'It's all right, you're a brave girl. It's all over now.'

NINETEEN

Home at last. Everything seemed quiet, but there was a strange car in the driveway. Ellie saw that Hawk-face had noticed it too. He parked to one side, with Judo close behind him. Ellie helped Ursula out of the car. The girl was as stiff as a Barbie doll.

Everything looked normal as they approached the front door, but Ellie couldn't help remembering that Charlie had not been at the drinks party, and therefore might have been somewhere else, making mischief. She remembered

Deep Throat's last threat to make Ellie pay.

She used her keys to let them in. Everything still seemed normal. In fact, there was a burst of laughter from the kitchen. With one arm around Ursula, Ellie followed the noise, to be confronted by as cosy a domestic scene as anyone could wish.

Kate was breastfeeding her baby, while the toddler lay in the pushchair, fast asleep. Rose was dishing out helpings of her beef casserole, while Armand and his large colleague from school were helping themselves to mugs of tea.

Rose, pink with pleasure, cried, 'What goings-on! Just like the old days!'

'Ah, food!' said Judo, sliding into a chair at the table.

'Come and join us!' cried Armand. 'The enemy came, broke in through the back door, and were conquered. They thought we'd be easy, so they'd hardly brought much of an arsenal with them. Just knuckledusters, a baseball bat and a rather wicked knife. But we were ready for them. I tripped one up, Kate swept the legs from under another who bumped his head against Rose's frying pan, Big Man here sat on them, and after that they didn't have such an optimistic view of life.

'We tied them up and put them in the larder, thinking we could finish our supper before we rang the police, but they made so much noise we had to get rid of them first. The police thought they were a couple of ordinary burglars till they saw the arsenal of weapons they had with them. They were, as they say, known to the police already. One is called Charlie, the other was someone he recruited in a pub just for this evening's little foray. All been tidied away now. So, how did the drinks party go?'

'Very well,' said Ellie. The girl within her arm shivered and gasped, all the stiffness leaving her body. As she sank to the floor, so Ellie found Ursula's weight had been taken off her.

Hawk-face lifted Ursula up. 'Where shall I take her?'

'I'll show you.' She led him into the sitting room, only dimly lit with sidelamps at that time of night, and pointed out the settee. He laid her down with care. Ellie took the girl in her arms, and Hawk-face left them to it.

Ursula wept till she was too tired to cry any more.

Rose came in with a tray of hot drinks and tiny sandwiches, saying that Denis and Diana had eaten with them earlier and now gone back to her flat, if you please, and who did they think they were, treating Ellie's home like a boarding house.

Ursula lifted her head, and blearily tried to smile. 'You've been so good to me. If it hadn't been for you they'd have got away with it. But what I'm going to do about Mia, I don't know.'

How like Ursula to think she had to shoulder her friend's burden! Ellie passed the cup of tea to her. 'I'll look after Mia.'

'Will you?' Ursula seemed doubtful. 'I'd like to, but I don't see how I can manage it, living down in Portsmouth.'

'Leave it to me,' said Ellie, thinking that perhaps this was God's way of making sure she used more of the vacant rooms in the house. And why not, anyway? Rose would love to cosset Mia, and if the girl had some IT skills they could pay her a wage of sorts for helping Thomas now and then, or she could work for Stewart, helping tenants to downsize or whatever. Just till she was strong enough to go back to university. Surely Thomas wouldn't object.

'Try to eat.'

Ursula took a few sips of tea, but couldn't eat.

Armand and Kate poked their heads around the door and said they rather thought they'd go home now, if it was all right with Ellie. Their large friend went with them, saying he'd doss down on their settee again as it was too late for him to get a train back home that night.

Judo came in, and hovered. Ursula gave him a weak smile, and a weaker 'Thanks'. He said he might ring her tomorrow, if she liked. She nodded, though not with any great enthusiasm.

Midge the cat came in, sniffed at Ursula's shoe, decided she was an all right person, and sat on a stool nearby so that she could stroke him if she felt so inclined. Which she did, eventually.

Hawk-face appeared with another hot drink, this time for Ellie, and a hot-water bottle for Ursula's feet. He removed himself to a chair in the shadows. Ellie considered that Hawk-face had more common sense than most.

At last Ursula roused herself. 'I must look terrible. So sorry. Made a complete fool of myself.'

'Bed, my dear. If you can bear to sleep in your mother's sheets.'

'I'd prefer, if you don't mind, and you'll probably think me very silly, but I'd like to go home to the flat, to my own bed.'

Hawk-face stood up, yawning. 'I'll see you home then. Sleep across your bedroom door.'

She giggled, weakly. 'Silly. I'd fall over you in the night, going to the bathroom.'

'Any time.' He smiled, and in smiling revealed himself to be a man of considerable charm. Which, added to his common sense, made him a rare bird in Ellie's book. And in Ursula's, too, it seemed.

'No funny business.' Ursula struggled to sit upright. 'I'm not in the market for a man.'

'I know.' He continued to smile, and Ellie speculated how long it would be before he made a move on Ursula. A week? Two? An hour?

He spread his hands, speaking to both Ellie and Ursula. 'A bachelor: gainfully employed, honest and well intentioned.'

'A third-year student, with her eyes on a career,' said Ursula, tossing back her hair but smiling. A tinge of colour returned to her face. Ellie considered that this exchange argued well for the success of a future relationship between them. Of course, there was an age gap, probably of about ten years. Did that matter? Probably not. Ursula had outgrown boys of her own age.

Hawk-face bent over Ellie. 'Are you all right, Mrs Quicke? It must have been quite a strain, all this. And your husband's away tonight, I understand. Can I lock up for you, or something?'

Ellie wasn't sure she liked being relegated to the status of being a weak and elderly grandma, but he was quite right; she did feel like one at the moment. 'I'll be just fine. You take Cinderella here home, and look after her. But I wouldn't move on her too quickly, if I were you. Give it time.'

'Oh, wise woman.' He picked up Ellie's hand and kissed it. Then gathered Ursula up, cloak and all. Ellie saw them out of the front door, making sure the deadlock was on and the bolts shot home. And did the same for the kitchen door, which wouldn't shut properly due to the ministrations of Charlie and his mate, so she put a chair under the doorknob to keep out intruders.

Rose was already in bed, with the television on.

Ellie returned to the sitting room to turn out the lights, thinking that this was the first night she and Thomas had spent away from one another since they'd got married. She missed him. There was so much she wanted to tell him about the evening, and how Ursula had acted. She needed to talk to him about Mia too. Would he agree to their giving the girl a home till she was able to return to university? She ought to be with people who cared for her and could help her back to normality.

She looked at the phone. She couldn't ring him now, could she? He would be busy with colleagues, discussing all sorts of important things that she would never understand. She had a horrid feeling that some day he would be drawn away from her into the upper reaches of academia, where she would never be able to follow him.

The phone rang. It was Thomas. 'Are you all right, my dear? I've been so worried about you.'

'I'm just fine. How about you?' She sank down on to the settee. 'How did the paper go?' Midge decided Ellie had settled down, so jumped on to her lap.

'They seem to approve. How's your cold? Mine seems much better.'

They went on talking, the house quiet around them, and the cat purring.